THIS BOOK
BELONGS TO

_____

_____

_____

Signed edition

Salley Vickers

November 2021

VIKING
an imprint of
PENGUIN BOOKS

The Gardener

ABOUT THE AUTHOR

Salley Vickers is the author of many acclaimed novels and short-story collections including the bestselling *Miss Garnet's Angel*, *Mr Golightly's Holiday*, *The Other Side of You*, *The Cleaner of Chartres*, *Cousins*, *The Librarian* and *Grandmothers*. She has worked as a cleaner, a dancer, a teacher of children with special needs, a university lecturer and a psychoanalyst. She now writes and lectures full time. Find out more at www.salleyvickers.com or @SalleyVickers.

The Gardener

SALLEY VICKERS

VIKING
an imprint of
PENGUIN BOOKS

VIKING

UK | USA | Canada | Ireland | Australia
India | New Zealand | South Africa

Viking is part of the Penguin Random House group of companies
whose addresses can be found at global.penguinrandomhouse.com.

First published 2021
001

Copyright © Salley Vickers, 2021

The moral right of the author has been asserted

Set in 12.5/14.75pt Garamond MT Std
Typeset by Jouve (UK), Milton Keynes
Printed and bound in Great Britain by Clays Ltd, Elcograf S.p.A.

The authorized representative in the EEA is Penguin Random House Ireland,
Morrison Chambers, 32 Nassau Street, Dublin D02 YH68

A CIP catalogue record for this book is available from the British Library

HARDBACK ISBN: 978-0-241-48279-7
TRADE PAPERBACK ISBN: 978-0-241-48280-3

www.greenpenguin.co.uk

*In memory of John MacAuslan, friend and neighbour,
who wanted more of Miss Foot,
and for his wife, Karen.
And for Bob and Anna Simmons, who helped to make
lockdown more paradise than prison.*

There's always another story, there is more than meets the eye.

— W. H. Auden

March 2019

You might suppose it would feel strange to write to someone I have not met; and yet to write this for you does not
feel strange. Mistaken as this may be, I feel I already know
you. Or know as much as I will ever know, because what I
have learnt is that none of us know much – about ourselves
or each other – and that all the certainties we construct are
apt to be toppled by reality.

What I shall try to do is describe, as I now perceive them,
the events which span seven years. Events in which my life
was changed so completely and unexpectedly that I feel
I should record them. I am aware that in trying to recover
any stretch of time my memory will sometimes be fickle,
often play false. In setting out thoughts and observations
and conversations as I recall them, much that I write will
be re-membered, that is to say, refashioned, put together
anew. But that is the case for all recollections and there are
those who say that reality is better served by fiction than
by facts – which themselves are subject to their own kind
of distortions and falsehoods. What I write is, I believe, in
essence true, if not in precisely quantifiable detail.

The story is an unusual one although it is at the same time, in many respects, a common one – this contradiction being, I imagine, the case for most human stories. But how to begin? You might say begin at the beginning, but it is difficult to say where or when a beginning starts. Does this story start from the point when its elements first emerged? But then I would have to be going endlessly back in time. Or does it start when I myself first began to look back and all the matters I here describe began to take a connected shape in my consciousness?

Whatever the case, it is a story you should hear; so, having no good answers to these questions, I shall begin instead with a place, an old garden, where in a sense everything began, where I began to understand certain things and where I also began to understand that there were many more things that I would never understand.

PART I

I

'I shall never be able to manage all this,' I said.

I was surveying the moss-bound humps and ragged stretches of knee-high grass in the garden's rolling lawn with a mixture of awe and resentment. Rampant weeds had invaded those parts of the flower beds that were visible behind the hunched mass of brambles. Vicious-looking nettles awaited, darkly baleful. Towards the further end of the garden, I could make out ivy-engulfed trees braceleted with evil yellow fungi, which put me in mind of Arthur Rackham. Aged six, I had a most disturbing nightmare after stealing a book of fairy tales from my sister, Margot – a handsome, hardback book which I'd coveted like mad, bound in red cloth with indented gold lettering and a picture on the cover of a weird tree-man with branches issuing wildly from his head and hands. It was an illustration of a witch, for a story called *The Two Sisters* (which is perhaps relevant), that prompted the nightmare. I have hated Rackham ever since.

My sister was with me as I pronounced this gloomy verdict. 'We can get help,' she said, with her customary confidence.

'You mean I can?'

'You'll find someone, Hass, I know you will, you're good at that.' Her exquisitely manicured hands made a gesture, as if to conjure out of the air a green-fingered genie. She's a beauty, my sister; she gets her looks from our mother. Smiling radiantly now, she added, 'It'll be a *project*.'

This word, I couldn't help feeling, was being deployed to put a gloss on what amounted to a sentence of hard labour for me and I was already experiencing a phantom ache in my back. *This is how it will be*, I thought: *I'll be left to the drudgery of daily life while she skitters off into her world of whatever it is she does.* I was never quite sure what it was that Margot did do but it appeared to pay.

After months of indecision, we'd put together the money left us by our father and bought Knight's Fee, a sprawling old house on the outskirts of Hope Wenlock, a village just on the English side of the Welsh Marches. The house was picturesque, described in the agent's blurb as a 'jigsaw picture house' (a term which for some time set me against it). What I found, when Margot having eroded my resistance I agreed to view it, was a redbrick half-timbered building covered in creeper with what the agent assured us were Elizabethan antecedents. He was wrong about that, but I suppose it's foolish to expect accuracy from an estate agent.

I had spent many restless nights inwardly debating whether or not to invest my legacy in a shared property. It was Margot's idea and for that reason alone my first

6

instinct was to reject it. But the house's size and relative cheapness were undoubtedly enticing. It offered over three times the space I could afford to buy on my own and for much of the time I would have it to myself while Margot was off in London. And I was not without private reasons for wanting to take sanctuary in the countryside.

'Well . . .?' Margot had said. 'Look, we don't have to live cheek by jowl. And if we find it doesn't suit us then . . .'

'Then what?' My sister's habit of not completing her spoken thoughts was in my experience designed to allow for later backsliding. She was like that: capricious.

But on this occasion she was prepared to spell them out. 'Then we can sell up. Nothing lost. We're bound to make money on it with all our improvements.'

'You mean your improvements?'

'Hass, don't be such a wet blanket,' she said, ruffling my hair. She's done this since we were children and it annoyed me even then. 'The place has fantastic scope. It could be amazing. And if it turns out we hate living together, worst case, it'll be an adventure. It's good to have adventures. It expands the horizons.'

'Horizons can't actually be expanded,' I said. I'm fussy about language.

Margot sighed. 'You know what? We *could* try to get on. It's not unknown between sisters.'

Writing this now it occurs to me that I was wrong: horizons can be expanded – it merely requires a change in your point of view.

Knight's Fee was a probate sale and had stood uninhabited for over two years while various legal complexities were being unravelled. Now the legatees were 'keen to get it off their hands before . . .' here the agent had hesitated, 'further unnecessary costs'.

'What costs?' I asked suspiciously. I was anxious about money. In those days I was always broke.

Margot supplied the agent with an answer.

'Council tax, insurance, stuff, you know . . . We were the same about Belmont Street, remember?'

My thoughts flickered back to our family home, the modest Victorian semi in Sheffield. Unlike Margot, I had not been anxious to sell; I would have preferred to hide there longer to adjust to the shock of being orphaned.

But this very different house was certainly appealing. In its decayed grandeur it stood for a way of life I could never before have entertained. We could, Margot pointed out, divide it if we chose to live separately. Only the extensive garden need be shared.

What that would mean, I was now ruminating, already prickling at the prospect, was that I would be the bloody toiler in the vineyard while Margot would sit in the garden, drinking and sunning herself, enjoying the results of my labours. Or showing it off to her London friends.

Familiar snakes of fury began to writhe in my stomach. I was insane to have agreed to this. Sharing with Margot in whose shadow I'd always lived, until she ran away from home. Even then, her lost presence had tainted the remains of my childhood – our mother daily disappointed by the post which brought no word from her favourite, keeping Margot's room a sanctuary, refusing to let me take it over: 'Margie might be back any day and you've made your room so nice with all your paintings, love.'

8

'Love' was what I was called when she was not going to let me have my way. It was some time since it had come to seem to me a term of abuse.

'You'll manage,' Margot said. 'You're brilliant at that.' I should explain that one of her methods for getting her way was a form of casual flattery. That this worked, even with me, fuelled one of my several sources of grievance. She stooped now and picked a dried stem of a plant and handed it to me. 'What's this?'

'I've no idea.' I twirled the seed head between my fingers, admiring the delicate fragility of the papery globe, and a mass of tiny black seeds showered out. 'It's like a fairy's pepper pot.'

'You should put it in one of your illustrations.' Margot turned back towards the kitchen. 'What's there to eat? I'm starving.'

The kitchen had no fridge, nor any of the conveniences commonly associated with modern life: washing machine, dishwasher – 'There's not even a proper stove,' I'd said, feeling defeated already when the removals men requested tea.

'Oh, come on,' Margot had said. 'It's fun. Like camping.'

When did you ever go camping? I thought crossly, filling a heavy enamel kettle with water that ran a sinister orange.

The electricity, despite our requests, had not been turned on so the electric kettle we'd brought was useless. Luckily, there was a functioning canister of Calor gas. I made tea for the men on an ancient hob with the long-life milk we'd brought with us in Margot's car. 'You'll need to get a car of your own here,' Margot had remarked.

I produced the sliced bread and soapy cheese and over-ripe tomatoes I'd bought from the village shop and, while the removals men were still unloading on to the drive, we ate outside in our coats at a rotting wooden table on rusting garden chairs. 'You'd pay good money for these in London,' Margot pronounced.

They looked to me as if they might disintegrate any minute. I didn't share Margot's design pretensions.

'They just need sanding down,' Margot said. 'We can repaint them.'

You mean I can, I thought, mentally resolving to buy some of the white plastic chairs I'd observed on sale at a nearby garage.

'This bread is poison to the digestion.' Margot flicked crumbs from the table.

'It was all there was in the shop. You can't imagine I'd buy this for choice?'

A cruel memory slid behind this protest. 'Sliced white toast with Golden Shred might be my favourite breakfast,' I had once proclaimed. It was on a ferryboat to France when things were different, when I was different. I was no longer that person. In those days I used to wonder if there is any essential us that survives all life's shifts and vicissitudes and if that's what people meant by the soul.

'I can bring decent bread back from London,' Margot said. 'We can bung it in the freezer once we've got one. The local produce is bound to be dire. But tonight we can go into Ludlow to eat. Don't worry, I'll pay.'

I brushed the remaining crumbs from the table and a robin dropped down. The neat rust-breasted bird with knowing black-bead eyes seemed a kind of ally. Margot's reference to money was reviving my reservations about the decision to share. She earnt a great deal more than me and I had already determined that if we did divide the house the services must be separated. In winter I often wear socks and sometimes a cardigan in bed. In my straitened circumstances I didn't fancy subsidizing Margot's fuel consumption.

The robin whirred on to the table and pecked up the last few specks of crumbs.

'It's like in *The Secret Garden*,' Margot said, at the very moment I was recalling the book myself. Margot is like that – she frisks your mind, helping herself to your thoughts before you can have them for yourself. 'I read it to you when you had chickenpox, do you remember?'

'Yes,' I said. 'And I also remember you slapping me.'

'Only because you kept picking at your scabs. I didn't want Scarface for a sister.'

There were several rooms on the second floor to choose from for our bedrooms. Margot chose the largest, which overlooked a grassy gravelled drive. I chose a smaller L-shaped room that had two windows, a corner window with a view of the far-off hills and a large bay, with a window seat, that overlooked the garden.

At one end of the long corridor was a bathroom with a massive claw-foot enamel bath and at the other a cramped little room, smelling of damp, with a stained washbasin and a shower. The shower was fitted with perished rubber tubing and the grouting on the tiles was black with mould.

'You take the shower room, it'll make your bedroom almost en suite. I'll make do with the bath,' Margot decided.

But this bit of Margotism I didn't mind. I preferred my room. I was taken by its odd shape and the fact that it looked over the garden. There was a book, *The L-Shaped Room*, which I had read after seeing the film which starred Leslie Caron. I had seen it during a British Cinema season at the NFT with Robert. *Mustn't think about Robert*, I tried to tell myself. But as you will discover, there is no power on earth that can unthink thoughts.

'You're frowning,' Margot said. 'You shouldn't frown so much. It's giving you wrinkles.'

'I've already got wrinkles.' I didn't have many but Margot's obsession with appearances brought out resistance in me.

'So no need to bring on more.'

'Oh, for God's sake,' I said, annoyed, I suspect, that she didn't contradict me about the wrinkles. 'You know I'm not like you. I don't care how I look.'

'You do,' Margot said. 'Everyone does. I'm just more honest about it than you.'

The removals van had brought the furniture from the family home in which our father had died. I had given up my rented place in London and gone to nurse him in his last illness, so anything I owned had been brought from there too. Margot was letting her London flat to a friend but she was keeping a room for herself when she was in town, so nothing much had come from there. 'It wouldn't suit the country anyway,' she had declared. 'It's mostly Conran or Heal's.'

We spent the afternoon rearranging the furniture that had been set down, under Margot's instructions, by the removals men.

'The rooms are so huge it's impossible to see where things fit,' Margot complained after we had heaved a heavy leather sofa from where it had been placed in a bay window to a position by the fire and then shifted it all the way back again. 'Shit, I've broken a nail.' She eyed the drop-lid oak bureau that had been our father's. 'I can't see where Dad's desk should go. It looks wrong there but where else could we put it . . .?'

I was remembering the last time I had gone to that desk to fetch some letters for Dad. He had still been alive, just. On the very brink between life and death and aware that he was about to die. What is it like? I had longed to ask. Is it like the moment when we emerge, still steeped in unconsciousness, into the new light of day – or that other moment, when we sense we are about to drop into the oblivion of night?

With a fascination that I was half ashamed of, I'd stood over my father, watching the purpled moth-wing eyelids flutter over his semi-slumbering eyes. His tall, bony frame had dwindled to become pitifully frail and skeletal and he seemed to have grown transparent, as if he were shedding mortal flesh ready to take flight.

'Think of me bound for the *swallow thronged loft*, Hass,' he said to me once when I had become tearful. 'No cause to fret. I'll fit in there.'

'Leave it for now,' I said to Margot. 'I'll find the right place.'

'If we don't do it now, it'll just get left and then it'll never be right. Strike while the iron is hot.'

'That doesn't seem an apt saying for the circumstances.'

'Hass,' Margot startled me with a sudden vehemence, 'I know you were ever so *noble* going to look after him but you don't *own* Dad.'

2

When I woke next morning, sunlight was blessing the bottom of my bed and I felt absurdly pleased at having judged the orientation of the room correctly. The glass in the corner window was old and flawed, with the result that the sun's rays passing through it were transforming that part of the room into a chapel of dancing light. I lay there contentedly contemplating the prospect of tea. Tea in the morning is one of those simple pleasures that can be relied on whatever else has crumbled or failed. But for the moment bed was a cocoon from which I wasn't ready to emerge.

The divan bed, brought from Sheffield, fitted snugly into the narrower portion of the L-shape, leaving just enough space at the side for whatever books I was currently reading. I have a habit of reading several books at once so by my bed there tends to be a tottering tower. After a while, the promise of a view began to draw me and I wriggled on my bottom, dragging the duvet, nearer to the window to inspect it.

With eyes scrunched, the hills did have a bluish tinge, as Housman's melancholy poem suggests, but when I relaxed my eyes they looked merely greyish-brown. *Perhaps*, I thought, *the 'blue' was a reflection of his mood. Blue is maybe more poetic – but grey and brown have their own poetry.*

As if chiming with this thought, a tree growing close to the window swayed in a sudden whip of wind and a compact little grey-brown bird shot from a branch. Like a sparrow but not a town sparrow. Dad's ornithology books were among the books I'd brought from the Sheffield house. *I could learn about birds here*, I thought.

I went downstairs in my fisherman's socks – I never wear slippers. The stairway was vast, with an anachronistic curving mahogany bannister, the kind a child would slide down. In my mind's eye, my infant self went whizzing past the sober middle-aged person padding down the dusty stairs to the hall. The latter person followed the ghost of my young self through to the beamed kitchen and into a cold scullery.

She would have liked this, I thought, *my young self: a proper old-fashioned scullery with a flagstone floor and a capacious pantry to maybe hide in.*

It put me in mind of one of Beatrix Potter's illustrations. As a child, I read her stories avidly but above all I loved the meticulous illustrations. The pantry reminded me of *The Tale of Samuel Whiskers*, which led me to think that given its age and recent neglect Knight's Fee might well house rats. I didn't much like that thought and it crossed my mind to maybe get a cat.

The pantry shelves held some empty Kilner jars, a double boiler and one of those umbrella-shaped devices used to protect food from flies. Several had expired on the netting. That there was a problem with flies was confirmed when I managed to force open one of the drawers of the built-in dresser which was jammed full of sticky brown fly papers. Also some old-fashioned carbolic soap, a dirty icing bag and some half-melted candles, which would come in handy if the electricity was not connected soon. We'd gone to bed by the light of our phones. I rarely use my mobile now but in those days I needed one for work.

I filled the kettle, lit the gas ring and opened the back door. In the pale morning light, the garden was a vista of greens. As if on cue, the robin dropped from a bush and hopped towards the door on legs that looked too brittle to support the stocky little body.

I found the bread Margot had objected to and watched while the robin briskly pecked up crumbs. It fixed me with its black-bead eyes and flitted off again.

The removals men had left piled in the stairwell an assortment of boxes. I ripped open one marked 'Shoes Miscellaneous' to find a collection of mouldy sandals – which I must have put away damp – someone's gold party slippers, Margot's old pink satin ballet shoes, which our mother had had framed, and several pairs of heels which I'd not worn since I left London. The tartan slippers – my last present to Dad, which I'd not been able to bring myself to chuck out – were there too and a pair of ancient Dr. Scholl's. I squeezed my feet in the bulky socks into these and stepped outside.

It was the first week of March. I stood on the lawn with the cold breeze painting my cheeks and breathed in deeply. Perhaps here I might begin yoga. I pictured myself on the lawn, hands supporting my hips, feet in the air. I'd considered starting yoga before so why had I not got round to it? The truth was I'd not been up to getting round to anything that might have been good for me. Unwelcome thoughts began to invade and I went back into the house.

Margot, in an expensive-looking angora dressing gown, was pouring boiled water into a jug. 'I couldn't find the cafetière, but we can make coffee Jane Austen's way.'

'What way's that?' Jane Austen was one of my favourite authors. I'd never heard of her having a special way with coffee.

'It's in one of her letters.' Margot poured out a dribble of coffee into a china cup and tipped it back into the jug. 'There, if you let it settle the grounds sink. I read about it somewhere.'

'Where?'

'A magazine. *Harper's*, I think.'

'I can't see *Harper's* running a piece on Jane Austen.'

'Don't be so snotty. *Harper's* has some very good writers. Here, have some coffee. Perhaps that'll put you in a better mood.'

The mug she handed me, decorated with the words 'Campbell's Soup', was the one our mother had used for surplus fat from our family Sunday roast. God knows why I'd brought it. Margot's cup was part of a gold-patterned china service which I'd donated to Oxfam. She noticed me clocking it. 'I could only find this cup in the box.'

'It's the only one left,' I said, sipping coffee. It was undeniably good. The Jane Austen method apparently worked. 'I got rid of the rest. That one must've got left behind.'

'Mother adored that tea service. It was a wedding present.'

'You weren't there, Marg. There was so much stuff to deal with. And no one uses tea sets nowadays.'

'I do,' Margot said. 'I loved Mum's china. You could've asked.'

She was right. I should have asked. It infuriated me when anyone took my wishes for granted. But I wasn't going to admit this. I'd single-handedly seen to the major part of the sorting out of the house and it had nearly finished me off. If Margot had cared about tea sets she should have bloody well come and helped.

We spent the day fractiously unpacking, placing and then replacing and then re-replacing all over again the contents of some of the boxes.

'I'm knackered,' Margot announced, flopping down on to a dusty footstool. 'Why did you bring this? It's riddled with woodworm. And why have we ended up with four tin openers and no corkscrew?'

'There are plenty of corkscrews,' I said. I wandered over to a bulging cardboard box and began to pick books out.

'Don't,' Margot commanded. 'It's pointless unpacking books till we have shelves.'

'I'm looking for Dad's bird books.'

Most of our father's books had come with us. I could find no one who wanted them – it's shameful how little books are prized these days. I'd contacted, without success, second-hand booksellers galore, and I wasn't going to send Dad's treasured library ignominiously to the dump. So I'd packed up his Loeb classics, with the red and green covers, his poetry books and all the hardback novels, even the collected Walter Scotts which no one nowadays reads.

I shall read these, I mentally determined. *All the books I've never read, and I've been saying I'll read one day when I get around to it, while Margot is off in London, I shall read.*

'When are you going back to London?' I asked, hoping not to sound too eager.

'Day after tomorrow. I'm taking a week off at Easter but till then I'll be hither and yon.'

A phrase she's aware I dislike. 'So will you drive?'

'I'll see how the trains are. But look, you'll need your own wheels. I don't want you relying on the Lexus.'

'I wouldn't want to. I'd be in dread of scratching it.'

'You better not!'

'I said I wouldn't want to, didn't I?'

Margot said she was taking the Lexus into Shrewsbury. 'I'm not wasting money on overpriced loo roll at the local shop. It won't have any decent cheese or coffee either.'

'We should use their shop, though. We're incomers. It'll alienate them if we don't.'

'We can use it enough to keep in with them.'

Why do I bother? I wondered. *She doesn't care what they think of us. It's all right for her – she isn't going to be here all the time.* 'I think I'll walk into the village,' I said, making an action of my thoughts. 'I want to put a notice up about the garden.'

'Good idea,' Margot said. 'But you'd better find something more waterproof than those dreadful sandals. I don't know why you packed them. That black stuff on them looks like mould.'

The route to the village was along a narrow road lined with blackthorn. The froth of white blossoms and the hawthorn, still laced with autumnal berries and garlanded with old man's beard, gave the hedgerows a festive appearance. The road itself was less appealing. Traffic had gouged deep potholes in the surface. There was no pavement and a couple of lorries thundered past, frighteningly close. I'd noticed this about the country: in some ways it's worse than town. Certainly you're often closer to traffic. Holding my breath as an oil tanker rounded the bend, expelling noxious fumes, I ducked under some wire fencing into a field. A stile at the far end suggested an alternative route to the village.

When I reached the stile, I stopped to survey the view. Beyond the next field was a copse, and some way beyond that I could see a crenellated church tower. Behind the tower were the blue-remembered hills that had cast their long shadow on Housman's spirits, still to my eyes lacking the poetic blue but nevertheless inviting.

A skein of geese in RAF formation flew overhead, their raucous honking strangely stirring in the still surrounds. *Dad would like it here*, I thought, jumping from the stile into a wet slurry of mud. *I wish you could visit, Dad, and yes, I know I'm only here because you're dead and if you were still alive I wouldn't be here in the first place. I wonder what you'd think of it all and what you'd make of me living with Margot.*

I believe now he might have been pleased. When Margot left home there was a part of him, I sensed, that felt relief. At least there was an end to our endless quarrelling. Our captious mother liked to pick fights but Dad hated rows and rarely allowed himself to get drawn in. 'Least said, soonest mended,' he said once when, infuriated by his passivity in the face of our mother's taunting, I asked why he didn't retaliate. 'But that only works if there's a willingness on *both* sides to mend, Dad,' I said to what I considered then his tame reply and he turned away from me as if I'd hurt him. I think now he might have been feeling ashamed.

He was an old-school male, brought up to respect women by his fiercely ambitious, acutely intelligent working-class mother, herself something of a tyrant. But for all that, I can see now he felt he was weak in never managing to temper his wife's moody, dominating character; and much as I loved him, I think, somewhere, though I couldn't afford to acknowledge this at the time – Dad being, then, my only ally – I felt let down by him because he wasn't up to protecting me.

I stopped challenging him once I saw he wasn't going to change. It's hard to come to terms with your parents' limitations; I have only just begun to do so now. And after our mother died there was no need for him to change. Free of her carping spirit, Dad was fine – certainly as far as I was concerned. We were always close in an unstated way and since he'd died I'd got into the habit of inwardly chatting to him. I was talking to him in my mind still as I crossed the field to a track that led into the copse.

The air among the trees was rich with the scent of rotting bark and decomposing leaves, which lay soft and thick underfoot amid irregular rugs of brilliant green moss. Passing a massive oak, rooted in skirts of emerald velvet, I stopped to run my hands over a moss-engrained burl. Ruskin would have sketched it. He might also have sketched the overhanging branch of a rowan, still ornamented with brilliant orange berries. I visited his house on

Coniston Water once and admired his skilful drawings of leaves and berries and flowers. As I was recalling this, the rowan swayed in a passing breeze, dropping on my head a few drops of rain or dew, as if in blessing. And I heard my mother's scornful tones, 'There's Hassie being fanciful again.'

The copse was more extensive than I had first supposed, more like a small wood or glade. Following the track, I came to a pool surrounded by clumps of hazel and holly and yew.

I've always had a thing for water: pools, streams, springs, lakes. I stared down now at my outline hazily mirrored in the pool. A reflection of someone reflecting. One of those everyday metaphors that have got into the language and are so blurred by use that few people observe them any more. Reflections require still waters. Still waters run deep. Perhaps here it would be safe to reflect.

The wood led into another field where sheep were grazing. A few raised tousled nicotine-white heads and stared at me with pale, deadpan eyes, then resumed methodically cropping the thin grass. Another stile took me on to a track which led down to a gate which in turn took me back on to a bend in the road from where the village was now in sight.

A customer was being served in the shop where I had bought yesterday's lunch. While I waited, I examined the produce: some overripe fruit and wilting veg, on the shelves a standard collection of tinned soups, baked beans, cereals, fizzy drinks, a rack of newspapers and magazines and by the till assorted sweets, raspberry laces, chews, flying saucers – Margot and I loved those as kids.

The woman behind the counter was joshing the young

man she was serving. I caught a glimpse of a packet of sanitary towels and guessed from the badinage that his wife had recently had a baby. The bell on the shop door sounded and an elderly woman wearing a brown tweed coat came into the shop as the young man was leaving.

'Good morning, Hayley, good morning, Steve,' she said, nodding at the young man. 'How is Jade? And the brand-new arrival? Feeding like a young gannet?'

'Mother and baby are doing well, thank you, Miss Foot.'

'A girl, I hear.'

'Yes. We're thinking of Molly.'

'Such glad tidings, new life, new promise. I shall call by later – if I may.' She inclined her head, acknowledging me.

'Hi, I'm Hassie,' I said, taking a plunge.

The woman stepped back to examine me before extending a gloved hand. 'How do you do? I am Phyllis Foot.' Her clipped tone left a space around each word as if she were an elocution teacher.

'Halcyon, strictly speaking,' I said, though I didn't as a rule like to give my full name. 'Halcyon Days.'

The slight risk of this revelation seemed to fly invisibly between us. Then she said, in an accent I think of as Edwardian, 'We have Greek names in common. Halcyon is new to me but it is a propitious name. Amusing with your surname. Someone had a sense of humour.'

'Yes,' I said. It was Dad who gave me my odd name. 'Though it can be a nuisance.' I felt a slight disloyalty to my father as I said this.

Miss Foot raised quizzical eyebrows and seemed about to speak, then merely enquired, 'Have you kept my loaf, Hayley?'

'Under the counter, Miss Foot. And your *New States-man*. That's five pound twenty.'

'Manners, Hayley. Miss Days was before me.'

'No, no,' I said. 'Please go ahead. I'm enjoying browsing. I – we – my sister and I, have just moved to Hope Wenlock.'

'Come and see me,' Miss Foot suggested once she had settled up. 'We are just past the postbox, a little way up Folly Hill – number seven, though it's hard to see under the creeper, but we are the house with the thatched porch and the green door. Don't be frightened of Alfred. His bark is infinitely worse than his bite, though that's not saying much as his bark is pretty frightful. My front door is always open but yell if you do come. I'm growing deaf.'

'She was my teacher,' Hayley explained as I offered up my purchases: two tins of baked beans, a jar of Branston pickle and a few of the firmer tomatoes. 'She taught all us village kids when we still had the primary here. To be honest, I'm still a bit afraid of her.'

'What happened to the school?'

'Cuts, what else. They have to bus the kids now to Shrewsbury, primary as well as secondary. It's a shame. It was great for us being able to walk to school and play out after with our mates.'

When I left the shop, I decided to explore the rest of the village. Along the main street I passed two other shops: a hardware store and 'A Stitch in Time', a shop with a bow window in which knitting wool and women's foundation garments, of a kind I supposed long out of fashion, were displayed. A snicket took me up a steep, narrow lane to a lychgate. A man was cutting the grass in the churchyard.

He paused as I came through the gate to wish me good morning.

'Hello,' I said. 'Is the church open?'

'Every day from seven till sundown.'

I now know that the name 'Hope' comes from 'hop', Old English for the side of a hill, and true to its name Hope Wenlock lies on the slopes of a small hill and the church stands towards the brow. Below me I could see, spread out like a map, clusters of trees and fields girded with hedges and stone walls where sheep and a few cattle grazed. 'What a lovely view it is from up here.'

'The church isn't bad either, we like to think.'

The man got back to his mowing and I went into the church, which had the peculiar smell of country churches: damp and musty but not unpleasant. There was the usual collection of postcards and leaflets and a pamphlet promising to tell me all about the church. I put 50p in the box and learnt that the church was St Michael and All Angels and boasted Saxon origins. These had been built on substantially by the Normans and more aggressively added to by the Victorians, who had introduced some garish stained-glass windows and ornate plaques commemorating local bigwigs. The Victorian floor, tiled in red and black lozenges, put me in mind of the hall in our house in Sheffield, where Margot and I, in our occasionally cooperative moods, used to play a complicated game with tiddlywinks. She invented it; she was clever at inventing games.

A simple stone tablet listed the names of Hope Wenlock's dead from the two world wars; I always find these moving. Hidden away in a high niche by where the bell ropes hung was a small stone-carved figure with a hand raised presumably in blessing. The features were so blunted that it was impossible to discern the sex. I consulted the pamphlet but while it was chattily full of other information there was no mention of the figure.

I sat for a while, observing a lozenge of semi-precious light, cast by the stained glass, dance on the smooth, worn wooden surface of the pew, and pondering, not for the first time, what people meant when they claimed to pray. I wonder if there is anyone who hasn't at some point of despair or crisis prayed; even Richard Dawkins must have given in at some point. But on the few occasions when I have in desperation resorted to prayer, I was conscious that these were not prayers that any divinity would be likely to be bothered with. Most prayers, surely, were wishful thinking, or requests to be let off crimes and misdemeanours. It was babyish to suppose a deity, even assuming there was one, paid any attention. If there was a ruling deity It must be like the weather, I had decided, indifferent to the clamourings of humankind.

When I came out of the church, the gardener was sitting on a gravestone drinking from a thermos. He waved the cup genially at me. 'Thirsty work. The first cut after winter.'

'The smell of mown grass is worth it, though,' I suggested.

'My wife, when she was alive, wore a scent called Mown Hay. I used to buy it for her from a fancy shop in London.'

'How nice.' His face was the sort I instinctively trust: mild and unassuming. I didn't confide that someone once used to buy me L'Heure Bleue. I never wear it now but that he had thought to buy his wife scent made me like him.

'She was worth it. I'm Peter, by the way. Peter Haycroft,

hence the scent. It was our joke.' He smiled a little mournfully.

'I'm Hassie Days,' I volunteered. 'My sister Margot and I have just moved into Knight's Fee.'

'It has a history, that house. I've some material about it if you'd like to know more. Well, I'd better get on or I'll be in trouble with the chief churchwarden. She's a martinet. The vicar's in mortal terror of her.'

'I've yet to meet him,' I said, adding quickly, 'Sorry, I should have said "or her". Is your vicar male or female?' I was being polite; I couldn't have cared less whether the vicar was a him or a her.

Peter Haycroft bowed slightly so I could see the spot on the top of his head where he was balding. 'You're talking to him. But today I'm the jobbing gardener. Our usual chap has done his back in so I'm taking his place. I can hear Audrey – that was my wife – telling me it's good for me. Good exercise.'

Trying to make up for any tactlessness, I said, 'We're not regular churchgoers but now we're here I'll try to come.' It suddenly felt important – like using the village shop. And while the whole time I'd lived in London I'd never set foot in a church, there had been a time when I had often visited cathedrals.

The vicar gave a rueful smile. 'Audrey used to say they should teach us "Get used to disappointment" at theological college instead of all the nonsense we were obliged to learn.'

When I got back to the house, Margot was preparing a salad.

'I found a Waitrose. Not quite London standard but not bad. I got my rye bread.'

'Thank God. I was on tenterhooks.'

'Don't be mean. You've no idea how my gut bloats with the merest hint of gluten.'

I didn't bother to say that rye flour was also glutenous. It was an argument we'd had many times before.

'Oh, and the electrics are on at last. I managed to order a fridge-freezer on my phone. And a washer-dryer. They'll plumb in the washing machine when they deliver, but we should find a local plumber and an electrician. How was the village shop?'

Which was when I realized that I'd forgotten about putting up a notice for a gardener.

3

The following afternoon, the washing machine was delivered by an overweight, elderly man and a well-muscled younger man who set about plumbing it in. I found Margot's habit of flirting with workmen tiresome so I left her to it and set out again for the village to see about an advert for a gardener.

I cut across the fields and through the wood with the beginnings of a sense of familiarity and, as happens once you've walked a route, I seemed to reach the village in a much shorter time.

Hayley was on her phone. She waved an explanatory hand, mouthing 'mother', so I entertained myself reading the headlines. The Prime Minister was having more problems with her MPs. I've never voted Conservative but I couldn't help having some sympathy for the woman who, it seemed to me, was struggling to do the right thing. *She's bullied by those men*, I thought. THERESA *DIS*-MAY the *Sun* mocked. Whatever you thought of the *Sun*, you had to admit it had a flair for headlines. I idly reflected that it might be fun to work for a tabloid. My own work was lonely. I was most definitely not looking forward to the manuscript waiting for me at home.

Hayley finished her conversation. 'Sorry about that. How you settling in?'

I said we were getting there and explained about the notice requesting help with the garden. I was suddenly assailed by an image of my father, sitting in his worn leather armchair, listening to *Gardeners' Question Time*. He loved the garden and apart from a bit of weeding, which I helped with when he was getting past it, I'd never bothered about our garden. I was overcome by a painful sensation, common at that time, of wanting to cry.

'I'm hopelessly ignorant about plants,' I explained.

'There's plenty here will be glad to help,' Hayley assured me. 'There's not much work around these days.' She produced a card and a pen and took a pound for two weeks' display. 'If you get no takers you can have another fortnight half price. If push comes to shove my husband'll give you a hand with the grass. There's plenty of it at Knight's Fee.'

I wrote out the postcard and Hayley stuck it up in the window beside cards offering ukulele lessons, art classes, over-fifties keep fit and some baby lop-eared rabbits (free to good homes). Also a request for work: YOUNG RELI-ABLE MAN, ABLE TO DO ODD JOBS. GOOD REFS.

'We'll need a mower,' I said, thinking aloud.

'Brian at the hardware up the street does mowers. There's places in Shrewsbury you can get one cheaper but you'll get brownie points in the village if you buy from Brian.'

The hardware shop had a notice 'Closed till Wednesday'. I'm a hopeless procrastinator and I had no appetite for the work I had waiting, so I wandered further up the hill towards where Miss Foot had said I would find her house.

I found it standing back from the road: a black-timbered cottage with a thatched porch on which a couple of doves were perching. Another jigsaw picture house, more so than Knight's Fee because you could see that in summer there would be roses blooming round the door.

As I approached, there was an eruption of barking and a large yellow Labrador raced towards me down the path.

Miss Foot appeared in the porch. 'Don't mind him. Alfred, shut up!'

Alfred leapt up at me enthusiastically. I'm a little afraid of dogs. Dog owners tend not to have much sympathy for this, so I made a feeble show of trying to pat the creature.

His owner must have sensed my apprehension because she came down the path and stuck an authoritative foot under his belly to lift him off. 'Poor misguided beast believes he's being welcoming. Come in. Alfred, you can stay in the kitchen.'

She took me into a room whose stone-flagged floor was covered with oriental rugs.

My first impression, which never quite faded, was of a kind of Aladdin's Cave. Masses of paintings, plates, clocks, carvings, musical instruments and I don't know what were crammed together on the walls; there was a good deal of mahogany furniture; a moss-green velvet sofa was set across an open fireplace in which logs burnt; a rocking chair and a small armchair in the shape of a shell stood one on each side of the fireplace where a gleaming brass coal scuttle and a large pair of antique-looking bellows stood. Over the stone fireplace hung a faded tapestry worked in blue and green wools.

'Take the shell,' Miss Foot indicated.

I sat down gingerly; the velvet appeared perilously worn. 'I hardly like to sit on this – it looks valuable.'

'My grandmother's. Most of my better things were hers. But I don't hold with treating possessions like museum pieces. Coffee, tea or a glass of wine? It's my own, rhubarb, but dry and I'm assured palatable.'

'Coffee, please, if it's not a nuisance.'

'Alfred, quiet!' There was indignant barking from the kitchen. 'My dear, you may trust me to only say what I feel. I'm like Alfred, too old a bitch to learn new tricks.'

I laughed at this. But I have an annoying way of colouring easily and felt I was flushing. To divert attention I said, 'Your tapestry is interesting. Is it of a hunt?'

'Also my grandmother's. As a child I used desperately to hope the deer got away. Now then, coffee. And I'll let Alfred out into the garden. He's annoyed at not being allowed to meet you.'

I heard her talking to Alfred and then the noise of a coffee grinder. I got up to examine the pictures. Some were old landscapes in time-darkened oils. Others were drawings of leaves, seeds and parts of flowers, labelled in a brown italic script. In one alcove hung a long silk scroll painted with an image of a tree.

'Supposed to be the tree of knowledge,' Miss Foot explained, kicking open the door and entering with a tray.

33

'Part of the haul my missionary ancestors brought back from the East.'

'Oh,' I said. I'd never met anyone connected to missionaries. 'How nice.'

'Hmm.' Miss Foot settled herself in the rocking chair and poured coffee into bone-china cups. One, I noticed, had a cracked handle which someone had mended. 'Not so nice for those my ancestors liked to call "the natives".' She passed me the uncracked cup. 'Most missionaries were sanctified robbers. Do you know the Noël Coward song "Uncle Harry's not a missionary now"?' offering a plate of crumbling digestives.

'No, sorry, I don't.'

'He's not fashionable these days. People don't like the voice, but he wasn't grand at all. Common, my mother would have said. A dreadful snob, my mother, poor duck. She never got over the fact that my brother Philip and I both became ardent socialists. You can put your cup there.'

This instruction was accompanied by a magisterial nod at a small table, inlaid with mother of pearl and set with marquetry.

'This is beautiful. I don't like to put anything on it.'

'That's my backgammon table. There's a mat in the side drawer, there. I don't suppose you play?'

I found a small square of material in the drawer worked in gigantic red cross-stitch. 'No. Sorry.'

'The mat was a present from one of my children. Michael Mason, a terror, but a heart of gold. He's a PE teacher now. People don't play backgammon here nowadays. A pity. It's an excellent game.'

'I'm afraid I'm no good at games,' I said. My mother

liked cards. When she was ill with the cancer that finally killed her she played patience, day in, day out. I found this peculiarly depressing.

'In the East, where it's still popular, backgammon is rather more than a game.'

'What is it, if not a game?'

Miss Foot took a biscuit and chewed thoughtfully. Looking at her flat, placid-seeming face, I realized who it was she reminded me of – the White Queen in *Alice*. 'They would probably say it is a philosophy of life. It relies on an interplay between chance – hazard, they would have called it in the East – and gaps. Not concepts well understood in the West but true of life, wouldn't you say?'

I was spared any need to respond to this by a scratching at the window. My hostess rose to open it and a skinny scraping of soot jumped down and crouched shuddering on the hearthrug.

Miss Foot greeted him. 'Hello, Mags. Formally he's Magwitch – I found him in the churchyard – but he mostly goes by Mags – Maggot when he's bad.'

'May I pick him up?'

'He's not very civilized. He can bite.'

I read somewhere that you can divide the world into Venice people or Florence people, Mozart people or Beethoven people, cat people or dog people. It's one of those nonsensical categorizations but for what it's worth I am a cat person. I presented the kitten with my hand, as I know to be the correct feline etiquette, and the kitten snuffed cautiously and then began to emery-board my fingers with his tiny rose-pink tongue.

'You seem to have passed the test,' Miss Foot said.

'Nelly East, who owned Knight's Fee, had a black tomcat she was devoted to and never had neutered. She rather lost her grip at the end of her life and by the time she died Wesley's offspring were running the place and many went feral. Mags will be one of Wes's descendants.'

Nelly is a name you don't hear of much these days. 'Nelly short for . . .?'

'I believe Ellen. But I only knew her as Nelly or Nell. She was an evacuee during the war and Arthur, the elder East boy, fell for her when she was still a child and she and her siblings were placed there. She came back to visit after the war and he married her, rather against the family's wishes. The Easts felt they were somebody because they'd lived at Knight's Fee for generations.'

'The vicar told me he had some material about the house. I met him in the churchyard, like Magwitch.' I'd scooped up the kitten, who had coiled himself into a trusting fur rosette on my lap.

'So you've met Peter, our atheist vicar.'

'Is he?'

'Well, judge for yourself: doesn't believe in the resurrection, doesn't believe in the Trinity, doesn't believe in hell.'

'I didn't think anyone believed in hell these days.'

'You obviously don't move in fundamentalist circles. My sister married one – a genuine fire and brimstone "Christian". My poor sister was named Patience and married to that poltroon she needed it. Happily, I need have nothing to do with him since she died.'

Our family went to church at Christmas for the carol concert, and sometimes not even then. That was more to do with my mother keeping up appearances. Dad was an atheist but not one who made a stand. 'I've not really thought much about religion,' I said.

'There's religion and religion, wouldn't you agree?' Miss Foot said. 'Have another biscuit.'

'I won't, thank you.' The digestives were extremely stale. But in case this seemed rude and because I was truly intrigued, I asked, 'Do you know why it's called Knight's Fee?'

'I have my own ideas. But for that you should see Peter. One of my former pupils who went on to read History and is now a professor did some research on the village. Peter has her paper.'

'Hayley told me you taught at the village school.'

'I've taught half the village. Hayley was a good girl. Not spectacularly bright but persevering. Perseverance gets you a long way.'

'You must have minded when they closed the school.'

She laughed, a surprisingly deep, guttural laugh. 'I managed to keep it open for longer than they bargained for by lying about my age.'

'How did you manage that?' It was hard to tell how old she was.

'Partly luck, partly sleight of hand. I – we – were born in what since Partition is Pakistan, where births were registered somewhat irregularly. My parents didn't get around to registering my birth until some time after the event and the year was registered incorrectly. By the time anyone noticed, it would have been a terrible business getting it altered, so it was left as it was with the happy outcome that I was able to retire late. How about you? I assume as a modern young woman you work?'

'Yes,' I said, a little reluctantly. 'I'm an illustrator. I wouldn't want not to work.'

'Quite right. Bright girls should be gainfully employed.'

'I wouldn't say I was especially "bright".' My sister was the clever one. She turned down an offer of a place at Cambridge and our mother never got over it.

Miss Foot was crisp. 'In my experience "bright" frequently means facile. Often it was my slower pupils who did better in the longer run.'

'I did do better later,' I agreed. 'I could have gone to university but I chose to go to art school.'

'Training in art is greatly undervalued,' Miss Foot asserted. It was apparent that my new acquaintance was not short of opinions. 'I was reading the other day that life drawing is a prophylactic against Alzheimer's. The coordination of eye and brain and hand is thought beneficial. What is your speciality? What do you draw?'

'It's not very elevated, I'm afraid. I illustrate a rather dismal series of children's books.'

'Would I know them?'

To my annoyance, I found I was reddening again. 'They feature an elf called Elfine.'

'No, I've not come across them.'

I was relieved to hear it. I'd already decided that I liked Miss Foot and wanted her to think well of me. 'In the past,' I said, 'people, well, children's authors anyway, had more line drawings in their books and I did some that were quite well thought of. I enjoyed doing those. Partly because I enjoyed the books.' I saw myself in Catherine Tenant's garden studio. 'But Elfine is dire. The writing makes me cringe. The publishers only use me because they know I need the work so I'm cheap. The books are too – cheap.'

'That's a shame,' Miss Foot said. 'Elves and fairies should be treated with proper respect. There's nothing whimsical about them. They can be quite vicious.'

As I was saying goodbye at the door the pair of doves flew down from the porch and sauntered along the path on their slender coral-red legs before me, pecking at invisible seeds.

There had been doves at Catherine's wedding. They had just come out of the church and Robert and I had been photographed, standing amid the cloud of doves. One had settled on my arm. I noticed then the fragile coral-red legs and the surprisingly tenacious little claws.

'Perhaps it's the Holy Ghost,' Robert suggested. We had only just met and I wasn't sure if he was joking.

Walking back through the wood, I stopped again by the pool.

Elfine's author had sent me a breathy synopsis of her heroine's adventures which were to be published in a 'Bumper' volume. One of these involved a pool with 'friendly frogs' and 'dippy ducks' and 'wise old water rats', that kind of thing. I don't mind anthropomorphism in the right hands but I found these mawkish caricatures inexcusable. I had developed an aversion to Elfine's author. I hated her for being a bad writer but also, I'm afraid, I hated her success. I had been successful once with more offers of work than I could take on but when I went to live with Dad I had allowed my professional life to slide. And when the state of my finances obliged me to go back to it, the publishing world had moved on, there were fewer illustrations wanted and those that were being commissioned were no longer in my style. All I had to keep the wolf from the door was Elfine.

Derek, my old agent, had retired during my stay with Dad and sold his business; the people who bought the agency were keener on money than on satisfying their clients' sensibilities. Derek not only knew how to sell my work but he also genuinely admired it and, as all creative people will testify, even a snippet of admiration is the manna that feeds us in the desert. It's hard to keep going without the nourishment of some form of acknowledgement. These days my star had fallen so far that I was looked after by a callow young assistant, who, I sensed, found my illustrations old-fashioned. It was she who had come up with the Elfine commission (probably to fend off my slew of desperate emails) and at first I'd been grateful. But by now the ersatz elf had come to seem a symbol of all that I'd lost and feared I would never have again, and I raged inwardly at this dereliction of fortune.

As I stood by the pool that day, I assuaged these savage regrets by amusing myself with thoughts of an illustration in which Elfine's tiny head was held under the water by her enemy, Travis the Troll. I had a soft spot for Travis and enjoyed fantasies of him polishing Elfine off. But if Elfine were taken out there would be no more work. The books were popular and the small publisher's revenue received a regular boost from Elfine's sales. I lamented the days of Catherine's well-written novels. But Catherine was how I had met Robert and I mustn't think about Robert.

I was feeling altogether happier about the decision to

live at Knight's Fee when I arrived back there. 'I've met three of the villagers now,' I announced.

Margot was in the scullery fiddling with the washing machine. 'I can't get these fucking controls on low spin. Who were they, the local yokels?'

I chose to ignore the 'yokels'.

'Hayley at the shop, then there's the atheist vicar and I've just had coffee with Miss Foot – she's called Phyllis but she's rather formidable; I didn't feel I knew her well enough to call her by her first name.'

'An atheist vicar is a contradiction in terms,' Margot said. 'It looks as if there's no hand-wash on this bloody machine. We won't be able to wash cashmere.'

'Woe is me,' I mimed beating my breast. 'What a tragedy.'

'Cow!' Margot said, chucking a sweater at me. 'You were very glad of the cashmere hat and scarf I gave you for Christmas.' This was true and I felt a little chastened. She compounded this by saying, '*And* I bought you a French *tarte au citron*, since you turn up your nose at gluten-free, so you can come down for five minutes off your ever-so-superior plane.'

She was right about that. I did with her tend to take the moral high ground.

4

Margot had set off back to London and Elfine's latest adventures were still unread. To fortify myself, I made a second jug of coffee and took my mug out into the garden.

I walked past the weed-choked flower beds and the broken trellis arches to the shed where I hoped to find tools. I found it by what must have been a nursery garden, where rotting posts lurched at crazy angles from which hung remnants of nets, once there to keep marauding birds from ripening fruit, now riddled with holes large enough for flocks to fly through.

There were two sheds, tacked lopsidedly on to each other. The entrance to the larger one was laced with spiderwebs in which many mummified corpses of flies were suspended. I lifted these carefully aside with a stick. Inside, it was pitch black. A switch produced light from a bulb dangling from a wire that would have put any health and safety officer into a frenzy.

Rusty garden tools were hung or stacked neatly around the walls: spades, forks, rakes, scythes, hoes, several sieves of different sizes, a saw, an ancient straw hat, an apron, stacks of terracotta flowerpots and a weighty garden roller. I thought what a good drawing all this garden equipment would make if I hadn't got Elfine hanging over me.

The second shed had no light but with the door open I could see more flowerpots, some wooden trays, a collection of empty jam jars, bundles of raffia and several grubby envelopes, yellowed with age. I made out 'sweet peas (mixed)', 'runners', 'parsnip', 'parsley', 'calendula', but on most the writing was too faded to be legible. There was a scent of earth. The potting shed, of course.

When I came out, a rabbit feeding among the tangled nets started away and a magpie flew screeching into one of the trees. One for sorrow. There ought to be a charm to *un*learn these unhelpful sayings. You really can't live sanely in a universe governed by magpies.

As the noisy bird flew away I heard, a little way off, another sound. It was November when Margot had finally persuaded me to view Knight's Fee: a day of thin sleet and cutting wind so we had not gone as far as the sheds when we viewed the garden. There was very little then that was pleasing to the eye: a stone wall that ran one side of the garden, on the other, an overgrown yew hedge, several trees which looked as if they might bear fruit; otherwise I had only noted a hideous spotted laurel (even in my non-gardening days I disliked variegated plants) and I seem to remember some bags of frozen compost, a pile of sand and some paving stones.

The garden had been described as 'extensive' with a

small estate agent caveat: *we are advised by the vendors that the garden was formerly well stocked.* It had been enough for us that Dad's legacy would provide sufficient space in the shared house. The state of the garden, well stocked or otherwise, had been of little concern.

As I ducked through a gap in a brake of thorns, my jersey caught and ripped a hole as I pulled away, lured on by a glimmer of water just visible through a screen of vegetation.

A stream. With luck, flowering rushes and minnows and tadpoles.

I was rejoicing at nature's unlooked-for bounty when a gleam of bright turquoise arrowed past and I cried aloud at this further gift.

'The most one can reasonably ask of life,' Dad said to me once, in a rare moment of self-disclosure, 'is for it to be lit occasionally by the sight of a kingfisher.'

'Why Halcyon?' Robert asked.

'It was my father's joke because of our surname. He was a birdwatcher. Halcyon Days.' I waited for him to look enlightened.

'Sorry, I'm none the wiser.'

'It's from the Greek. Halcyon days are, well, it's a term for a period of clement weather, but it's come to mean any good or propitious period of time. It's from a legend about a bird which by tradition was a kingfisher. Dad saw a kingfisher the morning I was born.'

I didn't at the time, but I've wondered since why he was out birdwatching and not with my mother or at least at the hospital. He was a dutiful husband and a loving father so it can only have been that she had not wanted him there.

'It suits you, with that beak of a nose.'

'Oh thanks!'

'I like your nose. It makes you look like a portrait of one of the Medici.'

'My mother never liked the name.'

Our mother had wanted a boy, who was to be called Harry. A girl was to be Harriet till Dad came up with Halcyon. For once, she let him have his way. I imagine she didn't much care as I wasn't the child of her dreams. In fact, I have wondered if maybe she hadn't wanted another child at all. As far back as I can remember my parents had separate beds.

'Silly woman,' Robert said.

She was silly. She never saw what a jewel she had in Dad.

'I think it was my father's way of, I don't know, blessing me . . .' Dad wasn't in the least religious, so I didn't know what I meant by this. I have a better idea now.

'I'd like to meet your father. I like the sound of him.'

'So you shall,' I said. 'He would like you too.' At least, I hoped he would. When it came to feelings, Dad was a dark horse.

Walking back to the house, I passed the sheds and thought what a good title *The Potting Shed* would be for a book of the kind I preferred to read and how unlike the title of the current Elfine: *Elfine's Extraordinary Escapades*. Even the word 'escapade' irked me.

But my moment of reckoning with Elfine was postponed as, reaching the house, I saw I had a visitor. A big man with cropped gingerish hair and a broad cheerful face.

'My wife said you needed a hand with the garden.'

'You must be . . .?'

'Russ. Hayley's better half.' His grin implied that this was not to be taken as more than a token sop to current social politics. 'I'm no great hand at gardening but I'm happy to help get the lawns in shape. The place's been neglected since the old lady passed away. Mind you, it was pretty rundown even before. She went a bit funny upstairs with her cats.'

'What happened to the cats when she died?'

Russ sliced a finger theatrically across his throat. 'Had to be put down. Mind you, some of them never got caught. You see her old tomcat's offspring around the village. Poor creatures. Not that I'm a cat man, myself. But I didn't like to see them taken off to the gas chambers.'

'I'm afraid I haven't got a lawnmower,' I said, changing the subject. I'd been visited by a vision of Miss Foot's little black kitten under the cosh. 'I looked in the shed but there's only a roller.'

Russ went to his van and returned with a machine. 'I do the maintenance for the hedges and ditches for the Council. And the kiddies' playground. Give me grass and I know what to do with it but aside from veg that's the limit of my horticultural skills.'

'I'd be very grateful for your help with the grass, Russ. I'm overwhelmed – it's way too much for me.'

Displacing again, I turned instead to the unpacked boxes and unwrapped a china shepherdess with a chipped nose.

'She's Dresden!' Our mother's face was livid. 'Have you any idea what that's worth?'

'Was worth,' my father had added, and winked at me with one of his discreet shows of confederacy.

Margot and I had taken the forbidden china ornaments from the glass-fronted cabinet that had stood for as long as I could remember in the sitting room. Margot had taken possession of the shepherdess while I'd been obliged to make do with the shepherd. We'd argued as usual, after Margot had mocked the shepherd for his blue knee breeches, and this had led to me swiping the shepherdess with the poker and chipping her costly little nose.

Unwrapping the ornaments from the box marked 'Fragile', I wondered, not for the first time, how my parents had managed the business of living together, when, as far as I could tell, they had really only met over the supper table, and I puzzled again over how our mother had come to marry Dad.

Why he had fallen for her was easier to guess. You could see from the old photos that she had been stunning as a young woman, with a figure – she was never tired of telling us – which had earnt her a bit part in a low-budget film. Her one moment in the limelight. But Dad, twenty years older, a Classics teacher in a comprehensive school, where he struggled to keep the subject alive – unworldly, vague, what could have been the draw? It must have been that, initially at least, she was impressed by his brains. If so, it hadn't taken long for disillusion to set in. For as long as I could remember, her eyes had been gimlets of reproach. There had been no softening in old age. Even at the point of death, the eyes staring up at me as I kissed her goodbye were glints of disappointment.

By the time I was properly aware of my parents, Dad

had retreated into a fastness of his own devising, pursuing activities that his wife wouldn't find threatening but took him out of the firing line: reading, listening to the radio, gardening, rambling, birdwatching. An image of him, binoculars round his neck, the field guide to birds stuffed into his haversack, sent me back to the book box.

The field guide was somewhere near the bottom, instantly recognizable in its worn covering of Christmas-holly wrapping paper. Leafing through the illustrations, I decided the little brown bird I'd seen outside my bedroom window was either a tree or a hedge sparrow. Beside the latter, Dad had written: *'sober and unpretending'* cf. *History of British Birds* by F. O. Morris. Sober and unpretending, much like him.

I was about to search the box for this *History of British Birds* when a shout at the kitchen door returned me to the present.

'I've started on the lawn but it's that overgrown it needs a strim first. I can drop by with a strimmer this evening.'

'Thank you so much, Russ. How much do I owe you?'

'Nothing. Call it a "welcome to Hope" gift.'

'Oh, but that doesn't seem . . .'

'It's in the Council's time. I'll come back after tea, if that suits . . .?'

When Russ had gone, I took the china figures through to the kitchen to wash, ranging them along the draining board to dry. They stood, their shiny china faces dripping and impassive, offering no hint of what they had witnessed down the years. 'Why am I keeping you?' I wondered aloud.

The battered bird book set me off on one of my fits of

48

self-reproach. I should have gone with Dad when he went birdwatching. He never asked but I knew he would have liked me to. And now I wondered why I'd never accompanied him. The unhappy truth, I concluded, was that I was pandering to my mother's tacit command that she come first in anyone's affections – even if, as was the case with me, they didn't come first in hers. So Dad, who made no demands, was left soldiering on, probably lonely, a recognition which made me wince now.

The bird table and the feeders he'd had hanging in our Sheffield garden had more or less disintegrated, so I'd left them behind. *I'll get a new feeder and attract more birds to the garden*, I determined. *They can be my private memorial to Dad.*

In his last months, I used to make cheese-and-pickle sandwiches and when he was up to it we'd have a picnic lunch in the garden, on the bench which he bought when my mother died. He claimed he had bought it as a memorial to her and was always vowing to have a plaque made for it engraved with her name. He never did and I wonder if he ever learnt to be disloyal enough to recognize that the bench was more like a thanksgiving that she'd finally left him in peace. I will never know because that is the kind of thing Dad would never confide.

I hadn't brought the bench from Sheffield either and now I began to wish that I had. The fact was, I'd become resentful over the whole business of clearing the house and by the end I felt too worn down to make decisions. There were several items I'd left behind that I was regretting, as well as any amount of rubbish I'd brought because I was past caring enough to filter it. Angered all over again – with myself, with Margot and bloody Elfine – I

49

made a doorstopper of a cheese-and-pickle sandwich and went outside.

The sun was thrusting pale probing fingers through the clouds, daubing the distant hilltops with smudges of light. As I brushed past a shrub it released a scent and I paused to inspect the flowers. A fine crown of yellow around a tangle of dark crimson.

I wasted more time searching the boxes in vain for a gardening book until thoughts of Elfine began to nudge uncomfortably. This is the problem with procrastination: you don't really escape the unpleasant tasks – they lurk in corners of your mind and loom up when you least want to confront them or hang around your bed at night, looking worse and worse.

'I *must* get on,' I rebuked myself, speaking the words aloud in the hope of galvanizing my failing will. Living alone, you get to talking to yourself. I hope it will be some time before you find that out.

But where was I to work? Although we had settled for bedrooms on the second floor, the house rose to a third, reached by two sets of twisting stairs. These had been too narrow for any of the furniture we had brought, so the upper three rooms held only the lumber left by Mrs East or her ancestors. In the first was a solitary tin trunk. Opening it, I found some old maps, a box of dusty papers and a child's hairbrush. In the middle room was a dilapidated rocking horse and an old-fashioned school desk and in the third, a fire screen displaying a bunch of variegated flowers worked in wool, two wooden tennis rackets and a basket that stank of cat.

I decided to make my quarters in the rocking-horse

room, which hosted the most light. The school desk was too low to be useful but I'd noted a folding table tucked away in a cupboard and the stairs were not too narrow to bring up Dad's oak desk chair. It would be cold below the rafters, but there was a socket for an electric heater and if my feet got cold – as they tended to while I worked – there were my trusty fisherman's socks.

A butterfly, its wings patterned like a tiny exquisite Persian carpet, flitted out from some dark corner and began to flap frantically against the windowpane. I shoved hard at the window, hurting my wrist in the effort to open it, but it was stuck fast.

I was downstairs in the pantry, hunting for some instrument to prise open the window, when there was a gentle tapping at the back door.

A young man, slight, dark-haired, bearded, shabbily but neatly dressed, with a scarlet muffler round his neck.

'It is about the notice in the shop.'

A foreign accent, though clearly with a fair command of English. *Maybe this is Young reliable man, able to do odd jobs. Good refs.* 'Yes?'

'I can help.'

'Oh good. Well, come in.'

I took him through to the kitchen, where he sat looking uneasily down at his feet.

'My shoes. I am not so sure they are very clean.'

'Don't worry. The floor is filthy. We've only just moved in.'

'It is you and your husband here?'

'Me and my sister. She works in London so I'm in charge of the garden. You know about gardens?' It seemed unlikely.

'I read books. I learn.'

'OK, good,' I said, trying not to sound discouraging. Again, he inspected his sandals. 'Where are you from, I mean originally?' I asked, hoping this didn't sound hostile.

'I am from Albania.'

Robert and I had once stopped in Albania to see the ancient site of Butrint on our way to Greece. The town where we stayed for the night was dingy and depressing, built in the old Communist mould, but I did recall a restaurant where the food was wonderful and the service friendly. 'I went there once.'

'Yes?' He sounded pleased.

'I enjoyed it.' He looked again at his feet as if unwilling to confront me with this lie. 'But the garden,' I said. 'Do you think you could really . . .?'

'Yes.' His eyes were painfully sincere.

There seemed nothing for it but to take him round the garden with the pretence that I believed he knew what was what.

'I dig these out?' he suggested, pointing to a clump of withered chrysanthemum stalks.

'I don't think so, not those.'

'But this here is good?'

'Not really, I *think* that's woody nightshade. It's poisonous.' He frowned and I said, 'There are lots of things my sister and I need help with. It doesn't have to be the garden.'

'I can help you with the garden.'

'Yes, I'm sure.'

'You may ask Miss Foot.'

'I'm sure there's no need but . . .'

'I am very cheap.'

I know what it is to sell yourself cheap. I began to have a fellow feeling. 'I'm so sorry, I forgot to ask your name. I should have said, I'm Hassie.'

'I am Murat.'

There was something formal in his speech and I found myself uncharacteristically formal in return. 'I am pleased to meet you, Murad.'

'It is Murat. With the "t".' Emphasizing the consonant, he revealed impressive teeth.

'I'm so sorry, Murat.'

I offered my hand, which he took with both of his and cupped it fervently. 'Hassie, is a common name?'

'It's Halcyon, really. It means, well, nowadays it sort of means a happy, peaceful time.'

'My name means "wish".'

'Then we both have promising names.'

'Promising . . .?'

'Hopeful. Good times.'

'Good times? Yes.' He smiled eagerly, again revealing the dazzling teeth.

Oh dear, I thought, *I expect I'll regret this but there seems no help for it.* 'So, Murat, how much do you charge?'

5

While Margot was off in London, I busied myself cleaning the house. I like cleaning – I find it therapeutic and as many artists will tell you (writers too, I am told) it makes for a wonderful displacement activity to avoid getting down to work. By the time Margot arrived back I'd seen off most of the cobwebs, polished all the furniture and washed all the uncarpeted floors.

She was back on Thursday evening bringing some rugs, several lamps, a coffee machine, a steamer, a NutriBullet and various beauty aids.

'My God, it's dusty here,' was her first comment, which annoyed me given the hard work I'd put in.

'I couldn't hoover. We're out of dust bags.'

'I'm thinking of getting a Dyson,' was all she said to that.

'Haven't you brought enough technology into the house? It's Jacobean, remember. What's that?' I asked, inspecting one of the devices.

'It's a sonic toothbrush. It whitens the teeth.'

Which brought Murat to mind. 'By the way, I've found a gardener.'

'One of the local yokels?'

'No. He's Albanian.'

'What's he doing here?'

'Much the same as us, I guess.' I had begun to fear that every arrival of Margot was going to produce this assault on my nerves.

'We're not looking for work. I assume he is.'

'Well, I've given him work.'

'Not full-time, I hope.'

'Of course not full-time.'

'Don't snap at me, Hass. It's a perfectly reasonable question. Look, I had these which are too big for my flat. They'll be perfect here.' She laid out a couple of rugs – one a silvery blue, the other faded rose and moss green. Margot did have taste.

'You have a great eye, Marg,' I said, feeling remorseful.

She looked pleased. She's lovely when she smiles. I must tell you, jealousy could make me unfair.

As if to confirm this, Margot produced a silver table lamp with a blue silk shade. 'I thought you might like this. You can have the blue rug too.'

'Oh Marg.' Compunction made me go across to kiss her – we didn't often kiss in our family. 'You smell divine.'

'Jo Malone. It's her new fragrance.'

'The vicar told me about a scent called Mown Hay.'

'Is he gay?'

'I shouldn't think so. He looks straight as a ruler. He used to buy it for his wife. He's a widower.'

'Aha! And he told you?'

'Marg!' I could tell what was crossing her mind.

'There are worse fates than being a vicar's wife.'

'He's pretty obviously still in mourning,' I said, hoping to nip this in the bud. 'He was clearly very attached to his wife. He spoke of her most fondly.'

Margot smiled her annoying knowing smile. 'All the more reason for him to need a replacement.'

I furnished the attic room with the blue rug and the baize-topped card table discovered in one of the cupboards, a little wobbly but perfectly functional once I'd secured the legs with tape. I had Dad's desk chair, my old Anglepoise for close work and Margot's silver lamp with the blue silk shade. The latter I placed on a nest of tables which had come from the sitting room in the Sheffield house and which Margot had rejected as 'twee'.

The lamp illuminated a painting I'd hung on the chimney breast: a young woman standing at an easel wearing a blue gown. The painting, by a Dutch artist, had been given me by Robert. 'She reminds me of you,' he had said.

'She's got her back to us. You can't tell what she looks like.'

'You were wearing that air-blue colour when we met. But it's her back that reminds me of you. Backs are very distinctive. Haven't you noticed?'

After that I did notice. Robert himself, when naked, had a particularly pleasing back.

I had planned to hang the painting in my bedroom, where, when I moved back there, it had hung in the

Sheffield house. But the attic was more private. Margot, who had dismissed the attic rooms as 'terrible' for her allergies, was unlikely to bother to often climb those stairs.

I havered over where to put Margot's lamp but the blue of the shade matched the girl's gown. I sometimes wondered if Margot ever wondered about Robert but I could never ask.

The first dove had fluttered off and another had descended and taken its place.

'The doves seem to like you,' he suggested.

'They can't both be the Holy Ghost,' I said, referring to his first remark.

'Maybe the Holy Ghost has multiplied. Maybe it's a case of parthenogenesis.'

The second dove gently deposited a gobbet of shit on to the sleeve of my blue silk dress. (I had hesitated about buying it – it was over my usual budget – but I was inwardly congratulating myself now that I had.) We both burst out laughing. 'I think that settles it,' I suggested.

'Who says the Holy Ghost can't have a functioning digestive system?'

'In that case it could hardly be a ghost, surely,' I said, trying and failing to find a tissue with which to clean my sleeve.

'Have you ever wondered why it's called the Holy Ghost?' he asked, taking my arm. 'Here, have this.' He handed me a handkerchief. 'I mean, why "ghost"?' he continued, steering me expertly by the elbow. 'Let's find another drink. I don't know about you but I'm allergic to cheap champagne.'

'Allergic?' I wondered if I dare keep the handkerchief but could think of no way of discreetly pocketing it.

'Not clinically. I mean I dislike the stuff. I suppose people feel they have to have it at weddings. But I'd have thought better of Alistair.'

'It's Catherine's parents who've organized the wedding.' I had met Catherine's mother – openly jubilant that her wheelchair-bound daughter was marrying at last – and had felt insulted on Catherine's behalf.

'I'd have thought at their age they'd dispense with all that faff. But people revert, don't they, at weddings and funerals? It's an archetype.'

'I suppose they do.' I wasn't sure what an archetype was. 'It's Alistair whom you know, then?' I asked, beginning to feel a thread of panic that my conversational resources would run dry. I wanted to stay talking to this man as long as possible.

'Yes. And you . . .?'

'I'm here because of Catherine.'

'I'm glad for him. He was miserable after his first wife died. He's so eligible he was besieged by predatory women, and we all feared for him. But she seems just right. And I gather she's very talented.'

'Oh yes.' Catherine was firmer ground. 'She's a very bright star in the children's literature firmament. But not at all up herself.'

'I should hope not. If she were, I would have to rescue Alistair.'

'I hope you won't have to do that.'

He had secured white wine for me and for himself a

glass of whisky, and to my delight seemed content to continue talking. 'I gather her MS comes and goes.'

I couldn't help recalling the upright young woman I had met on my very first commission. The horrible disease seemed to be more coming than going these days. 'It's a while since she's been able to walk. It's a dreadful disease.'

Beguiled by his interest, I said more than I had intended and in my maddening way I flushed.

'And what is it that you do?' he asked as I was searching about for something clever or witty to say to change the subject. I didn't think it quite right to discuss Catherine's medical condition with a stranger.

'I illustrate her books.'

'Ah, I've heard about you. You have that unusual name.'

'It's a nuisance sometimes. People always say *What?* And then make me spell it.' Now I feared I sounded prissy.

'It's a beautiful name,' he declared. And added, 'It suits you.'

When I next visited the shop, Hayley said, 'Did you get any takers for your ad?'

'Yes, thank you. I think you can take the ad down.'

'Who've you hired?'

But when I told her, she looked rather too obviously non-committal. 'He's got good references,' I said, feeling a little defensive. 'He says Miss Foot will vouch for him.'

'Right. I suppose if Miss Foot . . .'

I hadn't in fact checked these references, so I took the

opportunity to stroll up to the house with the thatched porch and the green door.

Miss Foot seemed pleased to see me. 'Come in. Shut up, Alfred! I'll throw him out.'

'Oh, don't on my account.'

'He'll just bark his head off. Coffee?'

When she returned from the kitchen with a tray, I was re-examining the drawings of plants and flowers that hung on one of the walls of her sitting room. 'Are these yours?'

Miss Foot set down the tray and came slightly ponderously over to join me. 'I like the discipline of copying nature. Or did before my hands became too arthritic. It's her design that I most respect. That seed head, for example.'

Squinting at the fine brown-ink script, I deciphered *Nigella*.

'Commonly known as love-in-a-mist. A heavenly blue and a generous plant. It self-seeds so one need never sow more than once.'

'It grows in the garden at Knight's Fee,' I said, resuming my seat in the shell chair. The black kitten was sitting by the hearth, paws neatly together. He had closed his eyes and was perfectly still, like a little cat effigy carved in stone. 'There're masses of those seed heads in the garden.'

'Knight's Fee has a splendid garden. Or did. Nelly was a great gardener but towards the end she let it run down. With a bit of labour it will come back.'

'That's what my sister, Margot, says. But she expects me to see to it.'

Miss Foot glanced at me. 'So you're the Martha?'

'If you mean that I usually end up doing the hard work. But I've hired someone called Murat to help me. He gave you as a reference.'

Miss Foot seemed to know all about Murat. 'He's a very decent young man and most conscientious. An Albanian is rather a fish out of water in Hope Wenlock, though I gather his family have settled in Corfu. Brexit hasn't helped but he seems to want to stay here.'

'I wondered how much he knew about gardening.'

Miss Foot glanced at me again and I saw that her eyes, which were rather small and hidden under the folds of wrinkles, were a hazelish-green. 'He's very willing. I am sure he will learn. I can lend you books if you wish.'

'That would be very kind.' I'd been cursing that Dad's gardening books had been among those I'd passed on to Oxfam.

My new friend went across to a laden bookshelf. 'I've wild-flower books too if you'd like to borrow any.'

I had a better grasp of wild flowers. 'I know quite a few through the Flower Fairy books.'

Miss Foot's face assumed an expression which I came to recognize. 'I don't entirely disapprove of them as they teach children about flowers. It's the illustrations I don't care for. Those winsome little fairies. Quite unreal.' She handed me a couple of books. 'That is a good basic book. And the other might be useful if you decide to revive the vegetable garden.'

I never got to open the attic window and when I next went up there the lovely Persian-carpet butterfly had died.

Its papery corpse lay on the window ledge, wings precisely folded back, showing their funereal underside. I was reluctant to sweep the delicate body away but disliked this visible reminder that everything passes.

'Isn't it terribly valuable?' I had asked Robert of the painting.

'No more than you are. In fact, *you* are invaluable.'

'Don't,' I begged. 'I don't like it when you exaggerate.'

'Why do you suppose that's exaggeration? You're my girl in the air-blue gown, the love of my life. And will be as long as I live.'

'Please, Robert, don't,' I said again. 'That makes me think of death. You might die.'

'Naturally I'll die, silly.'

'But you might before I do.'

'I expect I shall. I'm older than you.'

'I don't want to think of that.'

I left the butterfly corpse where it lay and got down to work.

Elfine had acquired a friend, Eloise, as insufferable as Elfine. I had already mentally changed her name to Elsie. Elsie was at least a down-to-earth name. Elfine's features and elfin costume were too well established to be altered without protests from her many young fans. But Eloise offered scope for artistic licence.

I was experimenting with sticking-out ears when Margot yelled, 'Are you coming down for lunch?'

'Just coming,' I bellowed back. The ears made Eloise look like Minnie Mouse. Unlikely that would be acceptable to the publishers.

'Are you coming?' Margot shouted again.

Only family members, I thought, running downstairs, *roar at each other like this.*

'Lunch isn't quite ready.' Margot was stirring soup. 'But your Romanian's here so I needed you to come and tell him what to do.'

'Albanian, not Romanian. I hope you were nice to him.'

'I'm always "nice".'

I didn't bother to contest this. 'Did you offer him tea or coffee or anything?'

'I was waiting for you. What are we paying him, by the way?'

'Seven pounds an hour,' I said smoothly and went into the garden.

Murat's plea of cheapness and his look of expecting rejection had led to my offering ten pounds an hour: London rates. Margot, if she were told this, would demur and I didn't want to have to defend my decision.

'You only do it to be thought well of,' Margot had said once, when, after a dinner of exceptionally poor service, I had left ten pounds which I could ill afford.

'I've been a waitress. I know how it feels.'

'It's a picture of yourself,' Margot said. 'Lady Bountiful. I wouldn't mind, it's your money, but speaking as your sister I'd rather you spent it on yourself.'

Murat was examining the long weed-ridden flower bed. Russ had been as good as his word and returned with a strimmer and followed this up with the Council's mower to give the grass what he called 'a first pass'. He had kindly helped me rub down a few of the less rusty garden tools and oiled the secateurs. I led Murat to the shed and pointed out the spade and fork and the wheelbarrow.

'Do you have any boots, Murat?' He was wearing open-toed sandals with no socks. 'Only, the beds will be muddy.'

He shrugged and shook his head.

'Maybe I . . . perhaps you wouldn't mind if I got you some wellingtons to be getting on with?'

'Wellingtons?'

'Boots to protect your feet. We don't want you chopping off your toes by mistake.'

I can't think what made me say this. That sort of heavy-handed humour is not like me at all. I suppose I was feeling awkward in the role of employer.

A look of alarm flashed across his face and hastily I said, 'Sorry, a silly joke. But look, if you know your foot size I can zip into the village and get some boots.'

He bent down, unlatched a sandal and balancing effortlessly on one leg wordlessly handed the sandal to me. Size 44, which I reckoned was 9 in British sizes.

'Would it be OK then if I went and got you some boots? I'm worried about your feet getting so cold and, well, muddy.'

I couldn't read from his expressionless face how he was reacting to this probably incomprehensible request. Still standing heronlike, on one leg, he bowed his head, as if surrendering to some unfathomable foreign ritual, and carefully replaced the sandal. 'Where would you like I start?'

'Maybe the long bed, where you were looking.'

We walked back to the flower bed and I pointed out some of the more obvious weeds. 'That's bindweed,' I explained. Bindweed, along with ground elder, had pretty well taken over the garden and had a stranglehold on the few surviving plants. 'And see there, Murat, those dead-looking plants with the bindweed round them, they're probably flowers, so if you could unwind the bindweed and dig around them. I don't know myself what they are. We shall have to wait and see.'

'Wait and see?' He smiled at this, showing the excellent teeth. 'I like wait and see.'

'He needs boots,' I explained to Margot. 'Can I borrow the Lexus to pop into the village?'

'The soup's ready!'

'It'll take about ten minutes there and back, and he's wearing open-toed sandals with bare feet. Apart from anything else, he'll freeze.'

'He might prefer his sandals. Have you thought of that?'

'We don't want him injuring himself.' Margot's firm had recently been sued by a cleaner whose leg had been damaged by an industrial vacuum, so I added, 'We're not insured.'

'OK. But hurry up. I'm starving.'

The trip to the village took longer than predicted. I called at the village shop – mostly to advertise the fact that I was making a local purchase – and was directed by Hayley to the hardware store.

'Brian there does wellies and you might get socks at "A Stitch".'

The hardware shop was full of the distinctive scent of brushes and doormats peculiar to such stores. Waiting while Brian was in the back room, I wondered again why it was so enticing. He emerged, waving a pair of green wellingtons. 'You're in luck, these are our last. I could only find one of the pair to start with but I tracked down the other in a size 7 box.'

The visit to 'A Stitch in Time' took longer.

A middle-aged woman, with the soft, over-powdered cheeks that always put me in mind of the fuzz on a peach, explained that she was not the owner, that the owner, Mrs Manning, was up in Manchester visiting her son and that she herself was not too familiar with the stock. I could tell she was one of those women who never stop talking. My attempt to get away was thwarted further when she insisted on phoning the owner to see if she could assist. Politeness obliged me to wait while at the other end of the line the owner went into an account about her son before getting around to the subject of socks.

'He's doing a PhD in Engineering,' the assistant, whose name I'd gathered was Iris, explained. 'She's ever so proud of him. Still fusses over him as if he was a school-boy.' She blinked nervously, sensing a possible disloyalty, and added, 'Oh, and Mrs Manning says we only do ladies' socks but to try Debs down the hill at Greenaways. She sells handicrafts.'

Greenaways was part of a terrace of drab, fifties-looking houses in the lower, less picturesque, part of the village. A young woman opened the door and I intro-duced myself and explained.

'I do sell hand-knits but not socks. But come inside and look if you'd like to.'

Diplomacy suggested that I say 'I'd love to' and I was

shown into a room where pottery mugs, knitted scarfs and bobble hats and a range of scented candles impressed with dried flowers were displayed. The walls were hung with some garish paintings executed in thick oils.

Looking about for a tolerable item, I hesitated over a candle.

'The candles aren't local. Everything else is.'

I assured her that I'd much rather buy something local and found I was staring at an oil rendering of a hillside. Clotted-cream sheep were distributed in blobs among rocks and hollows painted in unnatural shades of emerald and mauve.

'That's by our local artist. He paints in the Primitive style. Brilliant, isn't it?'

I agreed that it was remarkable and settled on a lumpen mug decorated with a crude depiction of a rabbit.

I found the Lexus being inspected by a gang of children. As I drew nearer, a small girl with white-blonde hair shouted, 'This yours, miss?'

Panting, because in my anxiety to get back to Murat and the garden I'd been hurrying, I said, 'It's my sister's. I borrowed it to buy some things from the village.' I don't know why I should have bothered to explain myself except that there was something commanding about the girl.

She stared at me pityingly. 'You'd do best to go to Shrewsbury.' She pronounced it as it is spelt, to rhyme with shoe.

'I prefer to shop locally,' I said, rather put out.

This got short shrift. 'The shops here are rubbish.'

One of the boys laughed rudely and another asked, 'Are you the lady's moved into Mrs East's house?'

'Yes.'

'She was mad.'

'Bonkers!' another boy said. He glanced anxiously at the first girl as if for reassurance he had said the right thing.

The girl, who had a pale, sharp-featured face and purple knees covered in scabs, nodded approval. 'She was crazy. She thought there were fairies at the bottom of her garden. Cray-*zee*,' she said again and as if at a signal the other children began to chant 'cray-*zee*, cray-*zee*' and laugh hysterically.

'Well,' I said, 'that isn't a nice thing to say. And I can assure you my sister and I aren't mad.'

I pushed past to get into the car and banged the door hard, a gesture which was wasted as the metal seat-belt clasp caught in the door so that I had to open it and bang it shut again.

I could hear the gang of children screeching with laughter and yelling demonically as I drove away. After trying so hard to demonstrate loyalty to my new location, I couldn't help feeling rather hurt.

When I got back, I found that Murat had dug over almost half the long flower bed.

'Goodness, Murat. That's amazing. You have done well!'

Among the weeds piled into the wheelbarrow were some clumps of what looked like perennials. But I said nothing. It would be more fun anyway to plant my own choice of flowers.

I presented him with the boots, which he accepted

solemnly, stood them neatly side by side on the lawn and continued to dig in his sandals.

'I hope I haven't offended him,' I said back in the kitchen. 'He's not put the boots on.'

Margot had finished her lunch and was doing the crossword. 'I did ring but you'd left your phone behind. Where did you get that awful mug?' – peering into my bag – 'The pottery's so thick there's no room for any drink inside.'

I had predicted this reaction and had been attempting to conceal the mug. 'Don't be such a snob, Marg. I bought it from a woman in the village – it's important we keep in with them.' In fact, I was annoyed with myself about the boots. I have a habit of giving things. I don't know why I do this as it often offends and very few people respond well to generosity.

'Anyway,' I went on defensively, 'I was obviously wrong. He's dug a hell of a lot of that bed. And in a very short time.'

'He's wiry,' Margot said. 'They get that way in the old commie countries. It's the discipline. Can you do this: *Dance with a sailor before everyone turns up*, ten letters?'

'He's from Corfu,' I said, 'which has never, as far as I know, been Communist, and you know I loathe puzzles.' The encounter with the local children had ruffled me and I was nettled at Margot's indifference to my efforts to win over the village.

I had finished the soup and was washing up when Margot, who had abandoned the crossword and was idly picking at candle grease on the kitchen table, announced, 'Oh, by the way, I've invited some people here for Easter.'

'Who? The house isn't nearly ready for guests.'

'I've ordered some beds – don't worry, they're on me. And I thought we could make the room next to the drawing room into a dining room. I've some sconces back at the flat I picked up ages ago in the Portobello Road. They'd go brilliantly there – we could eat by candlelight. *Très* romantic, *non?*'

'Fine,' I said in the brisk voice I adopt when she's being affected. It was the first I'd heard of any sitting room of ours referred to as a 'drawing room'. 'It'll be you not me having dinner parties. And the answer's *tarantella*, by the way.' I was about to sweep out with a rare feeling of triumph but was halted by a troubling intuition. 'Who is it you've invited?'

But in a split second I'd divined the answer.

6

Catherine put down the phone extension in her garden studio and said, 'That was Alistair wondering if you'd like to join us. We've got Robert Aitken coming for lunch.'

We had been going over the illustrations for Catherine's latest book, a story based around the Lollards and the anti-clerical movement in medieval England. There had been some uncertainty about the clothes I had drawn for the story's principal character, a boy called Ned whose family were not of the Lollard party.

There was never any tension in these discussions. We both enjoyed the animated to-and-fros and these recces, as Catherine called them, often continued long after a technical point had been resolved. Although I'd arrived just after nine that Saturday morning, by then it was almost one o'clock.

'Yes, sure,' I said, 'love to,' and hoped my face showed nothing more than polite pleasure at the invitation. The wedding had been months ago and I had heard nothing from Robert Aitken.

He had arrived already when I wheeled Catherine across the gravel to the house. I heard Alistair say something and then a deeper voice answer, which my body told me at once was Robert's. Both men laughed and I was instantly sure that Alistair was warning him of my arrival and that the laughter was about me. That this was not the case was apparent from the shock on Robert's face when I entered the room. He covered it over quickly, though not before he had noticed me clock it, and said, 'Well, well. The Holy Ghost at work again.'

'What's this about the Holy Ghost?' Catherine glanced between us.

Some instinct made me move swiftly into the accord that Robert and I learnt later to rely on. 'Just a silly joke we shared when we met at your wedding.'

'You aren't religious, for Christ's sake, are you, Hassie?' Alistair was a little drunk.

Robert and I exchanged a look and I discerned from this that he was feeling relief. Quite what was behind this feeling I wasn't sure, but I had already recognized that in an as yet undisclosed way Robert and I were in something together.

'Not at all,' I said. 'Just a bit of banter.'

The lunch was long, involving several bottles of wine, and afterwards we lingered in the garden. Other than his reference to the Holy Ghost, Robert directed only a few polite questions at me and appeared otherwise engaged in discussing with Alistair a walking holiday they were planning together in the Scottish Highlands.

'I'm glad Al has a walking companion,' Catherine confided. 'I don't want him feeling tied to my side.'

'Robert seems nice,' I tentatively suggested. To my annoyance, I felt myself blush.

Catherine glanced at me but all she said was, 'I hardly know him. Al's very fond of him. They're fellow Scots.'

Robert and Alistair were still deep in conversation in the garden when it was time for me to leave to catch my train. I gave a designedly casual wave in their direction, kissed Catherine goodbye and set off to walk to the station. I was slightly tipsy from the wine.

As I was about to cross the bridge to reach the station platform, a car drew up beside me and Robert wound down the window. 'Hop in. I'm taking you where you're going.'

'You don't know where I'm going.'

'Doesn't matter. I'm taking you there.' I climbed into the car. 'Where, so I can set the satnav?'

'It might be miles out of your way.' Against my own desire, I felt a weird need to put him off.

'England's not that large a country unless you're going to tell me you live in Gretna Green. *Do* you live in Gretna Green?'

This was delivered in such an accusing tone that I laughed. 'I live in Bethnal Green.'

'Slightly more convenient. If the M40's clear, we'll be there in under two hours.'

After a while I asked, 'Where do you live, if Bethnal Green isn't out of your way?'

'Did I say it wasn't out of my way?'

'No, but . . .'

'Are you going to challenge everything I say?'

'That depends.'

'And you seemed such an accommodating woman when we met at the wedding. Don't tell me I've been mis-led.' He always had the knack of making me laugh.

'Probably.'

Now it was he who laughed. As the car swung on to the motorway, he said, 'I live in London too. The other side but it's no big deal and it's pleasant to have company on a drive.'

'Yes,' I agreed, disappointed if this was to be all.

We drove some distance down the M40 till he said, 'I'm not being honest. I wanted to see you again. I hope you don't mind.'

'There's something I need to say,' he said.

We were sitting up in bed in my Bethnal Green flat. Robert had bought wine when we stopped for petrol at a filling station and we were draining the last of it.

'OK.'

'I have to say it now or I'll put it off and the chances are then I'll never say it at all.'

I was praying that this was going to be no more than, say, a case of chronic snoring or at worst a job that took him overseas. 'OK.'

'I'm married. And I'm never going to leave my wife. She's older than me and she took me on when I was a pretty shiftless young man with a criminal record and made me what I am today.'

I didn't say that I didn't have a clue what it was that he was today.

'She's my best friend as well as my former agent. She built a career for me as an artist –' so that's why he knew who I was, I thought – 'and everything I am and own I owe to her.'

This seemed definitive, if not – I inwardly recognized – unexpected. Very attractive men of a certain age tend to be married.

'It's fine,' I said and very probably smiled. 'I quite understand. And you can count on my discretion.' I began to clamber out of the bed but he pulled me back.

'No, listen. Please. It's like this.' He paused, apparently sorting out his thoughts. 'I love Laura but I'm not in love with her. I'm not sure I ever was. I was dazzled, amazed that this clever, sophisticated, *very* attractive –' why must he emphasize *that*? I thought crossly – 'older woman took an interest in me when I had a pretty low opinion of myself. I never want to hurt her – I know that's the kind of banal thing tossers say about their wives – but I don't. Since I'm coming clean, you should know that I did have an affair and Laura found out about it. I didn't exactly promise never to do it again but, well, her distress was pretty devastating, to me as well as obviously to her, and I really did feel as if I truly never wanted to do it again. Then I met you at the wedding and something, I don't know, clicked.'

I don't remember what I said to that. Nothing, probably. I seem to recall I was feeling strangely blank throughout this confession.

'Call me a coward but I walked away from it and from you. I asked Catherine, when I went to visit them soon after, very discreetly about you and she said that as well as being her best illustrator –'

'I'm her *only* illustrator,' I objected.

75

'OK – her only – but she clearly rates you highly as an artist and she also said what a very sweet person you were and how you had become a dear friend.'

'I don't know about "sweet".'

'Could you possibly shut up for five minutes while I get this off my chest and then you can say what you like, throw bricks at me, walk out . . .'

'I can hardly walk out of my own flat, unless you're thinking of squatting here.'

As I said this, a police car went by with its siren on full blast and we both started to speak at once.

'Sorry,' he said. 'You go ahead.'

'Nothing,' I said. 'I was only going to ask how long it will take you to get home. But by all means do go on with what you were saying . . .'

In the ensuing silence I could still hear the fading sound of the siren.

'Oh look, forget it,' he said. 'This was stupid of me. I'm sorry.' He got out of bed and stood there naked, his back to me. 'Would you mind if I took a shower?'

'There's a spare towel in the cupboard over there.' I spoke as coldly as I could. In those days, I had a notion that dignity mattered.

When he came out of the bathroom, his hair wet from the shower, I had dressed in a pair of very old trousers and a T-shirt stained with paint. 'Now you've decided to try and make yourself look unattractive.'

This was true, so I said, 'You don't know anything about me.'

He ignored this and said, 'It hasn't worked.'

'Robert,' I said. 'Please. Just go. It's fine. It's all fine, really.' I honestly believe I believed I meant this. 'We can forget about this. It's not important. But *please just go.*'

I was so heartened by what Murat had done in the garden that I spent the following morning digging out more weeds. I found this surprisingly enjoyable. Apart from the satisfaction of lifting deep-rooted clods of grass and winkling out the strangling bindweed, digging and hacking at dandelion roots did wonders for my pent-up destructive urges. I felt strangely calm after I'd bored down to the tips of their devilishly tenacious roots and wrested them out of the ground. Then there were the worms. Their pale-pink presence toiling through the earth was curiously gratifying. *There's a whole life there, beneath the world's surface, that I knew nothing of,* I thought. This isn't exactly a novel idea but it was new to me then.

'The garden's teeming with worms,' I told Margot when I came in, filthy but pleasantly tired and thoroughly pleased with myself.

'Fascinating.'

'Worms are good. They aerate the earth.'

'Thank you, David Attenborough.'

'Knight's Fee obviously has a reputation as a five-star worm Airbnb.'

Margot afforded me the faint smile she kept for jokes she didn't consider the slightest bit funny and continued studying a paint chart. 'How about one of these Georgian reds for the dining room?'

'But the house isn't Georgian. If anything it's either Jacobean or 1970s.' (I haven't explained yet that there's a rather ugly 1970s element to the house, which the Easts must have had tacked on in the days before planning officers ruled the roost.) I braced myself for what I guessed was about to be a battle.

'So? It's all kinds of styles so it can be any colour scheme. And red is so warm for dining.'

'I like plain white. White all through. Simple, plain white,' I added, deciding to be obdurate. I didn't want Margot feeling she could just take over.

'One, plain white is extremely dull and two, it's cold. This house needs warmth.'

'We can give it that with your rugs and things. You can put anything with white and it's easy to redecorate. And if you want something a bit different, we can use whitewash. I've heard it produces a lovely patina.' I was hoping that 'patina' would add panache to these claims.

'You can whitewash your bedroom. And your study. I'm painting mine yellow. It's conducive to thought. And before you start jeering, there's loads of scientific evidence for the effect on us of colour.'

I had been about to challenge 'scientific evidence' when it hit me that she was right. I used not to jeer. At least, I think I didn't.

'Perhaps,' I said instead, 'we could each take some of the rooms and do them up our own way?'

'I don't know. If I take the dining room you'll want the sitting room, won't you? That would be grim all white. Like a tomb.'

'You're thinking of whited sepulchres. They're white on the outside, not the inside. But you can have the sitting and dining rooms both.' I didn't really care that much about the colour of the walls; it was that I felt it prudent to peg out some safe territory for myself.

'If you're sure,' Margot said and went on hurriedly, forestalling a possible change of heart on my part. 'Tell you what, you paint the kitchen and the pantry. They're more your area and they won't look bad in white.'

In the months after my relationship with Robert ended, I would torment myself by wondering if I might have been better off letting him walk away that first night. What had averted this alternative outcome was my incorrigible curiosity.

As Robert was saying a muted goodbye at the door, and I had just delivered a designedly indifferent response, I was overcome by a desire to hear about the criminal past he had mentioned. I tried to bite it back but couldn't resist asking, 'What had you done that was criminal that your wife saved you from?'

For a moment he looked puzzled, as if he couldn't himself recall the occasion, and then said, 'Nothing heinous. A bloke I did some work for refused to pay me. I was livid – I was desperately poor at the time and reckoned I'd done a good job for him – so I broke into his house and stole his chequebook and wrote myself out the fee he had promised, plus a bit more, which was a mistake. I think if I'd stuck to the agreed sum nothing would have happened but, as it was, he called the police and I got clobbered when I tried to cash the cheque.'

'That sounds unfair,' I said, unaware that treacherous sympathies were mustering within.

'It was. Bloody unfair. But it was my word against his and he was a respectable gallery owner – I did the catalogue for an exhibition for him – and I was a mendicant nobody. I was given a suspended sentence but it still goes on your record. Why? Did you hope for something more glamorous?'

'Cold-blooded murder at the very least,' I said, fatally, as it turned out, because having once abandoned a defensive posture it is almost impossible to recover it.

By Sunday afternoon Murat and I between us had cleared the whole of the long bed. Even the ground elder seemed to have gone (although I was to learn that this was merely my horticultural innocence). The surviving plants, freed of weeds, looked frail and pallid, like people who had suffered a long sickness. The only ones I recognized were some ancient-looking roses, grown woody and leggy, and a few malformed hyacinths which had struggled up from hibernation and were poking warily above the earth. The tangled yellow shrub with the subtle scent, I learnt from Miss Foot's book, was a witch hazel, the species *Hamamelis vernalis* which, the book informed me, blooms in early spring. I liked the idea of witch hazel. *I'll buy more*, I thought. *I'll buy its winter-flowering colleague. And I'll buy a proper herbal.*

Russ had left a corner of the lawn unmown. He had strimmed it until he came on a crop of daffodils hidden in the long grass. Pale angelic blooms nodding on slender stems and brassier gold trumpets were now lightening that part of the lawn in a concert of yellows.

'There's been snowdrops here too.' Russ had pointed out the fine-cut, grey-green leaves. 'And I reckon other bulbs. I came here as a lad – in those days the family had a springtide fête affair for us locals. The edges of the lawns

I remember as a mass of bulbs. Crocuses and those little yellow fellows, I forget the name.'

'Aconites,' Margot said. She had come out to inspect. 'They're used in homoeopathy for anxiety if you're sallow-skinned. You should try it, Hass. That bed looks very bare.'

'There are plenty of plants in there,' I said, deciding that in this new environment I would become Zen and develop the art of patience. 'We'll have to wait till they flower to see what they are.'

But I liked the bare earth. The smell when it was newly turned put me in a contented frame of mind. I watched a portion of pale-pink worm, followed by a thicker purple portion, disappear into a patch of earth and an orange centipede emerge. The centipede made its way purposefully on speedy ticklish legs. What was its purpose? Did centipedes have a purpose? *Why not?* I thought. *Why shouldn't centipedes have a purpose every bit as much as we have? Or haven't*, I mentally amended.

'By the way,' Margot said, 'there's an offer in the *Sunday Times* this morning for camellias. You should plant some of those. They're winter-flowering and the colours are divine.'

That evening, Margot left for London. I'd been looking forward to some solitude, imagining myself settling down to a reposeful evening of cheese and biscuits and a book. *I'll embark on Walter Scott*, I had thought. But as is often the case with plans, in the event this wasn't what I found I wanted after all. I'd unpacked the Walter Scotts and the Dickens and Thackeray, but *Ivanhoe* was very heavy going.

I tried *Martin Chuzzlewit*, one of the few Dickens that I'd never got round to, but that bored me too. Altogether, I felt edgy and restless and drifted from room to room futilely rearranging things. *I have too many pointless things*, I said to myself. *I should be rid of them unless they're useful or beautiful.* (This, by the way, while a praiseworthy maxim, is for some reason impracticable.)

I attempted a fire in the sitting room but the paper simply flared up and died away and the kindling failed to catch. 'Chimney sweep' was on the list of 'things to do' that Margot had left me with. I unpacked one of the boxes of poetry but was then unsure where to put the books – and ended up repacking them less efficiently than before so that some were left spilt out untidily on the carpet. Even leafing through one of Dad's several copies of Housman, his favourite poet, didn't soothe me. It reminded me of the time I took him to the Stoppard play at the National with the brilliant Paul Rhys as the young Housman. The heart-breaking lines to Moses Jackson rang in my mind – and I had to put the book away. I was too familiar with what it meant to go *with half a life about my ways*.

This set me off on a train of thought that I knew would not end well so I went upstairs to my attic study, deciding that I might as well throw myself into work.

It was cold in the attic. I'd installed the fan heater brought from Sheffield, which we'd used there as a standby in case of frozen pipes. As I switched it on, there was a violent crack and all the lights went out.

There was no torch to hand and with no street lights outside the house was completely dark. Swearing loudly, to keep off any phantom bogles, I eased my way on my bottom down the narrow stairs.

The lights on the second floor had also blown. Margot had tracked down an electrician, but his number was in my diary in my bag in the bedroom.

I fumbled my way along to my bedroom and found my bag and my phone with its in-built torch, but of course it was out of charge.

It was clearly that kind of evening – the kind when Dad would have said 'the gods are not on our side'. There seemed nothing for it but to go to bed. But even that was unsatisfactory. I was cold. My feet were cold, my hands were cold. I hate being cold. Suddenly I wanted to cry.

'For heaven's sake!' I snapped at myself aloud. 'Pull yourself together!'

It had been raining earlier. Silver-grey raindrops had collected around the frames and were making rivulets down the glass pane. Beyond this, there was nothing but a blank night sky. No clouds. No moon. Clutching the duvet round my shoulders, I caterpillared down the bed to press my nose to the window.

There were not even stars, although, as my eyes adjusted, spangling shavings of light began to wink through the close veil of the dark.

We had gone back to bed and I had got out again to fetch a bottle of cognac.

'Why do you keep cognac in your wardrobe?'

'It was given to me as a present and I was saving it to give it to someone else.'

'Who gave it to you? Not a rival, I hope?'

'You don't have a rival. It's a sort of standby, in case.'

'In case of what? Do you always give away your presents?'

'Sometimes I do, if someone else would like them more than me.'

'I'm not sure what I think about that.'

'What I think about it,' I said, 'is that if ever there were an "in case" this is it. I bloody well need a brandy.'

'Count me in. It's been a fair old roller coaster for me too.'

Trying to undo the brandy, I cut my hand on the stupid plastic they stick round the top and swore.

'Come here, you're bleeding.'

'It's fine,' I said, licking my palm. 'It's nothing.' I tend to lick any cuts.

'Let me do that.'

'It's OK, I've opened it.'

'Not the brandy.'

He took my hand and gently licked the ball of my palm where a bead of bright-red blood had formed. 'Now it will be fine.'

I sloshed out liberal measures of cognac and handed him a glass and he leant across to clink mine, so that I could smell his distinctive musky scent. Why is it that the scent of a desired body is so utterly slaying?

'Here's to us.'

'Are we an "us"?' I asked. This was betraying a dangerous vulnerability but I couldn't help it.

'Christ, I hope so after all this. You don't want to chuck me out again?'

'No,' I said. 'But . . .'

'But you'd like to know more?'

'Yes.'

'And we can't let sleeping dogs lie for a while?'

'Well . . .'

'No, listen. It's OK. What do you want to know?'

'Whatever you want to tell me.'

He placed his two hands flat against my cheeks and gently turned my face to his. 'That's a bad answer. I don't at present, my darling, "want" to tell you anything. What I "want" is to lie here beside you, enjoying this rather good brandy – you must be nuts to be thinking of giving it away – and then I want to make love to you again. And possibly again after that. So if you want to know more, you'll have to ask.'

'OK,' I said. 'How about a compromise. We make love and then I'll ask.'

A while later I said, 'Why was your wife not at Catherine and Alistair's wedding and why wasn't she there at lunch today?'

'Have you been wondering that while we were making love?'

'No. I said I'd ask what I wanted to know once we'd made love.'

'Oh God, so you did. I need to pee.'

Coming back from the bathroom, he stopped to look out of the window. 'It's a pity you can hardly ever see stars in London.'

'They're there, though, anyway, aren't they?'

'The illusion of them is. What we see, when we can see them, is no longer there. Don't you find that odd?'

'Are you trying to tell me something?'

'Only that I find it interesting that we live by illusions. We set such store by what isn't actually there.' He got back into bed and said, 'Another spot of cognac wouldn't come amiss.'

I poured out more and he lay there, balancing his glass on his chest, not drinking. I was wondering if I'd already spoilt things.

'Laura wasn't at the wedding because she was in New York. She might not have gone anyway. We don't necessarily do things together. When we got together first, she said to me, or something like, "I'm older than you and I already have a circle of friends. It's not that I don't want you to meet them. They would and will like you, and they will be happy for me. But you will need your own friends and to follow your own interests and inclinations."' He paused to sip. 'I was put out by this initially. I felt jealous of her friends and insecure – as if she felt me not good enough, or too young and unsophisticated to be seen with. But after a while I saw the wisdom of it and in so far as we have worked it's partly for that reason.' He took another sip of brandy, as if egging himself on with little incremental rewards. 'She's a wise woman. But of course it has had its dangers, of which you were one.'

'And the other woman you had an affair with.'

He frowned at this. 'Yes, and her.'

'But you don't want to discuss her?'

'I don't. But I shall. I shall because it's best to get everything said at the start.'

'You sound angry,' I said, hoping I didn't sound as if about to cry.

'No. Not angry. Not really. A bit defensive and also . . .'

'What?'

He sighed. 'This woman – I liked her a lot and I dropped her rather brutally and it's not something I'm desperately proud of. So I don't like talking about it, but I will. You see what an effort I'm making for you?'

'I'm sorry. I shouldn't have asked.'

'Don't be. It's your right to ask. How else can you judge if this is what you want to embark on? I'm trying my best to be fair.'

'Now I feel bad.'

'Listen,' he said, 'I'll tell you. I don't want to, but . . . She was a friend of Laura's – that was why it was so wrong of me. But Laura almost pushed her into my arms. She was – is, I suppose – my age and we met at a point when the age difference between me and Laura was beginning to tell. Laura tore a tendon in her leg and so had to cancel a walking holiday we'd planned and at the eleventh hour she suggested Ellen – that's her name – go with me instead. She was on her own after a long relationship had ended and Laura is like that – generous, always wanting to help. I say "generous" but it's a quality which, to be frank, can piss me off. I wasn't keen. I hardly knew the woman. In fact, I was embarrassed at the prospect and tried to resist but Laura said I was being mean-spirited and I tended to give in to her because – well, because she was – is – generally nicer, better-natured than me and usually knows best – at least, I thought so then. Ellen and I ended up walking all day together, then eating dinner together, and one evening we drank too much together and the rest you know.'

'How did Laura find out?'

'In what I gather is a not uncommon way. She read a letter from Ellen.'

'So she suspected?'

'She insisted not. She said that I must have wanted her to find out because the letter was apparently in my jacket pocket, though I didn't recall leaving it there.'

She did suspect, she was snooping, I thought, *and either he doesn't know her that well or he doesn't want to know.* But all I said was, 'And *did* you want her to find out?'

'Not as far as I could tell but how far is that? How do we know what we really want or know? It's a conundrum. Not one I'm equipped to answer. It's true I felt relief that it was over.'

'Because you were tired of her?'

'Tired of the deception, certainly.'

'And will you become tired of the deception in my case?'

'You know,' he said, 'this is why I didn't want to have this conversation.'

'But we're having it, so will you? Will you become tired?'

'Not of you. I can't imagine that. You're . . .'

'What? What am I?'

'I'm not a poet, my darling.'

'And I'm not especially beautiful. Or clever.'

I was fishing of course but all he said dully was, 'I don't know what you are to me, Hassie. The best I can say is a fit.'

'As in a state of madness?' I said this deliberately, to hurt myself. I do that. Or I did.

'No,' he said wearily. 'Not as in mad. As in a match. As in a glove.'

'But what about the deception?' Against all my desire, I pressed him. 'You got tired of that before. You might again.'

At this, he got out of bed and went back to the window and stood there looking out. Condensation in my uninsulated flat had made water collect on the windowpane. Light from the sodium street lamps below gleamed on the planes of his naked buttocks and back. As I stared at his body, a smattering of light, caught like a lone star in a drop of water, hung there, then ran down the glass, a slow bead of silver against the dark.

'There *is* a star,' he said, not turning round. 'Just one. Just one star that isn't really there.'

'You look like a marble statue,' I said. 'By Michelangelo or someone. I'm sorry. Forgive me. It's me that's mad, that's having the fit. Please come back to bed.'

7

The clocks had gone forward and with the passing of the vernal equinox the days were opening up, growing longer and lighter.

Murat had made great strides in the garden. Often we worked in it together, he mostly silent while I made the odd neutral observation so as not to appear standoffish. I felt safe in his company. He made no demands and I liked watching him at work. He moved with a graceful efficiency, stepping lightly around the plants and handling them with a dextrous care that I found quietly attractive. I was impressed at his willingness to learn and at how rapidly he had acquired a feeling for the garden. I was discovering that, unbeknown to myself, I was one of the all-too-many who, while congratulating themselves on a universal democratic tolerance, had in fact been harbouring a racial prejudice: I had assumed that a handsome young Albanian would have no interest in or facility with plants or gardening.

By now he was coming several times a week. At first, I tried to limit his visits. With Margot contributing proportionally less of his pay – thanks to my deception – I'd become anxious about the cost. When I tried to explain this to Murat, he said, 'Give me an amount each week and I will come when I can.'

'You mean you'd rather I paid you a wage, the same amount each week?'

'Yes. The same each week and then I will come when I can.'

'But how much ought that to be, Murat?'

'Maybe what you can pay. I will come anyway.'

I reported this conversation to Margot, who said, 'He sounds unusually sensible.'

'Unusually compared with who?'

'Compared with "whom", isn't it, as you'd be the first to tell me? I don't know – compared with most people you deal with. Don't jump on me all the time, Hass. It's tiring.'

One mild afternoon, Miss Foot dropped by in a racy-looking sports car with its hood down.

'A Mazda MX-5 convertible,' she said. And when my face must have expressed surprise, 'It belongs to my brother Philip's son's eldest. He keeps it in my garage as I no longer run a car and I'm under orders to take it out every so often to keep it ticking over.'

'Where is your nephew?'

'Great-nephew. Burma, currently. He's in the poverty business so he moves about.'

I was pondering how he came to own a sports car if that was his line of work when Miss Foot appeared to read my mind. 'The sports car goes with the poverty. Don't ask me how they hang together. Some psychological compensation, I imagine.' She was admiring of the progress in the garden. 'You *have* done well. I begin to see its old outlines.'

'That's mainly thanks to Murat. Would you like tea?'

The afternoon was warm enough for us to drink tea in the garden. I brought out a tray with my mother's surviving teacup and the lumpy rabbit mug.

Miss Foot nodded at it. 'You've discovered Debs at Greenaways.'

Margot, who was about to go off to Shrewsbury, had appeared in the garden to ask if I could think of anything else we needed. She acknowledged Miss Foot with a conspiratorial laugh. 'My sister's sucking up to the locals.'

The laughter was not returned. 'Of whom I am one.'

'No offence meant. I'm Margot, by the way.'

'Yes, I assumed you were.'

'And you are . . .?'

'This is Miss Foot,' I interposed.

'Oh yes. The schoolteacher.'

There was a quelling silence. *Why must she adopt that crass tone?* I thought. Then Miss Foot inclined her head and enquired, 'And your own line? Or are you a lady of leisure?'

Margot laughed the laddish laugh I found particularly grating. 'Chance would be a fine thing. I'm in finance. Must dash. Nice meeting you.'

There was another pause until there were sounds of the Lexus pulling out of the drive. I suddenly felt protective of my sister. 'I think Margot worries I may seem patronizing, buying things like this,' I said, waving the rabbit mug.

Miss Foot appeared to be about to say something and then apparently thought better of it. 'Sensible, I should say. I've lived here over sixty years and taught half the village and it took a good twenty of those before they ceased to see me as an interloper.'

'I bought the lawnmower locally too, from the hardware shop.'

Murat had accompanied me and had spent an embarrassing amount of time comparing the Hope Wenlock mowers with the models on his phone. I described how, after selecting the one he declared the best bargain, he had haggled, most skilfully, with Brian over the price.

'How did Murat come to be here, do you know? Hope Wenlock seems an unlikely place to settle but I haven't liked to ask.'

'The usual reasons. He fell for a girl whom he met while she was on holiday in Corfu. They had an affair, she brought him back here and they married. He was living with her in Ludlow where she runs a tea shop. And then, as happens, she met someone else and poor Murat was out on his ear. He was devastated. So devastated he unbent enough to confide in me. He's a proud man. But it helps that I grew up in a Muslim society.'

'Oh dear,' I said. 'What a horrid story.'

'But hardly an atypical one. As old as the hills, in fact.'

'Sad, though.'

'Sad is not the worst thing, is it?' To my confusion, I began to blush furiously but she appeared to be examining some narcissi that had come up in the corner of the

93

lawn. I'd not realized that narcissi have such a divine scent. 'He plays backgammon with me,' she added.

'I remember you mentioned backgammon,' I said, relieved at the change of subject. 'It must be nice to have someone to play with.'

'Better than "nice". It's good for me. It keeps me on my mental toes.'

'You strike me as already on your toes.'

'Thank you. The usual methods one reads of, exercise, crossword puzzles . . .' I made a face. 'You don't care for them? I don't either. Backgammon is my preferred stimulant. It takes effort to keep the aging mind from closing down. But you're too young to have noticed.'

'No,' I said, 'I think I know what you mean.'

'Are you familiar with the poem *The Ship of Death*?'

'I don't think so.'

Disconcertingly, Miss Foot suddenly pronounced, '*O build your ship of death, for you will need it* . . . D. H. Lawrence.'

'I'm afraid I've only read *Lady Chatterley* and mostly for the smutty bits at school.' I was slightly embarrassed at this dramatic performance.

If Miss Foot noticed this, she was undeterred. '*For the voyage of oblivion awaits you.* I don't care for his novels,' she continued. 'I don't believe he really liked women. All those cocks and cunts are a parade to show off what a jolly broad-minded fellow he was. The poetry, however, I do like. But to my mind, growing old is not so much a matter of building a ship as of clearing the decks.'

I was going to learn to sail once, I remembered.

*

94

'I have a yacht,' Robert said. 'And a houseboat.'

'Golly!'

'What does that mean?'

'It means I didn't realize you were so well appointed.'

'Why, thank you, ma'am. I am, as you say, exceptionally "well appointed".'

'Not that kind of "well appointed", show-off. I mean I'd no idea you were so propertied.'

'I'm not. Laura owns the house. And the Dorset cottage. They were both hers before I came on the scene. I bought the boats to have somewhere of my own. The houseboat's my studio. The yacht's strictly for pleasure. I like being afloat. I always have. I nearly joined the navy.'

'Why didn't you?'

'Why doesn't one do anything? Didn't get round to it? Too undisciplined? I would have kicked up like hell at the rules.'

'Iconoclast!'

'You bet. But anyway, it's sailing that I like, the wind in the sails, the closeness to the water. Sailing gives you time for reflection. I like that. I can take you sailing. Can you sail?'

'Speaking of ships,' Miss Foot said, 'you'll have discovered the stream. Nelly used to hold a paper boat contest for the village children when the Easts held their Midsummer's Eve parties.'

If that was the case, I said, the stream must have been faster-flowing then. It was now overgrown with reeds and clogged with weeds. We strolled down to inspect it.

By now there were marsh marigolds growing there and

kingcups, bold as brass. 'There've been tadpoles,' I told her. The discovery of these had caused me childish excitement. 'We used to catch them, my sister and I, but we had no pool to put them in and they always died.' It was grisly, seeing their little black bodies floating in the water, or lying inert at the bottom of the jam jar. 'I always longed for frogs.'

'Excellent for the garden, frogs. Have you encountered any of Nelly's toads? She was very proud of her toads. One old chap, who had his quarters by the potting shed, I used to call Mr Jackson.'

I said that I hadn't met any toads yet but I looked forward to meeting one and that I too was partial to toads, thanks to Beatrix Potter.

Walking back, she pointed out an insignificant-looking plant, growing in some profusion in one of the beds Murat and I had still to clear. 'That's enchanter's nightshade. It isn't nightshade at all. Nelly cultivated it, though most regard it as a weed. It's said to have magic properties.'

'What properties?' I was taken by the name.

'You can look it up in my herbal. Remind me next time you visit.' Which reminded me that I had still to get myself a herbal.

We stopped by the old nursery garden, where Murat had taken down the rotten posts, removed the torn nets and weeded and hoed the ground ready for replanting.

'What will you grow here?' Miss Foot asked.

'I'm not sure yet. I've bought masses of seeds.'

These too had been bought at the hardware store. I had found these purchases strangely thrilling. The neat paper packets, with their tempting pictures of tomatoes and cucumbers, lettuces, sweetcorn, celery, cauliflower, artichokes, peas, cabbages of all hues, beans of all sizes and the faintly sifting contents, had stirred me: they seemed a cornucopia of fertile promise.

'We need glass,' Murat informed me. 'To germinate seeds.'

He had commandeered one of the gardening books Miss Foot had loaned me and was following its guidance to the letter. Margot, who was present during a vegetable conference one Saturday morning, remarked, 'When he talks about carrots, he's got a sort of fanatical gleam in his eye.'

'Don't be absurd, Marg. He's just keen. It's touching how much it matters to him.'

'I'd be careful if I were you. You know nothing about him.'

'I do.' I felt doubly indignant as this was in fact the case. I didn't know much about Murat. Like me, I sensed he liked to keep himself to himself. 'Miss Foot plays backgammon with him,' I said, slightly plucking at straws.

Margot treated this with one of her dismissive gestures. 'I wouldn't pay any attention to that. She strikes me as a bit bonkers. Bossy, unmarried, intellectual women go that way.'

'Has it crossed your mind that *we* are unmarried?'

'We're not intellectual. At least I'm not. And we're still in our prime.'

'I've rarely met anyone saner than Miss Foot,' I said angrily. I didn't bother to challenge her pose of not being intellectual.

'You've met hardly anyone, Hass. She reminds me of that History teacher with a moustache we had at school who was in love with Robespierre and spat when she talked.'

This was Miss Cudlipp. I'd always felt sorry for the way the other girls mocked her and said, not entirely untruthfully, 'I liked her.' I was offended too by this caricature of Miss Foot. She did have a vestigial moustache but she certainly didn't spit. And being dark, I'm always in a slight dread of a moustache myself.

'Really? Or were you just sucking up? Be careful, that's all I'm saying. For all you know, he could be a criminal or a terrorist.'

'Margot! That's an appallingly prejudiced thing to say.'

'Well, he's Muslim, isn't he? I assume so if he's Albanian. And Albanians, by the way, are known as the gangsters of the Balkans.'

'Who says so? And since when were you an expert on the Balkans?'

Margot shrugged. 'I have friends in high places.'

'What does that mean?'

'It means I know someone who works in Montenegro. The Albanian diaspora there is known to be heavily involved in organized crime.'

I had risen from the kitchen table where we were having this exchange and I was so incensed at this I believe I actually stamped my foot. 'That's like saying because I'm British and a woman I'm like, like . . .' as so often at these moments I couldn't immediately think of a sufficiently objectionable person – 'Margaret Thatcher. Or because you're British and blonde you're like Myra Hindley,' I said, warming to my theme. 'You can't condemn one man on an unconfirmed prejudice about a whole country. Murat's had a horrible time. Miss Foot says his wife brought him back here to live with her and then kicked him out. If anything, he should be prejudiced against us.'

'How do you know that's true? It could just be a line. I wouldn't trust a batty old spinster to recognize a criminal or a terrorist. He could be storing bombs in our shed. Have you given him a key?'

I had. A padlock, bought also at the hardware store, ensured that the shed was now secure with the new lawnmower safely stored inside.

'For God's sake, Marg, of course I have. Otherwise he'd have to come to me all the time to get the tools.'

'Well, if you'd rather be blown up in your bed or held to ransom by a gang of crack dealers than be troubled for a key . . .'

'Oh Marg!' This was a depressingly familiar pattern. Margot said something exaggerated to wind me up, I rose to the bait, Margot then had to pursue it as if she meant it and we ended up really at odds. Did family relationships ever change? Could they? Maybe not. Maybe this whole experiment of living with my sister was doomed. For a moment there spun in my mind the multiple occasions when we had argued. And for what? And why? Nothing changed. Not really. Not people, anyway.

Trying to recover the situation, I heard myself become pleading. 'I like Miss Foot. I know she can be a bit peremptory, but she's entitled to be, she's old. She's very knowledgeable and she's kind. She's been kind to me as well as Murat. I trust her and I trust Murat. She's a friend and – and he is too.' This wasn't quite the case with Murat. But I think this was maybe when I realized that I should like it to be.

'If you say so. Personally, I thought she was rude.'

There was a silence, during which I felt my heart beating faster. 'Marg, are we always going to quarrel?'

'That's up to you.'

'It's up to both of us, isn't it?'

Margot had turned away, I thought, in anger, so I couldn't for the moment see her face. She turned back and I was astonished to see she was crying. 'I know you resent the fact that Dad left the same to me as to you.'

'What?'

'I know you gave up your London place to go and look after him. But you're self-employed. I couldn't leave my job.'

'Marg! I know that. I didn't expect you to.' Was that quite true? 'Dad didn't either.' That was certainly true. Dad was always scrupulously fair.

'But you feel that you deserved more of his money.'

'What *are* you talking about?' I was furiously indignant now. I didn't think to ask myself why.

'And of course we all know you were his favourite.'

'So? You were Mum's.'

'Christ, Hassie,' Margot said. 'Are you going to hold that against me for ever? Why the fuck do you think I ran away?'

8

'Come to the houseboat,' Robert had said.

And I had cautiously asked, 'Isn't it too close to home?' As a rule, any length of time we spent together was when Robert had reason or impulse to go abroad and Laura either could not or chose not to accompany him. The houseboat was moored on the canal in Little Venice, the neighbourhood of their house, and while I was aware of the boat, in all the time we'd known each other I'd never once visited Robert there.

'Laura will be in New York from Friday and I'd like you to see it.'

'What about neighbours?'

'What about them? You can come under cover of darkness wearing a false beard and leave at daybreak disguised as a washerwoman.'

'Be serious. I don't want to rock the boat.'

'You won't rock *Sal*. She's steady as a rock.'

'*Sal* – is that what the boat's called?'

'*Salad Days. Sal* for short. See, she even shares your sur-name, so you have to come. It's written in the stars.'

'Written in water, surely? But OK, I'll come.' As if I really needed persuading.

'Don't forget the beard.'

It was dusk when I rang him and he came whistling along the towpath to meet me.

'What's that you were whistling?'

'Do you like my whistle? I'm rather proud of it.'

'I'm impressed. You're a man of parts.'

'I'm glad you recognize it.'

He took my hand – he had a warm, dry grip, which I found profoundly reassuring – and led me past a string of moored barges to a long, low boat which I could see was painted green and gold.

'Green for salad?'

'The choice of name wasn't mine but you can't change a boat's name. It's unlucky. Mind the steps down, they're steep.'

I took in the interior with pleasure. It was like him. Like the secret Robert, whose nature, it pleased me to suppose, was only vouchsafed to me. The cabin, lit by lanterns, was also decorated in green. Long green cush-ions lined the benches. There were potted plants but no other ornaments except for his own work. An easel dis-played a print of what I recognized as one of his abstracts, *Lime Street*, a complex mosaic of a variety of greens.

'Did you ever use an easel?' I had once asked.

'Before the computer programmes became so sophisti-cated, I did.'

At one end of the boat there was a neat galley kitchen. At the other, a study area where I saw his open laptop.

'Were you working? I don't want to interrupt.'

'I was sending Laura a couple of my latest ideas. She's showing them to a textile designer who might take them up for his new collection. There's money in textiles.'

He kept Laura's name current in our exchanges. Not extensively, but enough to remind me of that first conversation when he had stated his terms. I should have been used to this by now. It had not lost its power to needle me but I understood why he did it, if not always liking that he did so.

I turned physically a little away, as if by this I could also distance Laura. 'No bed?' I suppose I was reverting to my own claims.

'Of course there's a bed. Would I ask you here without one? Here!' He pulled a lever and a bed unfolded smoothly from a wooden panel. 'A double. Comfy too. Try it.' He pulled me down to join him, kissing my forehead. 'Would you rather eat first? I've eggs and parsley – I can make you one of my famous omelettes.'

I lay there, deliberately unresponsive. 'Why are they famous?'

'They aren't yet but they're sure to be once you've tasted one.'

'Idiot!' Everything was suddenly all right again. 'Yes please to an omelette. A salad too if you've lettuce.'

'A salad on *Salad Days* is naturally available. Shall I cook now or . . .?'

'No. Later, please.'

*

Murat and I were enjoying a confab. This had become part of our ritual, with both of us making excited suggestions. No, I should rephrase that. He was never excitable; he was always apparently very composed.

'I like salads,' I said. 'Let's grow plenty of lettuce, all sorts. And tomatoes and cucumbers.'

'They are better in a glass house.'

'Greenhouse. They're called greenhouses.'

'Why? They are not green.'

I hadn't ever considered this. 'I'm not sure, Murat. Maybe because people grow green vegetables in them.'

'We can grow them in there,' he suggested, pointing through to the scullery. The wide window ledges of the scullery faced south-west on to the garden.

'Good thinking. But, you know, I was half wondering about getting a greenhouse.'

Murat's topaz eyes visibly brightened. If he ever expressed emotion it was with his eyes and, observing them now, I recalled Margot's comments and felt some relief that she wasn't there. 'There is an offer at the garden centre for Easter.' He produced his phone and flicked through a series of images. 'See here?'

'I've no idea how much they cost.' I began to regret raising this possibility: it was unlikely I had the means to make it materialize. 'What price are they? Expensive, I bet.'

'Not too much if we buy one to build.'

Margot wouldn't be happy about that 'we', I thought. 'We can go and look, by all means, but I'll have to check with my sister before I can make any decision.'

To my astonishment, when Margot returned and I mentioned the greenhouse, she was receptive to the idea.

'I'll give it you as an Easter present if you like.'

Since Margot had never given me anything more expensive than a dressing gown, I felt I should put her in the picture. 'According to Murat, the cheapest, and that's a self-build, is fifteen hundred quid.'

'That's OK. I'm getting my end-of-tax-year bonus next week. Go ahead. I assume the terrorist can build it for you.'

Grateful as I was, I couldn't help frowning. 'Don't, Marg. I know you're joking but don't.'

'Who says I'm joking?'

'I do.' I certainly hoped she was. It wasn't always easy to tell with Margot. She had some unsavoury-sounding right-wing friends. 'For one thing it's illegal. And racist. And also quite unjust. Supposing someone heard you?'

'Who's going to hear me? But OK, I won't if it bothers you so much. Just be careful, that's all.'

Although I harboured no fears about Murat, I found myself waiting till Margot returned to London before arranging to go with him to the garden centre. She had made me self-conscious about my efforts to befriend him. He was always most courteous but had remained distant and I didn't want to appear patronizing or to impose. I had begun to relax when I gardened and was relishing the peace of his company. Aside from this, and his recently acquired expertise over greenhouses – about which I knew nothing and the merits of which I was quite incompetent to judge – I needed him for transport.

I had not got round to buying a car. Miss Foot had offered to ask her great-nephew if I could use his, but given my recent history, which had left me crushingly insecure about my general competence, I was too worried about damaging it. Better, I told her, for me to find an old banger.

But no old banger had yet been acquired. I had come to the conclusion that I barely needed a car, preferring to shop for my supplies in the village, and Murat, who had the use of a van owned by the builder with whom he lodged and for whom he did odd jobs on the side, seemed happy to drive me.

'He's not paid properly by that man,' Miss Foot had objected when the builder's relationship with Murat had come up in conversation. 'It's rank exploitation.'

Miss Foot, I had discovered, cherished radical opinions, which were kept well stoked with examples of capitalist iniquity culled from the BBC and the daily press. Margot, with her quick instincts, picked up on this and remarked one day, 'I can just picture the old bat knitting at the guillotine while the poor monarchists rolled by in their tumbrils.'

(When, much later, and very circumspectly, I presented Miss Foot with a polite version of this opinion, she said, sharply, 'Not at all. *A Tale of Two Cities* is one of my favourite books,' which struck me as a not entirely relevant objection.)

It was nearing the end of March and the countryside was sounding with courting birds. Lenten lilies, the pale wild daffodils that made Wordsworth's heart dance, were silently trumpeting their annual revival and when I walked to the village I found patches of scented white violets. Life affords few blessings as sweet as these.

The roads were hedged with catkin-laden hazels when Murat and I set out. They showered benedictions of yellow pollen on the van as it brushed the branches over-hanging the narrow lanes. As we drove cautiously along – Murat was respectful with the builder's property – great drifts of primroses on all sides were reflecting back the renewing spring light.

'Would you mind if we stopped for a moment, Murat?'

He pulled up a track and parked by a gate. I got out and leant on the topmost bar, breathing in the clean air.

The lower slopes of the nearby hill were a milky way of pale flowers. I gazed, letting my eyes unfocus, trying to melt into the sunlit vista and dissolve out of my separate-ness to be absorbed into the dappled landscape of yellows and greens. *I could die here in this meadow and be perfectly happy*, I thought.

Into this thought, a memory – a kaleidoscope of memories – flickered.

As children, Margot and I used to go primrose picking when we picnicked by Padley Gorge. We bound the pink fleshy stems with strands of knitting wool, wrapped them in wet moss peeled from the rocks in the brook and packed them, with cold hands, into empty sandwich bags.

Once I cut myself jumping on to a rock and we had watched, fascinated, as the bright blood dripped from my toe into the racing springtide water.

'We might secretly be adopted Russian princesses,' Margot, who had just learnt about haemophilia, had announced, 'and you might bleed to death.' I'd been brave about the cut foot, but this made me scream and my mother slapped my bare leg and told me not to be hysterical. It was not the thought of haemophilia that scared me but the thought of being adopted, which was odd when you think about it. You'd imagine I'd have been glad not to have been my mother's child.

It wasn't frowned upon then to slap children as it is now. Maybe it was illegal now to pick primroses? Too bad, I thought as I climbed over the gate and stooped to pluck a single bloom. As a child, I loved the delicately elusive scent.

'You like these flowers?' Murat had climbed the gate to join me.

'They're called primroses.'

'They are roses?'

'No. Not at all. But I agree, it's strange that they are called prim roses. Maybe because they are prim.'

'Prim? What is that?'

How to explain prim. 'I suppose a bit fussy.'

'Like your sister?'

I hooted. 'Not like Margot. More like Miss Foot.' Though that wasn't accurate either. She was far from prim.

'Miss Foot is not like your sister.'

'No. Not at all.'

He looked at the flower in my hand. 'You would like it for the garden?'

'I would, yes, but . . .'

Before I could stop him, he had dropped down and begun hacking around one of the plants with a knife produced from his jacket pocket.

'Hey, Murat! I don't think that's allowed.' But the plant was already half out of the ground.

He was looking up at me, anxious. 'You don't want me to?'

'Well, we really shouldn't but as you've already dug it up . . .' With so many primroses, could it really matter?

Back in the van, he asked, 'I will not get into trouble for the plant?'

I had gleaned from the odd remark that, despite having been married to a British woman, his legal status in the UK was unclear. Perhaps the marriage wasn't recognized. Or perhaps the immigration regulations in view of Brexit had already been tightened. I never pursued this, deciding that ignorance was the safer path. Whatever his situation was, I could see he needed reassurance. 'Don't worry, Murat. If anyone is to get into trouble it will be me. But we'd better not dig up any more wild flowers.'

I amused myself as he restarted the van with the thought that Margot would be made most uneasy by that 'we'.

The visit to the garden centre went well. While Murat inspected greenhouses and made notes on his phone, I patrolled the rows of tempting plants and shrubs, spoilt for choice. After a good deal of havering I settled on some lupins and poppies, some white foxgloves and peonies, several varieties of salvia (which I had formerly known of only in their ugly municipal form), phlox and Canterbury bells. All good old-fashioned cottage-garden flowers.

I found Murat studying packets of slug pellets in the goods and tools section, where I bought some secateurs and, because I fancied the look of them, a clutch of bamboo poles. I was tempted to buy fish blood and bone fertilizer, which seemed like ingredients in a witch's potion.

This was vetoed by Murat. 'It is cheaper on Amazon. The slug poison too.'

'OK, but I don't want any poison used in the garden, Murat.'

He shrugged, implying it was on my head, and because I didn't want to seem to be putting him down and because the visit had gone well and I was hungry, I offered, 'Lunch?'

But not at the garden centre café, I decided, which was packed with young mothers with under-school-age children and elderly couples trying to avoid them, the better to enjoy their child-free retirement. Instead, I suggested we drive till we came across a country pub.

'Lunch is on me, Murat.'

'Excuse me?'

'I mean, I'm paying for lunch. And you must let me pay when you fill up with diesel. It's the least I can do for your driving me here.'

We were more than halfway back to Hope Wenlock when I spotted a sign. 'Look, Murat, there's a pub by that church. Shall we try there?'

It turned out to be a dismal choice. There were some desiccated-looking Scotch eggs, which Murat obviously couldn't eat. I had one and it was most unpleasant, while he had a bag of crisps and a roll filled with limp lettuce and squishy tomatoes. We ate in the 'garden' – a patch of yellowing grass demarcated by an ugly chain fence. The toilet bowl, when I went to the Ladies, had plainly not been cleaned for some time.

A spreading yew, visible just beyond the churchyard, suggested an alternative spot to pee. 'Just going to stretch my legs, Murat.' He looked puzzled. 'A short walk. I shan't be long.'

Beyond the yew, the bank appeared to drop away. Having peed, I scrambled down to where, thanks to slippage, the ancient roots of the tree were exposed and had formed a natural basin. I parted the ferns and the ivy and peered down into a pool of muddy water. Above it, a lichen-covered stone tablet was set into the ground.

The engraving was faint under the lichen but, peering down and squinting, I just made out an S and what was either a W or an M. There were other characters faintly discernible but they were too eroded to read.

9

'What were you whistling?' I'd asked that evening Robert came to meet me on the towpath.

'You don't recognize "I Love a Lassie"?'

'I've never heard of it.'

'An unforgivable hole in your cultural repertoire. It's part of my Highland heritage.'

Robert often whistled. We were visiting a cathedral once and he was ticked off by a priest for whistling a bit of the St Matthew Passion, which made us laugh.

People don't whistle much these days. I thought of this when I met the vicar one Saturday with a copy of *The World of Fine Wines* in his hand. He was whistling – I recognized 'Where Sheep May Safely Graze' – but he stopped when he saw me and waved the magazine. 'My secret vice.'

'I won't give you away. I'm glad we've met. I wanted to ask if it was OK for me to come round to find out more about the house.'

'Surely. When would suit you? Wednesday is t'ai chi –'

he pulled a face – 'Audrey got me into it, so I try to keep it up, but . . . and this Friday it's the book club. I don't suppose you'd like to join? We're a mixed bag.'

I'd sampled a few too many book clubs. 'What's the book?'

'*The Mists of Avalon.* Not my cup of tea, to be frank with you, but don't give me away. The churchwarden – the one who's my particular nemesis – chose it and is very keen. I have to say I prefer a cosy murder myself.'

I said that I had often wondered why fictional murders were so reassuring and he offered that he'd often wondered this himself but had never come up with a satisfactory answer. I pretended an engagement for the book club night but accepted an invitation to call by the vicarage later that day.

'If you come after Evensong, it'll be drinks time.'

Miss Foot had rung to say she was thinning her lily-of-the-valley and should I want them there were outcasts to spare. She was hard at it, kneeling by the flower bed by the porch, when I came through the gate.

'I've set some aside for you. They're a heavenly flower with a delicious scent but rampant colonizers. Hitler had nothing on them.'

She wrapped the plants in an old copy of the *Guardian*.

'They're best moved in autumn but this time of year is fine too while they're still dormant. Keep the pips moist till you plant them. Coffee? I'm fagged out.'

The black kitten was asleep by the fireplace. When I sat down he sat up, sprang gracefully on to my lap and began to treadle my skirt with his claws.

'Mags wants to be your familiar,' Miss Foot observed.

'When did they stop burning witches?' If anyone knew, she would.

'As late as the early eighteenth century. Round here, on the borders, where they followed the old religion long after the country was Christianized, there were plenty of solitary old women who could have been denounced as witches. I would have been, sure as eggs.'

It had been crossing my mind that with no immediate family – other than the brother she sometimes spoke of – and her marbles almost shockingly intact, my new friend must sometimes miss a more intellectually challenging society. She had been welcoming to me as a newcomer; but she had also taken very little time to become confiding. As I now know, this happens in a country community, where other people's business is considered fair game. But I had a feeling, even back then, that Phyllis Foot thirsted for novelty and in a guarded way might be lonely, though I was sure she would deny it were I tactless enough to suggest this.

'My sister has asked some people to stay over Easter and I'll be a little outnumbered. Might you like to come to dinner one evening to give me moral support?'

For the first time in our acquaintance, Miss Foot looked surprised. 'I should be delighted if you think I can be of use. Though I am sorry you should feel outnumbered – that's an uncomfortable position to be in.'

Her expression was a touch stern, so I said, hastily, 'It's not Margot's fault.' I'd witnessed the antagonism spark between the pair of them. 'She doesn't know that I'll mind.'

'And you can't tell her?'

'Not really. They're . . . they're friends of hers and she wouldn't understand.'

'When should I go?' I asked, pulling my frock back on over my head. It was silk, patterned with pansies in glorious shades of blue and gold, a wild extravagance bought in the name of love, though thanks to love I'd not spent much time in it.

'No need till early evening. I'd say stay another night but . . . you know, Laura is flying in early and –'

'Yes, yes, I know,' I interrupted, failing to suppress an uprush of resentment. 'I know your rules dictate you be there when she arrives.'

'I'm sorry. It's not easy for me either.'

'I should think not, having to leap like a rampant stag from bed to bed.'

'Halcyon Days! You know I don't.'

'But you must sometimes. You can't just –'

Now it was he who interrupted. 'I'm not going to have this conversation. You're saying this to hurt yourself. How I am with Laura is what works with Laura. You know why. I'm bound by a certain loyalty to her. It may be a pretty ropey loyalty but it's what I've said I shall stick to. I'm with you because I want to be and for no other reason and if that's not enough then –'

'No,' I said, desperate to avert whatever he was about to say that might menace our love. 'It is enough. I'm sorry. I'm sorry, really.'

'Don't be. I understand. In another life . . .'

'But there never *is* another life,' I said miserably. 'I don't know why anyone says that.'

'We – I – say it because in our imaginations there are other lives. The imagination has a reality. Sometimes a greater reality. Look at art.'

'What about it?' I didn't want to be treated to a lecture.

'A work of art doesn't exist on the normal plane but there is a sense in which it has a reality more enduring . . .'

Now, I thought, *he's turning me into an idea, as if I'm some elevated concept like universal suffrage or liberty.*

'I don't give a *fuck* about art,' I shouted. 'I want you to fuck *me*. I want you back inside me so I can remember it all tonight and all tomorrow and all the next day and the day after that, so I can forget this fucking stupid bloody conversation that I wish I'd never started.'

I was sobbing and he put his arms tight around me so I could smell the engine oil on his rough Aran jersey. 'My darling, that can happily be arranged.'

Later, we embraced tenderly, the abrasive exchange – if not forgotten – put away for the time being.

'I'll go now. But I forgot my washerwoman disguise.'

'I don't think you'll need it. But to be on the safe side, much as I hate to, I'll let you go alone.'

He kissed me and blithe within the ark of my recovered happiness I climbed the steps to the deck and jumped on to the towpath.

A group of people were just rounding the path at the river's bend.

'Sherry?' the vicar enquired. 'A cliché, I know, but some of my parishioners expect it.' He sighed. 'I do my best to live up to the image but . . .' He seemed unsure how to complete this effort at confiding, waved a hand towards a corner cupboard and said in a brighter tone, 'Anyway, more exotically, I can offer you gin, plain and simple, the sloe variety, made by my tricky churchwarden, but for all that fairly drinkable, Scotch, Campari and soda, brandy, with or without ginger, and there's lager and a decent Riesling in the fridge. I can open a bottle of red if you'd prefer that. Or, scraping the barrel, there's some dubious slivovitz we brought back from Croatia with which Audrey used to lace the Christmas pudding – I can't say I recommend it, but there's no arguing with taste – *de gustibus non est disputandum*, you know.' He laughed uncertainly.

The poor man is shy, I thought. *I bet his wife managed the socializing. I bet she kept the place in better order too.*

The room would have been comfortable but there was a neglected look to it. The pictures on the walls hung slightly askew and on the desk there were empty cups with dried coffee dregs and a dirty wine glass on the mantelpiece. A baby grand in the corner was very dusty; clearly it was not being played. There was a photo on it of a smiling, dark-haired woman with a pretty face. His wife, I guessed; the piano must have been hers.

'A gin and tonic, if you've tonic, would be wonderful,' I said, removing a pile of magazines from a chair in order to sit down. 'It's ages since I had one.'

(The last time was at the theatre with Robert. I could remember the gin but not for the moment the play.)

'I have practically every last possibility an alcoholic might require. Not that I'm suggesting you are one. Audrey used to say I hovered on the permanent brink of alcoholism but I bested her every Lent by giving up completely.'

I accepted a lethal-looking G and T. 'Isn't it Lent now?'

'Surely, but with Audrey gone I've no need to prove myself. There are pluses in losing a spouse. Not many, I grant you, but there's a certain freedom.' He nursed his glass of Scotch, musing.

'Yes, I can see that,' I agreed.

'I'm a fully paid-up card-carrying member of the Society of Cakes and Ale.' He gave another uneasy chuckle. The kind of heavy-handed humour his wife would probably have chided him over. I saw with a pang there was a sprinkling of dandruff on his black shirt. She would have seen to that too. 'I've never regarded abstinence as a sign of godliness,' he continued. 'Quite the contrary. Some of the least Christian people it's been my misfortune to meet have been abstainers.'

Remembering how Miss Foot had described him as an atheist, I wondered if I could ask about his beliefs. But given that ours was such a recent acquaintance it would have seemed forward, so I changed the subject to what I had anyway come to ask.

'Knight's Fee – I looked it up – was a remuneration given to medieval knights in the form of plots of land. Is that why the name?'

'You'd think so.' The vicar waved his glass towards the desk. 'There are some copies of old maps there for you and it is the case there were fields and woods that do seem to have been attached to a building whose footprint stood more or less where your present house stands. But in fact the name is a corruption, or rather a foolish gentrification. I've dug out all the papers. Here.' He presented me with a manila file.

'May I borrow this?'

'It's yours, my dear. Arthur East lent me all the bumph when I had the foolish idea of setting up a local historical society.' He sighed smilingly, which reminded me of Dad: rueful but resigned. 'One of my many mishits here. Oh dear.' He poured himself more whisky. 'Audrey was always ticking me off for trying. She didn't like me to be disappointed, you see.'

I did see. 'Of course. But it's good that you tried. I'm sure people were grateful.'

'I'm not sure about that. But I feel it's an aspect of my pastoral duty. Still,' he brightened, 'we have the book club. And next month we're doing *Lolly Willowes*, one of Audrey's choices, which we never got round to, so perhaps I might persuade you . . .?'

'Of course,' I said. I had been feeling bad that I'd spurned *The Mists of Avalon*. 'I don't know the book but of course I'll come.' I had already formed a favourable impression of his wife's taste. 'But you were saying about the material on the house.'

'Ah, yes – when Arthur died, Nelly didn't want the stuff back. So I kept it. And I've added to it slightly. Bits and bobs might be of interest.'

'And the name?'

'Now that *is* fascinating. It was originally Wight not Knight. Some arriviste East felt that making it Knight's Fee gave it a spot of class. Entirely spurious but very English, don't you think?'

'I suppose it is.'

'There's no evidence of any forsoothing knight-at-arms alone and palely loitering. I'm part Scottish, which, as Audrey used to say, I retreat into when I want to distance myself from English class snobbery.'

'I had a Scottish friend who was very proud of his Celtic blood.' God knows why I said that. Probably because I'd just recalled the play where I last drank gin and tonic. It was *The Cherry Orchard*. You may not know this play yet but it ends with the felling of an ancient cherry orchard. It's quite a humorous play in parts – certainly the author thought so – but the ending is very poignant. Thinking of that final scene of wanton devastation touched a sensitive nerve.

My remark seemed to touch a sympathetic nerve in my host. 'We Scots now, our blood is a mix of the Picts and the Gaels. No doubt with a dollop of Roman legionary thrown in. This is why racism is so absurd. Anyone British is bound to be a cocktail. Speaking of which, ready for a top-up?'

'Thank you.' I had drunk the gin rather too fast with the result, as often happens, that I was keen for more. 'I used to illustrate for a children's novelist who wrote historical fiction. There were wights, I seem to remember, in her books. It means fellow or bloke, doesn't it?'

'Middle English for a chap, yes. Who was your author?'

I told him and his face lit up. 'A great favourite of Audrey's. She also loved Rosemary Sutcliff who, you will know, wrote a book called *Knight's Fee*.'

'The only ones I've read are *The Eagle of the Ninth* trilogy.'

'Audrey had everything she wrote. She gave a copy of *Knight's Fee* to Arthur, who was most put out to learn that the ancestral knight was simply wishful thinking and I'm sure never read it. The Easts were a pretty stuffy lot. We – Audrey and I – always felt Nelly's dottiness was a form of protest.'

'Was she really dotty?'

'Audrey knew her better. She was more at ease with Audrey. Not too keen on the dog collar.' He unconsciously tugged at this offending item and gave his nervous little laugh. There was something very moving about seeing the gold wedding band sunk into the flesh of his finger. 'Nelly was fanciful, certainly. But not clinically mad. One can go a touch rogue, you know, when untethered from one's life partner. Although in Nelly's case it was that she saw things, I never quite . . .'

Again he petered out and his mild-featured face became mournful. No stranger to the outcrops of grief, I felt moved to say, 'Might you like to come to dinner with me and my sister? We've guests staying over Easter. Phyllis Foot has said she'll come and it would be lovely if you could too.'

'I'd be delighted to come. Thank you, my dear, thank you.' *Audrey would be pleased*, I thought. *I bet she worried about him when she was aware that she was dying.* 'Phyllis,' he went on, 'is an old friend, though she does rather take me to task over what she sees as my dereliction of Christian duty. I never quite understand why since she's not a Christian herself.'

'Isn't she?' I was surprised to hear this, but I was learning that Miss Foot was not easy to categorize.

'Not a bit of it. Rather anti if anything. But she considers that as I am, officially so, anyway, I should keep up to the mark. I'm afraid I *am* rather inclined to fall short, you know. Story of my life.'

He looked just like an old tortoise, the way his neck crumpled into his dog collar. 'She is rather formidable,' I agreed. 'I called her Phyllis just now but in my mind she's always Miss Foot.'

'That's the schoolmarm in her. It took Audrey years to take the plunge and call her Phyllis. But she was a great teacher – really great. And although she can be picksome, as Audrey would have said, behind the sharp edges beats a kind heart. She ran a tight ship at the village school but for all that the children were, in the main, devoted to her. Especially the more backward ones. A velvet heart in an iron glove, I used to say.' He smiled wistfully at his own lame joke.

'I don't think she likes my sister much,' I confided. 'It's why it would be a help if you were at dinner too. Not that that's the reason I –'

'My dear, don't apologize.' He patted my arm. 'I'm practised at acting as social wadding. It goes with the territory, you know. I'll fend her off at the pass if she threatens to ride one of her hobby horses. Has she bullied you into playing backgammon yet?'

'I'm hopeless at games. But she plays with my gardener.'

'Yes, I was glad to hear you'd hired Murat. He's a nice young chap and I'm sorry to say there's quite a bit of unchristian prejudice in the village – or, I regret to say, in some cases *Christian* prejudice.' He sighed and said, 'When Audrey was alive we used to hold poetry evenings and we tried them once on Rumi. I courted Audrey on Rumi.' He laughed and went a little pink and then said, 'They paid lip service to the idea that in principle we share a God with Islam but by and large, you know, the

British tend to feel that Jesus Christ was white and would have voted Conservative.'

Which made me think of my mother. 'In Sheffield, where I grew up, there was quite a bit of prejudice.'

'I think it's the fact that he's foreign labour rather than the religious issue that's the problem locally. An Albanian in a Shropshire village is rather an anomaly and work here is in short supply. And then,' he went on, looking doleful, 'the village was pretty much Brexit to a man.' He paused, then added, 'I'm *so* sorry, I should have said "or woman". Forgive me.' He frowned and then, becoming flustered, added, 'Not that I'm saying Brexiteers are racially prejudiced. Not at all, I mean . . . Oh Lord, this is the kind of pickle Audrey used to warn me against getting myself into.'

He sat fiddling with his wedding ring and looking so downcast that I hurried to say, 'Really, it's OK. I haven't any special views about Brexit. I didn't even bother to vote.'

This wasn't quite true. I did have views – but none sufficiently important to detain me. I didn't vote because it was the day I broke down and took flight to Sheffield. For ever after, when all the rest of the country would remember it as the historic occasion when they voted to leave the EU, it would stay in my mind as the date for me of a far more significant parting.

'I'm all in favour of immigrants, though,' I added. 'Especially when they're like Murat. They strike me as much harder workers than the British. I'm not sure what the country is going to do without them. I mean, no one but Murat answered my ad.'

I was mildly drunk as I walked back from the village by

the road. Although the days were growing longer, darkness had fallen and, familiar as the way through the wood had become, even with a torch I wasn't quite confident of taking it alone.

As I left the village and was walking carefully along the main road, slightly fearful I might not be safely visible to passing traffic, something large and white flew straight at my face and I ducked and cried out.

Only an owl. White, so a barn owl.

'Ghosts, country people used to suppose them,' Dad told me when, one holiday, we had been similarly startled. 'Nothing to be afraid of,' he had said, 'unless you're a mouse or a shrew,' and most uncharacteristically added, 'Your mother, mind, might not be so safe.'

But my nerves were jangled and I was alarmed to see as I neared the house that the lights were on. I opened the back door, tensing my shoulders against an intruder.

A voice from the kitchen called out, 'Hass?'

'Marg, what are you doing here?'

'Hass, what are you doing here?' Margot turned back to the couple behind her on the towpath. 'This is my sister, Halcyon, aka Hassie. Hassie, Nadia and Julian.'

'Margot!' It was months since I'd heard from Margot. Since her flight from home we'd meet only occasionally, though we still phoned from time to time.

'Have you been to see Robert Aitken too? That's where we're heading now.'

There was no point in denying this: they had witnessed my flying leap from the boat. My mind froze with shock. Somewhere I registered that I'd physically paled.

I managed to come out with a lame-sounding, 'Catherine asked me to bring something over. She and Robert are friends – colleagues, I should say.' *Keep it simple*, I inwardly cautioned myself. *Don't over-elaborate.*

'My sister illustrates Catherine Tenant's books,' Margot explained. To my surprise, she spoke as if this was something she was proud of.

The woman said nothing but stared at me. She was tall and imposing, with one of those bony faces that are inherently beautiful but with something latently cruel about them. The man, older and wearing expensive Ray-Bans and ripped designer jeans, said in a bored tone, 'So, another artist.'

'Julian is an art collector,' Margot explained. 'They're here to look at Robert's work.'

'Oh, right.' I had my back still to the boat and was thinking fast. 'Actually, there's something else I should have asked . . .' Before the others could move, I sprang back on to the deck.

Robert's head and unclothed shoulders appeared through the hatch.

'Robert,' I said. I felt I was enunciating unnaturally and tried desperately to inject into my taut vocal cords a note of casual insouciance. 'Sorry, I forgot. Catherine wanted me to ask about that printer you mentioned. If you could let her have the details, or if you've got them here, I can take them now. This is my sister, Margot, by the way. It seems she's also coming to see you with some friends.'

'Small world,' Robert said. 'And you are . . .?' He stared at the strange couple.

'I'm a *very* old friend of Laura's from way back.' It seemed to me that the woman had glanced again in my direction. 'Nadia and Julian Dufort. Laura suggested as we were in the neighbourhood you wouldn't mind. We did ring.'

'I keep my phone off when I'm working,' Robert said. 'When did you speak to Laura?'

'I texted her in New York to say we'd be nearby and could we drop in. Julian collects modern artists so, given the link, we hoped we might parley directly with the horse's mouth, so to speak.' Nadia laughed as if she had said something witty. I could see that Robert's grey-blue eyes, so lately turned with ardour upon my body, had turned repelling and cold.

Nadia stopped laughing. 'Laura was your agent, wasn't she? She said she was sure you wouldn't mind.'

'He's a new client,' Margot confided to me. I was thankful that she had moved down the path away from the others to take a call on her phone. 'I've been given his portfolio to look after. Bit of a step up, actually. We're on the way to a drinks party that my boss is giving so I'm only here for the ride. Loaded,' she mouthed, nodding towards Julian.

I had turned away from the boat but heard Robert say, 'Sorry, but my wife has led you astray. She's not been my agent for years. I don't deal myself. Everything goes through my current agent.'

Looking discreetly round, I saw he had remained stock-still, half out of the hatch, with his lower half hidden as if he might be a merman. I wondered if it was as obvious to the others as it was to me that he was naked.

Embarrassment is contagious. There was an uneasy hiatus.

Then Julian said, 'Sorry, old man, led astray by the women. I'll look up your agent. We'll leave you in peace for now.'

A couple of cyclists ringing their bells aggressively obliged everyone to stand back, allowing me a chance to call, 'Robert, I'll tell Catherine you'll send her the stuff on the printer, shall I?' and make my getaway.

I began to walk back along the towpath when my elbow was seized in a tight grip and my heart lurched painfully against my ribs.

Nadia was smiling; but her pupils were sharp points of accusing needles. 'Don't hurry off, Halcyon. Why not, now we've met you, come along with us, unless you're going on somewhere? In that gorgeous outfit, you look as though you're already dressed for a party.'

'Thanks,' I said, 'but I'm meeting my girlfriend.' God knows why I said that – Margot would certainly tell them that I wasn't gay.

10

It had been news to me that Margot was, as she put it, 'dating' Julian, a term I suggested sounded ridiculous in anyone over forty. 'Don't be such a prune,' she said to this. 'You're beginning to sound like your schoolmarm pal.'

This state of Margot's affairs had emerged some weeks earlier when she had ambushed me with her announcement that she'd invited guests for Easter. A lightning image, of the kind I am often visited by, of that fateful encounter by Robert's houseboat had presaged my hunch about the identity of these guests. What I had not anticipated was this further intimacy with Julian. I didn't like the idea at all. In fact, it filled me with alarm.

'Julian asked me to keep it quiet while he disentangled from his wife.' Nadia with the armour-piercing eyes and the nails-of-steel grip. 'If she'd got wind, she'd have taken him even more to the cleaners. I know what you're thinking – I'm only interested in his money.' This was too close to the truth for me to acknowledge. 'He's actually a very interesting guy. I like that he's rich – I'm not a hypocrite – but I wouldn't be with him if money was all he had going for him.'

'Good. I'm glad for you.'

'You're not. You've gone all weird. They parted perfectly amicably, so you needn't get all moral with me.'

From which I thankfully concluded that Margot at least had remained ignorant of the nature of my relationship with Robert.

But the prospect of renewing acquaintance with a player in the terrible fallout of that evening was destabilizing. I considered bolting for the Easter weekend; but I had made very little progress with Elfine, so money was tight, and where, when it came to it, could I go? Also, I didn't fancy being driven out of my own home by Julian – whose wake bore the memory of Nadia and the ghostly Laura. Laura had Robert; I was damned if I was about to let her invade Knight's Fee. In the end, I determined to grit my teeth and stick it out with Phyllis Foot and the vicar as somewhat inadequate allies. And the idea of the radical Miss Foot and the rich aesthete Julian communing over dinner was amusing.

Margot, when I told her who would be joining us, made a bit of a fuss.

'They'll be rather out of their depth. I must say, I think you might have at least discussed it with me first, Hassie.'

'How out of their depth? Miss Foot went to Somerville and I think the vicar was at St Andrews.'

'You know that's not what I meant.'

'Well, I've invited them now so too bad.'

*

129

It was quite late on Good Friday when Margot arrived from London with Julian. During the day I'd developed one of the raging stomach aches that since childhood have attacked me when I'm anxious, so I had an excuse for having gone to bed early before they arrived. I made sure to be up well before them the following morning and spent the day with Murat in the garden, while Marg took Julian off for a walk to a pub in a nearby village, so I was spared a communal lunch.

When they returned, and Margot found we were out of butter, I volunteered to walk into the village to buy some in order to avoid tea with the gay couple who were arriving later that afternoon. As I'd met them before, this couldn't seem rude and my plan was to delay meeting Julian again for as long as possible.

That evening, I spent as much time as I could first in the bathroom and then getting changed into clothes that would spark no memory of my lovely pansy-patterned silk. My hair had grown long, longer than in the Robert days, and I twisted it up into a bun and selected my most camouflaging clothes. Inspecting my predominantly beige image in Margot's bathroom mirror, I was satisfied that I was unrecognizable as the woman whom Julian had encountered by Robert's houseboat. I couldn't help thinking that Robert, seeing me in these clothes, would have demanded I take them off.

I waited to come downstairs until Margot yelled 'Drinks', downed a glass of champagne, courtesy of Julian, and took myself off to the kitchen with the excuse that I was preparing the vegetables. Once there, I topped up my courage with the cooking brandy Margot had bought for the coq au vin. By the time Miss Foot and Peter drove up in the vicar's old Morris van I was slightly sloshed.

It was two years and nine months since I'd seen Julian, on the occasion which marked the beginning of what I'd come to call 'the end'. I had banked on the brevity of our encounter, and Margot failing to remind him that we had met before, and was relieved to note that he showed no sign of recognizing me.

Margot had gone ahead and painted the dining room a deep red. I had to acknowledge that with the candles in her sconces lit and casting a diffuse light the room did look inviting. She had laid out the long table with white napkins and jam jars full of wild flowers and had hung the walls with old prints which she had brought down from London. It was apparent to me that she was out to impress. I understood this but at the same time I was scornful. I did not consider Julian someone worth bothering to impress.

Peter had brought a bottle of wine from the old vineyard at Wroxeter. 'Roman Red, not half bad, the Romans knew their roads and their wine. I thought your guests might like to sample something local.'

Julian made an ill-disguised grimace in Margot's direction and she removed the wine to the kitchen. Some grand vintages that Julian had brought with him were already open on the table.

During the first course I made as few remarks as I could politely get away with. Conversation was stilted and – there was no other word for it – dull. Dull as ditchwater, though was ditchwater really 'dull'? One of those phrases, I found myself reflecting, that needed updating as nowadays ditchwater would be deemed full of environmentally fascinating life. I also found myself, when I managed to relax a little, regretting that I had set Peter to monitor Miss Foot. Whenever she showed signs of becoming amusingly insistent, there he was, dutifully ready to pounce on the conversation and supply pastoral oil.

'We had some interesting discussions about diversity in our Lent group,' he said, intercepting a diatribe that Miss Foot was poised to deliver about the government's mishandling of Windrush. And when she started on the follies of modern education, the poverty of the GCSE syllabus and the deplorable state of teaching at universities, he launched into a history of the village school. 'My friend here was for many years our school mistress, and a terrific job she made of it, but before that I'm sorry to say . . .'

I began to inwardly speculate on why so many good people are dull. The saints, or anyway those I'd heard of, sounded to my mind passionate, eccentric, bad-tempered even – so perhaps they were not especially 'good' after all. Julian was neither good nor dull; for the most part, I decided, he was boring. I entertained myself considering what made for bores and concluded that they drill into your mind, interfering with your own thoughts, while dull talk merely slides off the mind, leaving your privacy relatively undisturbed.

Julian's only noteworthy contribution to the conversation was, when Peter had finished his account of the local school, to stare at him and then ask, 'Have you ever been in the presence of real evil?' When poor Peter laughed awkwardly and said, 'Oh, I think very few people are truly evil, you know,' Julian smiled a horribly supercilious smile and resumed the expression of contemptuous hauteur which was the ruling feature of his face.

God knows what he had to feel so superior about. It was a not uninteresting question but it was posed with the intention of causing discomfort. Anyone could see Peter wouldn't recognize evil if it slapped him round the face. Give me dull people any day. On the whole, the dull do no harm.

Margot, meantime, was uncharacteristically docile. She was wearing ridiculously high-heeled sandals, had drenched herself in Jo Malone and done something unnecessary to her eyelashes. She has naturally thick eyelashes and adding to them makes her look like a Barbie doll. She had made an excellent dinner – she's an accomplished cook when she chooses and Julian, I was informed, was 'picky' about his food. Apart from drip-feeding him flattering remarks, she made little contribution to the general conversation. Margot's no fool and I found this performance dismaying. How little it requires to satisfy a narcissist, I thought sourly. It can only be his gilded portfolio that's the attraction – unless, I suddenly wondered – though it seemed improbable in one so etiolated – was Julian perhaps a demon lover? You never could know what people were like when it came to sex, because appearances really are deceptive; *or rather*, I amended the thought, *you can never know what people really want from sex.*

An almost physical shudder accompanied the memory of a moment with Robert. 'I was right about you,' he said that very first evening in bed in my flat. 'You looked so demure in your air-blue gown, I had a shrewd idea of what that disguised.' This was exactly the kind of memory

I didn't want to be having. The effect of having Julian here. Damn his horrible bloodshot eyes.

'Am I right – we consulted a Pevsner before coming – that your church has Saxon origins?' Stuart, the younger of the gay couple, was asking.

Peter began to supply the history of St Michael and All Angels in too much detail, at which Miss Foot jumped in with a move to embark on an account of pagan rites. 'The fact that it is on a hill suggests the church may stand on a much older site of pre-Christian worship.'

Stuart's partner, Chris, attempted a diversion with a question to the vicar about the Anglican Church's current policy on gay marriage, which Peter tried gamely to field though it was apparent he was at sea. Through a miasma of abstraction I heard Miss Foot interject, 'Peter, at the last synod the matter of LGBT rights . . .' before mentally ducking out again.

As Margot was clearing away plates, a familiar name penetrated my haze. Stuart was addressing me, revealing that at an earlier stage of his career he had been in publishing and had known Catherine Tenant. 'Such an early death. I assume it was the MS?'

'Yes,' I agreed. 'Or a consequence of it. It tends to make you vulnerable to respiratory disorders. We were all terribly sad.'

I was more than sad. I had been devastated when Catherine's husband rang with the news.

'My God, why? How?' I had said, appalled. Catherine was the first person to die whom I truly loved. I wonder if this is something like the first time one has sex – a cracking of some evolutionary innocence, so that the world outside one's own self-centred concerns changes for ever.

'Pneumonia. It was very quick. One day she was in hospital, the next morning she'd gone. I never even got to see her before she died.'

I had cried and cried in Robert's arms. 'She was my dearest friend and I don't have many. None like Catherine anyway.'

'Darling,' he had said. 'I know. I do know. But you still have me.'

But I had Robert no longer.

'You illustrated her books,' Chris was observing, politely bypassing the Anglican Church's policy on homosexuality.

At this point, Margot appeared with a cheeseboard. 'She's an extremely talented illustrator, my sister.'

'My wife loved your illustrations,' the vicar gallantly contributed.

Conversation halted again until Miss Foot gamely supplied, 'Indeed, they do you credit, my dear. Quite in the Charles Keeping style.'

'He illustrated Rosemary Sutcliff's books,' Peter volunteered to the rest of the table, doggedly pursuing his role.

'Thank you,' I said, 'but you're flattering me, Phyllis. I'm nowhere near Keeping's standard.' I was not at all relishing this turn in the limelight. Julian had removed himself to the garden to smoke and I didn't want him returning to have his memory jogged.

There was a further lull, while I sensed everyone scouring their minds for further potential topics of conversation.

Margot had gone to summon Julian. As they were

returning to the dining room, Peter was saying, 'She was another of Audrey's heroines.'

Resuming his seat, Julian enquired in his bored drawl, 'Who's that?'

For God's sake, Peter, I inwardly urged. *Drop it.* 'The blue cheese is local,' I said brightly. 'It would go well with Peter's wine. We think it better than Roquefort, don't we, Marg?'

Marg, to my annoyance, failed to grasp this baton but instead picked up the breadbasket and smilingly handed it round in her faux fifties-housewife guise.

With all the insensitivity of the professionally virtuous, Peter ploughed on. 'My wife, bless her. She was a great reader. We've been discussing Catherine Tenant for whom Hassie, here,' he patted my hand affectionately, 'drew most delightfully.'

Dear man, he thinks he's being helpful, I reminded myself. Another silence followed, while we all listened to the slight clicking of his jaw as he chewed a slice of rye bread.

'Ah, yes,' Julian said suddenly. His pale-blue eyes had been fixed across the table on Peter, and now with a swivel of his neck he turned the hard-boiled gaze on me. 'I was trying to recall where I'd seen you.' There was just the sliver of a beat, during which it was as if someone was directing an electric current through my body. *Save me*, I prayed.

'At Aitken's barge, wasn't it?' Julian continued, reaching for the wine. 'Must have been, what, two or three summers ago?'

'But how?' I asked desperately. 'How did she find out?'

'That snake Nadia. She reported your presence on *Sal.*'

'But I could have been anybody. Why did it follow from that that we were having an affair?'

'Laura knows I let no one aboard *Sal*. I allow her, only very occasionally, and she's not been there for years. It's my sanctuary. It's a measure of your place in my heart that you're allowed there.'

Were allowed, I thought bitterly. *And if that is the case, and she knows it, why advise Nadia and Julian to visit him there? Laura must have already suspected. Nadia was sent on purpose to spy.*

'And you've admitted it?'

His expression became defensive. 'If you recall, I was bollock naked when they turned up. The reptile Nadia spotted it. And I'm a bad liar. Women intuit these things and Laura's no exception. You know that. You do too.'

I could hardly deny this given my speculations. 'So what are we going to do now?'

Foresight can be a cruel gift; I had already rehearsed the answer many times: he would continue to see me but more and more nervously; the meetings would become more erratic, incrementally more strained; he would become costive with his time and we would more frequently quarrel over missed opportunities or cancelled plans. Finally, he would find it all too much and, feeling frantic, I would sense him drawing away.

What would happen thereafter I had not been able to quite phrase to myself – or face.

'We shall carry on seeing each other of course,' he said, but already his tone had become cautious. 'We must be careful, that's all. More careful.'

'How can we be more careful? We thought we'd been so before.'

'I don't know, love.'

'Love' – that fatal term of supposed endearment, which for me signalled its very absence. Coming from him, it cast a mortal chill.

'You never call me "love".'

'I do. Of course I do.'

'No you don't. "Darling love", "My love", "My sweet love" is what you say.' I was standing in a dwindling light on very thin ice, while all around I could hear ominous cracks. 'And "love",' I continued, striding out into the inhospitable dark as the ice gave way beneath my feet, 'is what my mother called me when she was refusing me something I really wanted.'

And now, I said to myself, *he'll rebuke me*.

He sighed. 'Oh Hassie, you're being childish.'

Julian had emptied the bottle and I had risen from the dinner table, on the pretext of fetching more wine, and retreated to the kitchen to attempt to recover my presence of mind or at least a semblance of it.

I stood there for some minutes collecting my thoughts. Then, seeing Peter's bottle of Roman Red unopened, I attacked it with the corkscrew. I'm not sure what was in my mind. Some sort of revenge on Julian, I suppose.

On my way back to the dining room, I encountered Miss Foot in the hall.

'The lavatory . . .?'

'Next door on the left.'

She paused a moment, weighing words. 'I like your gay friends,' she announced at last. It was evident that the point of this pronouncement was in what it omitted to say of the other guest.

Back in the dining room, standing behind Julian so my face could not be studied and apparently engaged in refilling his glass, I produced the question I'd steeled myself to ask. 'So how are Laura and Robert? Are you still in touch?'

The unimagined end had taken its time – and then its toll. My heart had been rubbed raw by the constant craving, the ceaseless thoughts of Robert; the weight of my anguish seemed to hang heavy on every breath I took. By night, I hungered for his body, eaten up by longing; by day, I was so absent that others began tactfully to avoid me, suspecting some struggle with mental illness. It didn't matter, nothing mattered, for every look that wasn't his was to me one of indifference – were I to encounter it, I knew that his look, drained of all that had sustained me, would kill.

I tried to wrench my life round into a new pattern, one in which Robert was no longer my sun and moon, the source of my light, my measure of the months and years. It was failing in this so repeatedly, so wretchedly, that had led to my flight to Sheffield, to my father – under the cowardly cover of filial concern for what seemed likely to be his last illness. Only from my father could I be sure of a sufficiently reliable affection, one that would never through its removal destroy me; only in his company, old allies as we were from the silent, conspiratorial days of my childhood, did I feel the smallest bit safe.

There, for the last eighteen months of my father's life, I tended him with such love and solicitude as I had it in me left to bestow. And he had rewarded me with his gentle gratitude and with occasional hints – more in his mildly enquiring looks, in what was not rather than in what was said – that he was aware that all was not well with me; always tactfully, bless him, he was the soul of tact, my father, and for that I offered up silent thanks. My father, who had bestowed on me my strange name, was providing me to the best of his ability with a version of those mythic halcyon days.

And then he died – and I had to start the business of learning to live all over again.

That I had done so, however feebly, was in part thanks to Margot. My sister's insistence that we move to Knight's Fee had turned out to be a nudge towards what had begun to revive if not yet restore me, not that I expected ever to be restored. But here, modestly, in measured medicinal doses, I had begun to fashion another, different way of life. A life which had begun to show the green shoots of an ordinary, everyday pleasure in a new simplicity, without the racing currents of desire and the necessity of a seeming reciprocity which I had no wish to reinstate or revive.

I had enjoyed my straightforward acquaintances with the villagers; I had enjoyed chatting to Hayley, hearing about her mother's new diet, her sister's tricky marriage to an alcoholic and how she, Hayley, was grateful that, thanks to a drunken father, Russ didn't drink; I'd enjoyed, with appropriate sympathetic interjections, hearing about their daughter's disastrous boyfriend, who was caught selling drugs, and Russ's addiction to *Breaking Bad*, from which, Hayley felt, given the boyfriend, her daughter should be shielded; I'd enjoyed calling by at Debs' to buy a hand-made card for a friend's birthday and adding my name to the petition to fight against the bus cuts; I'd enjoyed shopping at the 'Stitch' and buying a pair of Shetland gloves (reduced from £15 to £9.99) and hearing how the owner's son was coming along with his PhD. I'd even come to quite enjoy swapping 'artistic' reminiscences with Jim Bell, Hope Wenlock's pipe-smoking local artist, whose clotted-cream sheep and violent purple hills made him almost as much money as I earnt with Elfine.

It was fun buying seeds at Brian's, where I also bought a green watering can, because it looked so like the one in *Peter Rabbit*, a doormat with WELCOME on it, which Margot found 'vulgar', and a long feather duster with which to tackle the numerous cobwebs, which she dismissed as requiring 'a French maid's outfit complete with fishnet stockings'. All this was my new world – parochial, maybe, but parochial was what was seeing me through and I had come to value, even to cherish it.

The relationship I had with the villagers may have been superficial but I was learning that the superficial can be soothing, especially when all parties want only to be neighbourly and be free to get along peaceably with their lives. I wanted nothing deep, nothing that would summon my passions, which had burnt me so badly. I had found a friend in Phyllis Foot, another in Peter Haycroft, and neither were the sort to probe. In fact, when I considered it, they were the sort who themselves disliked being probed, private people with their own private worlds and only a mild, if any, curiosity about mine. They were kindly disposed, their demands were few and those they had were ones I was happy to meet. Above all, I had my garden, bounded by a stream which was visited by a kingfisher, and, to help me with it, a courteous and unobtrusive gardener, who had his own sorrows and fears to contend with, who left me to my solitude and seemed to want nothing but the same unruffled tranquillity for himself.

In short, I had found a haven and now here at my dinner table sat this agent of fate come to herald a new devastation.

'Oh didn't you hear?' Julian's languid drawl was intoning. 'Robert and Laura parted.' He turned to proffer his empty glass. For a second his expressionless eyes held mine. 'Laura kicked him out. From what I gather, not before time.'

I continued with consummate care to pour Roman Red into his glass while the brave new world I had been patiently constructing splintered into tiny shards around me.

PART II

11

Phyllis Foot and I were sitting in deckchairs enjoying a spell of sunny weather and the distinctive scent of mown grass. Murat had finished mowing the lawn and was digging in horse manure round the new roses we'd planted in the long flower bed. One of the several robins which parcelled out the garden between them was following in his wake, picking at the fresh-turned soil.

We had been drinking tea and had fallen into a comfortable silence. Then 'You are looking better, my dear,' Phyllis offered.

Easter, symbolically, had fallen on the first of April and the temperature had dropped to a level that seemed to me an appropriately bad joke. On Easter Sunday, I walked to church for the service, as an act of friendship for Peter rather than from any spiritual inclination. The church, alight with spring flowers – daffodils, forsythia, pussy willow – looked charming and the congregation, the children bearing bunches of wild flowers, had got themselves up nicely too.

Phyllis, wearing a surprisingly chic little hat which, she told me later, she had bought on a school trip to Paris, beckoned me over to her pew.

'I thought you weren't a Christian,' I said.

'Easter was celebrated here long before it was a Christian festival,' she said, in what I inwardly referred to as her schoolmarm voice. 'But you have been misinformed. It's the Church I quarrel with. I am all in favour of Jesus. Anyone who can summon a god of love and mercy who has stood the test of time is fine by me.' She must have observed me looking at the battered Bible she had open on the pew as she added tartly, 'You seem surprised. With some obvious reservations, I'm in favour of the Bible too. I've agreed that provided I am permitted to use my King James version I will read one of the lessons, John, chapter twenty, one to eighteen, verses I am fond of.'

Peter delivered a trite sermon on the empty tomb, on which Phyllis offered a critical commentary as we walked together back down the hill.

'I'm devoted to Peter but he hasn't a thimbleful of imagination. The empty tomb is a metaphor.'

'Is it?'

'The stone across the mouth of the tomb.'

'And . . .?'

'Think about it – a marvellous image of all the resistances and defences that imprison us – apparently intractable and unyielding but rolled away in a trice once the angels are let in.'

I didn't ask if she believed in angels. It seemed likely,

given her other cranky beliefs. I was feeling tomb-like myself so these wise words, if that's what they were, fell on deaf ears. Somewhat resentful ones, too. The church was unheated and the weather viciously chilly. I had already started a cold that day, which went on to develop into a bad cough, which in turn worsened and was finally diagnosed, when I agreed to a visit to the local GP, as 'one of those viruses', the effects of which lingered long after the obvious symptoms had disappeared. A general mood of slack weariness overcame me, I felt persistently done in and slopped about with a listlessness that was compounded by having Eloise, whose features I'd yet to determine, hanging over me.

My low spirits were accentuated by the burgeoning life around me. It has never surprised me that most suicides occur in the spring. *See, see, this is life*, the natural world seems to cry, admonishing those of us who are failing and faint of heart. *What price your miserable creeping existence compared to our ruthless ever-recurring beauty?*

Margot, when she returned from London, was first worried and then annoyed. 'I'm beginning to think you don't want to recover,' she complained after I'd rejected various alternative remedies and had turned down an offer of a visit to consult some health guru in Presteigne.

'Marg, the thought of getting dressed and travelling all that way . . .'

'Really, Hass, if you got yourself into some halfway decent clothes, you'd feel better. You look like an old-age pensioner, moping around in those terrible tracksuit bottoms. I can see your knickers through them. And those dreadful Dr. Scholl's . . . I thought I'd chucked them out.'

I'd deliberately fished the sandals out of the bin. It wasn't clear, even to me, why I was wearing them.

'And speaking of knickers, I threw out the ones you'd left to go mouldy in the washing machine.'

'What! Why?'

'Apart from the fact that they'd begun to stink, they're old ladies' knickers. And the white ones had gone all blue from being washed with jeans. You must never wash knickers with jeans. The dye can give you a vaginal rash.'

'Margot, I've never in my life had a vaginal rash and no one but me sees my knickers.'

'There's a lot of rashes about with these industrial dyes. And I see your knickers and I don't like to think of you in them. I've left a new pack on your bed – all cotton but not so big they'd fit a bargee's arse.'

I felt I should be annoyed by this but I was too lack-lustre to mind. 'As long as you've replaced the ones you've thrown out.'

'I bought two packs. You can have both. I've drawer-loads of knickers.'

I was praying that would be it but she was all set on one of her improving crusades. 'And it wouldn't hurt to brush your hair. You look like shit. You need to get out. Go and see some of your new pals, the precious villagers you were so keen to get to know.'

'Do shut up. I don't feel up to doing anything yet.'

Margot was quiet and then announced, 'I know what you need – a love life. You're sex-starved.'

This finally roused me. 'For Christ's sake, Marg!'

'What's the matter? It's perfectly normal. Women need

sex as much as men. More, in some cases. What about the vicar? He fancies you. Julian thought so too.'

'That's crap. And anyway, how could Julian possibly tell? Half that evening he was out in the garden smoking.'

'He's astute,' Margot said. 'He sussed you don't like him.'

'I barely know him.'

'Doesn't stop you disliking him. You went all weird when he was here.'

Please, please stop, I inwardly begged, but said, 'That had nothing to do with Julian. I couldn't give a fuck about him.'

'What is it then? I'm worried about you. You're not eating either. You can't afford to lose weight. You're developing jowls.'

'It's the book.' Desperately, I resorted to Elfine. 'It's getting me down, that's all. And I don't give a monkey's about getting jowls.'

'You don't want to look like a bloodhound. And you should dump Elfine. You hate her and it's bad for you.'

'You know I can't afford to,' I said resentfully.

'You can't afford not to,' Margot said. 'And I'm personally taking those dreadful Dr. Scholl's to the dump.'

But Margot didn't – how could she? – understand.

A few days after the dinner party, when Margot and Julian and the gay couple had returned to London and there was no chance of being overheard, I dug out my address book and looked up the number of Catherine's husband, Alistair.

We had fallen out of touch. Alistair had acquired a new

partner and together they had decamped to France. Robert and I had visited them once in their rural home near Autun. Alistair, who knew Laura only slightly, would, Robert assured me, be perfectly safe with our secret.

I had not taken to the new partner but, as Robert implied, she was culpable of no crime more heinous than that of not being Catherine. Catherine had been both my dearest friend and source of my best work. It was a loss I found impossible to overcome and no amount of French food in a tasteful French farmhouse could reconcile me to Catherine's replacement.

'I know it's unfair but I can't like her,' I confessed, and Robert kissed me.

'That's because you, my darling, are incorrigibly loyal.'

'The pot calling the kettle black?' I suggested, allowing myself a touch of waspishness. His constancy in loyalty to Laura remained a thorn.

So what had undone that seemingly indissoluble bond? And why had he not at once got in touch with me when that long-standing loyalty was no longer required?

For some days I chose to continue in ignorance but a need to know the worst is almost irresistible and the affinity that Robert and I shared had always, I believed, run on truth.

The first time I rang the number in France I put the phone down before it could be answered. The second time I hung on, heart thudding sickeningly, until a voice with an English accent answered. '*Oui, allô.*'

Even then, seconds passed before I managed, 'Alistair?'

'Who's this?'

'It's Hassie. Halcyon Days. Catherine's . . .'

'Of course I know who you are. Hassie, how nice to hear from you. What a nice surprise.'

We exchanged further pleasantries before I got round to the point of my call. Then, very tentatively, 'I wondered if you had heard at all from Robert.'

'Rob? Sure.' His voice had become careful.

Courage, I told myself. *Be brave.* 'I met someone recently who knew his wife and heard, at least that's what he suggested, that they have parted.'

A telling silence, then, 'Sorry, there was someone at the door. I believe that is the case.' The tone was very cautious now.

'Alistair, can you tell me what happened? I promise to be discreet.'

There, I had said it. And I waited at the other end of the phone to have my heart smashed into fragments all over again.

That the severity of the viral infection was a consequence of what I had learnt from Alistair I never doubted. If the first loss had deranged my wits, the second did for my health. It was not news to me that the body is in thrall to the mind, or whatever passes for it; but by now the state of my own mind was a puzzlement. In all the bleak nights after my flight to Sheffield, I never once dreamt of Robert. Now I dreamt of him all the time: in one dream I was begging him to hold me tight, tight against his own body, and in the dream space I felt him, as he pressed against my breasts, belly and thighs, grow hard with desire; in another dream, we were making love, not once but many times over – as we had on those occasions when we were able to

151

scramble together time enough to do so. Never before could I recall a dream in which I felt the sexual act so explicitly and physically. From these dreams I woke bathed in a sensual nimbus, whose effects so deeply perfused my body and limbs that it took sometimes half a day for the radiant warmth to fade. And then I was cruelly returned to the wan world, where Robert was missing – where Robert had proved false.

That these spectral dream events so exactly matched my most blissful recollections gave them an extraordinary dual valency: for on the one hand they almost perfectly re-enacted moments of intensely fulfilled desire and on the other they seemed like the cruel mockings of a hollow cosmic laughter, the deceiving tricks of some malign invisible power, with their lack of any real-world lasting validity.

For the brutal truth was that Robert had been free – free as a bird, from what Alistair had divulged – to come to me if it had pleased him.

I could get from Alistair no clear sense of what had occurred. He was reluctant to say more than that Julian was right: Robert and Laura had parted. He gave nothing more away, nothing about the cause or nature of the parting, adding that he saw very little of Robert these days. I concluded from this that whatever had happened there had been some crisis in Robert, a falling away from all his old ties. Had he wanted to, it could hardly have been easier to find me. He had my phone number, which had never changed – my unwillingness to use it on moving to Knight's Fee had something to do with the months I had spent anxiously consulting it in the vain hope of a message. My last communication to Robert had been a letter that, to ensure its anonymous arrival, I sent via his agent, in which I had spelt out my plans. *I am going for the time being to look after my father.* To this I first added *who needs me more than you apparently do* but I thought better of it and rewrote the letter, omitting anything that could be taken for a reproach.

I hesitated over how to end what might be his last taste of who I was, but finally wrote: *You once suggested that you would like to meet Dad. If you still feel you would then you will always be welcome and will find us at the below*, and appended the Sheffield address.

So there was no excuse. No Hardyesque opportunity for a malign fate to craft a lovers' misunderstanding. If there had been misunderstanding it was on my part: I could only conclude that in the end he simply didn't love me.

'Or maybe just not enough?' Phyllis Foot suggested.

It was the oddest thing that, sitting in the garden, still feeling weak as a kitten, I found myself confiding in my relatively new friend. The scent of the new-mown grass had led naturally on to the subject of Peter Haycroft. I mentioned how impressed I had been that he bought his wife scent, adding that the Haycrofts struck me as having been an unusually happy couple, and Phyllis had mentioned the critical attitude of some of the village towards the vicar's untidy appearance, explaining that this had become noticeable since his wife's death.

And perhaps because I was considering my own unmarried state, or because of my enfeebled condition, I followed this, most uncharacteristically because I dislike nosiness and was never as a rule a nosey person, with, 'Did you mind never marrying?'

Phyllis's face looked for a moment even flatter and paler than usual. 'Why do you assume I never married?'

I blushed deeply and was startled by a loud laugh.

'Your face! Of course you assumed . . . I did marry once, as it happens. A result of a misunderstanding with a young person. I never intended us to marry.'

'But then why did you?' liberated by the laughter, I felt able to ask.

'I hadn't grasped how essential it is to say everything one needs to say from the first – in any sexual relation-ship, that is – or perhaps in any relationship that might become important. I was still a victim of the unfortunate delusion that one must be polite. A mistake but, in fair-ness to my younger self, a common one.'

'Someone once said that to me,' I found myself confid-ing, 'that you had to say everything that had to be said at the beginning or it would be too late.'

'And it didn't help?' The hazelish-green eyes ceased to look amused.

'No.' Suddenly, I felt all the constraints formed by the long habit of secrecy drop away. What did it matter now what I said or whom I told? I no longer cared. It wasn't the case that I no longer cared for Robert; sadly, I couldn't envisage a time when that would be true – I say 'sadly' though I doubt that I wanted then to let that go – but I no longer seemed to care what I said about him. At least to Phyllis Foot who, despite all appearances, was neither a virgin nor a spinster.

'There was a man,' I said, 'I fell in love with and I believed was in love with me. But he was married . . .'

'I see,' was all my companion said for some time.

Phyllis Foot listened without interruption until I said, 'So you see, in the end I had to accept that he simply didn't love me.'

Which was when she said, 'Or maybe just not enough?'

'What could stop him once he was free?'

'Any number of things. Shame for one, at having let you go in the first place. Some feeling that he deserved punishment for having let two women down. The minds of men are often opaque to women. I'm aware that's old-fashioned and sexist.'

As she spoke, she bent a little towards me and the fine-set opal brooch that she customarily wore on the lapel of her grey jacket gleamed with a flash of fire. It sparked alight some forgotten words, which at the time I didn't stop to consider or construe. I was too set on clinging to the seat of the high horse of my misery.

'I knew Robert. Better than anyone, he claimed. I can't imagine either of those being reasons to stop him if he loved me.'

'Did you really know him, my dear? I'm inclined to think we know no one that well, given how exceedingly little we often know ourselves. And "love", well, it's a flexible matter at best, wouldn't you say?'

I was assailed by a fierce desire to dispute any suggestion that Robert's failure might have any mitigating reasons. 'Maybe,' I half conceded, secretly riled. I was unwilling to be freed from my wounding hook. 'But he could, *should* have written. He had my address. He swore we would never lose touch.'

She nodded, as if in agreement, but then said gently, 'In my experience most promises have loopholes and even the most honourable may finesse a way through them.'

I was saved from making an abrasive retort by Murat, who was approaching with a trug of forget-me-nots, a gift from Phyllis's garden.

'I have dug in the manure. Will I plant these now . . .?'

'Thank you, Murat, but I'll put those in myself. Would you like tea?' He never accepted these invitations but I always made a point of asking.

'Thank you. I have some more work with the vegetables. I am sowing spinach and kale.'

'That's great, Murat. Thank you.'

'I have also sowed tomatoes. They are in the kitchen.'

The greenhouse promised by Margot as an Easter present had never materialized. Murat had asked about it and I had had to explain that it was in my sister's gift and, since I couldn't afford the purchase myself, we would have to make do and wait. I should have known better than to trust this sort of careless gesture from Margot but it annoyed me on Murat's behalf. He was most attached to his vegetable garden.

He started towards it but turned back. 'The seeds are by the window,' he said. 'Remember to water.'

'Of course.' I was careless too in my way. I'd been remiss with his courgettes and was aware that I was receiving a tactful reprimand.

'I can't tell you,' I said, when Murat had gone, 'what he's done. He's sowed, I don't know –' I ticked off on my fingers – 'beetroots, carrots, Swiss chard, leeks, turnips and heaven knows what else. And he's laying a terrace with the old paving stones we found when we got here. It was his idea; he has a wonderful eye. I'd never have got the garden into any shape without him. He's been a godsend.'

What I didn't say was that I was grateful to Murat for providing an avenue of escape. I wished that I had never raised the matter of Robert's dereliction with Phyllis Foot. Now that I had, it was no longer safe within the vaults of my private consciousness.

12

Margot had not brought Julian down with her since the Easter visit and was spending more time, to be with him I assumed, in London. So I had Knight's Fee for longer spells to myself.

There remained in me some profound resistance to recovery. But in body, at least, I grew stronger. Living, as someone has said, is something that goes on happening in spite of yourself.

Margot's speculations about the vicar and my own over-confiding conversation with Phyllis Foot had left me disinclined to see either of my new friends. And my other acquaintances were not draw enough to make me want to linger long in the village. I began to regret my decision not to buy a car so I could drive out and walk on Wenlock Edge.

On Wenlock Edge the wood's in trouble . . . another of Dad's favourites. It struck me anew as feeble, as well as some-what disloyal, in all this time not to have explored those hills that formed so impressive a part of my daily horizon.

Dad would have been the first up there in his walking boots.

But in his honour I had fitted out the garden with hanging feeders and bird tables and instead of walking the hills I now began to study the birdlife. With only the birds as companions, I felt safe – safe from prying eyes or attempts at understanding. And I began to see why Dad had been drawn to birds. They were a respite from the problems of relationship. At the same time, they were a kind of relationship because they were life – but in forms from which one could suffer no harm. And birds, he told me once, are very old: the oldest surviving species of prehistoric times. There was something oddly calming about that.

It was apparent that, having had the place to themselves for over two years, the birds considered the garden their own. With Dad's binoculars I learnt to recognize all the common garden species. Blackbirds, thrushes and wrens were already familiar to me but now I learnt to distinguish blue tits, coal tits and great tits, and one day my heart was lifted by a flock of long-tailed tits, with buff-rose breasts and fine black markings, that arrived to swing in the branches of the alder trees that grew near the stream. Finches of various stripes, chaffinches, greenfinches and scarlet-topped goldfinches were regulars, and I became extremely fond of the little brown hedge sparrow, or dunnock, one of which had greeted me from the cherry tree my first morning at Knight's Fee. Those modest grey heads, whenever I saw them, somehow conveyed the essence of Dad.

Once, I walked down to the stream to find a heron hunched in the shallows, gravely inspecting the water for fish. I sat watching it for some time before it hiked up its long legs, extended huge wings, flapped clumsily upwards and flew off, its neck folded back on itself like a tuba. And one enchanted night I thought I heard a nightingale sing and down the years I heard Dad telling me, 'It goes *'jug jug'* *to dirty ears.'* That might have been wishful thinking; I've never heard one here again.

But since that early sighting, there had been no sign of my kingfisher.

There were other birds I began to be able to identify as I walked through field and wood to the village when I needed to shop: raggedy-winged, gregarious rooks, solitary crows, kestrels (which led to my rereading 'The Windhover'), lone kites, an occasional trim-bodied sparrowhawk. But the garden was my small private paradise which I felt honoured to share with the birds.

A kind of ritual established itself: early each morning, I would go outside in my nightclothes and stand barefoot in the dew-drenched grass and the tremulous dawn light, letting the silvery birdsong rinse my ears and the clean morning air fill my lungs and the sun or wind or rain bless my skin. It was at this time of day when I felt as if I were in touch with some larger, stranger reality, which lay behind the appearance of things, the hidden forces at work beneath nature's surface, and although I never consciously framed the thought there was a sense that if I stood there long and quietly enough, I might become sufficiently attuned to its mysteries to see into its heart.

Then I would go back inside, make a pot of coffee, heat milk in the copper-bottomed milk pan, put on boots or sandals and with my mug of coffee make a tour of the garden, inspecting what was coming up or coming out, what was spreading or burgeoning, what needed taking out and where and what I might replant.

I had planted out Phyllis's forget-me-nots, which she'd handed me with a characteristic 'Sorry to give you more invaders. These are worse than lily-of-the-valley but they make a heavenly ground cover and they do fill the gaps and keep down the weeds.' They were already weaving a blue and white brocade around the roses I had ordered – after an enjoyable evening scrutinizing a gardening catalogue – on which healthy-looking buds had formed. Foliage like fine green lace promised further blues from the self-seeded love-in-a-mist. The oriental poppies, bought at the garden centre, had spread their veined hairy leaves and the lupins and the foxgloves were pushing up tender-budded spires. Other perennials, from Nelly East's time, were re-emerging: paddle-shaped hollyhock leaves, delphiniums, red-hot pokers and a plant that I liked especially and learnt had the exotic name of Solomon's Seal. But happy as I was to see all this, what was most thrilling was the sight of the seeds Murat and I had sown germinating in the darkness of the potting shed.

One morning, about to enter the shed to inspect the seed trays, I heard a noise.

'Murat?' Early bird as he often was, it was early even for him.

No reply. Perhaps a fox had got inside. Murat had found one there one morning and suggested another lock was needed. Cautiously, I pushed the door ajar.

There was a scuffling and a small body shot past. Not a fox. A child. A girl – the slenderest slip of a girl in shocking-pink shorts with a dandelion-seed cloud of white-blonde hair.

'Hey!' I called and belted after her. Fleet as the girl was, her flight was halted by the stream. As I reached its banks, I saw her trying to wade upstream to where it flowed beyond the territory of the garden. 'Hey!' I yelled again. 'It's OK. I'm not cross.'

She turned back and I saw she was the girl who had been rude the day I bought Murat's boots. The child was so small that, shallow as the stream was, the water came up to past her waist. As she stood there, a shaft of sunlight lanced through the overhanging willow and lit up her features, so that what I had first seen as pinched and feral seemed transformed. A heart-shaped face, milk-white skin and blue veins tracing her temples like some latter-day princess; her hair caught in the sun formed a bright halo around her head and cast a rippling golden pattern across the water. She was so slight she might have been one of Elfine's elves.

'Would you like a biscuit?' I called, thinking we might make friends.

The girl stared scowling, most un-Elfine-like, then wordlessly began to wade towards the bank. She scrambled out and I saw that beneath the streaks of mud her knees were as bruised and scabbed as before.

'What's your name?' I hoped I sounded unthreatening. Having no children of my own, and with no close friends with children, I was a little unsure how to proceed.

The girl looked down at her sopping trainers. One had a hole in it and the toe poking through was painted with a chipped blue varnish. 'Why?'

'Sorry, I should have introduced myself first. I'm Hassie.'

The girl didn't look up but began to wring out a leg of her wet shorts.

I abandoned any further attempt at introductions. 'Let's go up to the house and get you dry before you have a biscuit.'

I found a towel and one of my own T-shirts and persuaded the girl to go to the bathroom to change. She emerged in the T-shirt, silently handing over a wet bundle of knickers and shorts.

'Shall I dry these for you?' No reply. 'Or put them in a bag for you to take home?'

The girl said nothing to this either, but she nodded. She nodded more emphatically when offered milk and biscuits. Happily, there was real milk in the fridge. Margot only drank oat or almond milk and I often didn't bother to buy ordinary cow's milk for myself. I suspected that any alternative version of milk would count against me with this child.

The girl had emptied the glass of milk and wolfed down two chocolate digestives before I spoke again. 'Sorry if this is a rude question – shouldn't you be at school?'

I was prepared to be rebuffed but she appeared unfazed. 'I'm off sick.'

'Nothing too bad, I hope?'

'A migraine.'

'I've never had a migraine but I'm told they're nasty.'

'My mum has them. They run in our family,' the girl announced with pride.

'But you're feeling OK now?'

The grey eyes in the pale face became wary again. 'If I get one in the morning I have them all day. Sometimes I have to lie down.'

'I see,' I said. I thought I probably did. 'Would it be OK to ask what you were doing in my shed?'

The expression darkened. 'Why?'

'No special reason except it is my shed. Our shed, I should say. Mine and my sister's.'

'My nan says it's not trespass if you don't do no harm.'

'Your nan is right. There're some interesting things in there if you like flowers.'

'What?'

'Some seeds growing. Would you like to see them?'

She frowned and said without enthusiasm, 'All right,' eyeing the packet of chocolate digestives.

'Have another,' I invited her. 'Better you eat them than me.'

'Why?'

'I don't want to put on weight,' I laughed, as I thought, encouragingly.

The girl closed her eyes, patently wearied by this pathetic attempt at ingratiation, and extracted two more biscuits from the packet. She ate greedily, cramming them in so that her mouth and chin were smeared with chocolate as we walked back down to the potting shed.

Murat had arrived and was unlocking the tool shed.

'Hi, Murat. I'm bringing – um . . .' gesturing at the girl, 'a visitor to look at your seeds.'

Murat graced her with his beatific smile, at which the girl muttered something inaudible.

'Sorry?' I bent down to hear better.

'I *said* I got to get back to my nan's.'

'You don't want to see the seeds?' Among her peers, as

I had witnessed, the girl was a leader and this could maybe set a trend. Here was a chance to bring brave new opportunities to the village children. A good cause into which I could put my battered heart.

As if in concord with these thoughts, Murat produced a seed packet from his jacket pocket and dropped down to the girl's level. 'Would you like to help sow these?'

His brown face, with the topaz eyes and narrow, slanting cheekbones, had something of the other-worldly quality of some Eastern saint found on an icon or ancient wall painting.

The girl stared steadily back and as I observed her slight form, with its angelic halo of spun-gold hair, and the figure of the dark young man, kneeling as if in supplication, there began to weave in my mind an alluring image: a gardening school for deprived local children, with Murat in charge of lessons and myself presiding, offering an environmentally creative outlet for youth and winning the gratitude of Hope Wenlock.

The girl turned and looked up at me with her candid-seeming grey eyes. 'Fucking paedo Muslim,' she pronounced, before zipping away back down towards the stream.

13

I spent the days that followed in a state of bleak despondency. The conversation with Phyllis and Margot's hints about the vicar had already prompted a distaste for Hope Wenlock society and the ugly comments flung at Murat by the blonde child deepened this sense of alienation. I had gone after her, as she fled along the stream, but past our garden its channel narrowed and was so overgrown with brambles that I felt unequal to fighting my way through and was left frustrated, vainly hoping that the vile little creature had been scratched to death.

I have made a classic mistake, I told myself. *I've fallen into the trap of supposing I could escape my fate by the mere physical act of moving. I am fated*, I decided, *to deceive myself.*

For days I wallowed in this self-pitying mood – mooching about, not getting on with Elfine and worrying about money. I hadn't so much as glanced at the manila file on the house's history, passed to me by Peter Haycroft, but noticing it where I had slung it on Dad's desk, and feeling disconsolate and thoroughly bored with myself, I carted it off to bed one evening to read.

The file contained copies of old maps depicting the land that had once belonged to a previous house; the current house, it appeared, was a relatively parvenu building, Jacobean, only constructed in the 1600s. It was a much earlier dwelling, now long gone, on the site of which the current house stands, that had been known as 'Wight's Fee'.

According to Phyllis's former pupil, it was not 'fee', as in a reward, but 'fey', which appeared to mean bad luck or ill fortune. 'Wight's Folly' was what, in essence, the house had been called. Obviously, I bitterly decided, it was to be my folly too.

That night I lay for hours, my limbs still aching from the debilitating virus, rehearsing all the bad decisions and wrong turns that had led me to take up residence in Knight's Fee.

I awoke the following morning, limbs still aching, to sounds in consort with the previous night's mood. The weather, which had begun the month so benignly, had turned foul. Bad weather in May is inevitably more depressing than in February. A screeching wind was hurling white blossoms from the wild cherry outside the corner window, making a mock snowstorm. Browning petals had stuck to the wet pane. They seemed to me obscure messages left by a malign nature.

I pulled on the tatty cardigan that doubled as my dressing gown and went through to the part of my L-shaped room that looked out over the garden. Rain was pelting the flowers in the long bed and the phlox and salvias and Canterbury bells I had lovingly planted had been flattened, as if battered senseless by a vicious hoodlum. 'I know how you feel,' I commiserated with them, through the glass. 'Beaten. Thoroughly beaten.'

I went downstairs, stubbing my toe painfully on the way, loaded a tray with teapot, milk and the remains of the chocolate digestives, and climbed wearily back to bed, toe smarting, legs aching.

God, I feel old, I thought. *Forty-four and already past my prime. I wish I was fucking dead.*

(I'm sorry about all this swearing. You probably won't approve, and I promise I didn't swear all that often, but I'm trying to be honest with you here.)

The tea, usually an unfailing comfort, which loyally I'd bought from the village shop, was a brand that I'd forgotten always tasted slightly of fish, the milk was soya, which I frankly detest, the biscuits put me in mind of the horrible blonde child, and *Wuthering Heights*, when I tried to return to it, had lost its appeal. It was a favourite novel, one I've read many times. But that morning *Wuthering Heights*, with its ghosts and the coincidence of Nelly Dean's name, had become a sinister reflection of Knight's Fee.

As part of my general malaise I had begun to hear voices at night. Mostly they seemed to be coming from the garden but sometimes from nearby. Once, I was sure I heard someone crying and got up, feeling scared, and forced myself to search the house. There was nothing and I dismissed these eerie sounds as a barn owl's screeching or foxes barking and my imagination, fuelled with, let's face it, too much of Margot's cheap cooking wine, working overtime. But that morning I did begin to wonder if the spirit of mad Mrs East, like the ghost of dead Cathy Earnshaw, could be haunting the house. A vision of the imploring, ghostly Cathy, as her wrists are rubbed brutally over the window's jagged glass till they run with blood, came back to me with more than usual horror. I was not especially superstitious, but I had always believed, like Dad, who wasn't otherwise in the least given to the irrational, that places bear the mark of those who have inhabited them and that passing generations leave a lasting imprint which has its own intangible reality.

Unable to settle in bed with these uneasy imaginings, I ran a bath in Margot's bathroom, accidentally tipped in half a bottle of her outlandishly expensive bath oil, found that the water had run too cold to enjoy the bath, swore violently, clambered out, bashing my shin on the cast-iron side, and collapsed on the floor, sobbing.

But crying never helps unless there is someone there to hear you.

Sitting on the bath mat, wet and cold, my shin bruised and bleeding, I heard first a tapping, then a knocking and finally a rattling at the back door.

Bloody hell, Murat.

I'd not seen him since the episode with the girl, when I had felt too appalled, too embarrassed, to do more than offer weak-sounding apologies. I would have to find a way of trying to make up for the disgraceful remarks. But remorse weakened rather than strengthened my will and I felt too defeated to attempt to make amends. What could I say? This was all my own doing. Margot was right: my desire to be thought well of by the locals was vain and inane.

Hugging my shins and rocking from side to side, I sat

like some inmate in a nineteenth-century lunatic asylum – praying for him to give up and go away. I'd left my pyjamas in my bedroom and Margot had removed for washing all the towels.

When enough silence had passed, I crawled naked, fearful of being observed, along the corridor back to my room, pulled on random clothes and went downstairs. Stealthily opening the back door, I found a tray of bedding plants.

'Oh shit!' In my dismay I spoke aloud.

'Excuse me?'

'Murat? I'm so sorry. I thought you'd gone.' More coals of fire: he was bearing, like some sacrificial gift, a second tray of plants. 'I'll be out in a minute when I've had coffee. Would you like some?' He never accepted coffee so this was safe.

With great care, he placed the tray of plants down beside the other and came through to the kitchen waving a brown paper bag. 'I will make you Greek coffee. I got it ground in Ludlow.'

Where the abandoning wife lived. 'That's very kind but . . .'

'In Corfu, I drink this many times a day. You have a small pan?'

Obediently, I fetched the copper-bottomed milk pan and watched as he filled it with water and spooned in the finely ground coffee, as if he were making a potion for a spell. 'Now,' he said, 'we boil this and add sugar.'

'No thank you, Murat. No sugar for me, please.'

'Yes,' he smiled, authoritative. 'You must have sugar. It is how it is made.'

He set the pan on the stove and lit the gas. A delicious smell began to percolate through the kitchen.

'It's good . . .?' He smiled again. I was trying to think if there was something to offer him other than chocolate digestives – tainted by association with the horrible child – when he handed me another bag. 'Cookies.'

Macaroons. I took one and bit into it. Slightly chewy and sticky as macaroons should be, with plenty of almonds on top. 'These are my favourites, Murat. How did you know?'

Of course he didn't, couldn't have known.

'They are mine too here,' he said simply. 'I miss the Greek pastries.'

I must get Margot to bring some baklava next time she comes, I thought.

The dark, aromatic liquid rose three times boiling in the pan before Murat requested cups. He poured out the coffee and I sipped the strong, sweet brew in silence. A feeling of peace began to seep through me. 'Murat, you're a magician – this coffee is delicious.'

'You know, I do not miss my family in Corfu, but here I miss the coffee.'

Outside, the rain-charged wind slapped blossoms furiously against the kitchen window. 'The weather too you miss, I should think.'

'Yes, but here is better for the plants.'

'What are the plants you brought in those trays?'

'Maybe they are not so good. But Brian is selling them now and I thought . . .'

'Yes, yes. You were quite right, Murat. We must support Brian. But –' an idea struck me – 'maybe it is time we went back to the garden centre. If you are free and the weather is better, we could go tomorrow or the day after.'

The rain had cleared. The countryside from its recent drenching was shining; stately horse chestnuts, alight with flowering candles, spread fingers of tender, translucent green over the blossom-laced hawthorn, which hedged the narrow lanes. Through the open window of the van I could smell the musky scent of the may as we rattled past. It was no longer primroses but banks of butter-coloured cowslips illumining the waysides. Lambs sprang in the air, all fours at once, or skittered and raced each other across the fields. In the wide sky, a pair of buzzards calmly wheeled.

I pointed them out to Murat, showing off the lore acquired through studying Dad's book. 'Look, Murat, up there. Buzzards. Birds of prey.'

'Excuse me. For prayer?'

'Oh, no, not that kind of pray. They kill mice and small birds.'

This time, on reaching the garden centre, we instinctively hunted as a pair, with me pointing out possible purchases and Murat taking pictures and researching them with an app on his phone.

He persuaded me to buy a kit for testing soil and became enthusiastic about an offer of twenty-five bags of compost.

'Isn't horse manure better? I thought we had a ready supply of that?'

'It is good to have some of this in case.'

'In case of what? Oh never mind.' If twenty-five bags

of compost would make him happy ... I felt better. Everything felt better.

We were in the same boat, Murat and I. He had been abandoned too, by the fickle Corfu tourist. Dissimilar as we might seem, misfortune had forged a link between us. Elated by this recognition, and to demonstrate my sense of camaraderie, I slid a hand under the crook of his arm.

He gave no outward sign but an instinct made me disengage my hand. I shouldn't have presumed. However amiable his behaviour, he could hardly not have reacted to that child's vile words. I vowed to find a moment to raise it again. *But not now*, I decided. He was busy searching on his phone for a hydrangea with pendulous white and lime-green blooms.

'Have you found it, Murat? It's rather lovely.'

'Magical Moonlight it is called. But it will not do well in our soil.'

'We haven't tested the soil yet.' I indicated the kit, waiting to be paid for.

'Miss Foot lent me hers. I have already done one test. It is alkaline. But we should test again. I think her kit is out of date.'

'Would you mind,' I said, as we left with the twenty-five bags of compost, two white lilacs, some honeysuckles and a variety of lavenders in the van, 'if we stopped on the way home? There's something I want to look at again. It's near that pub where we had lunch. But we won't eat there this time.'

'No Scottish eggs today?'

'Yes. I mean, no. No Scotch eggs. Peter, the vicar,

suggested a pub not far from here where he claims they serve very good salmon sandwiches.'

Lunch was much pleasanter this time. While we ate smoked-salmon sandwiches, Murat described to me his two elder brothers, who ran a bar in Ipsos, and his young sister, who worked in a nail salon in Corfu Town.

'Do you miss them?' I asked.

He shrugged. 'Not much. Not really. I like it here.'

In spite of the horrible child? I thought but didn't say. I didn't want to taint the cordial atmosphere.

We drove back and together we lugged the twenty-five bags of compost, first out of the van and into the wheel-barrow and then down to the shed, before I asked him if he would mind clearing more of the vegetation overhanging the stream.

He had already cleared our banks but since my failed attempt to catch the horrible child I had decided to see about clearing it beyond our boundaries.

He looked worried. 'It is your property?'

'No. But it seems a shame that it's so overgrown. I'd like to be able to explore it.'

'But it is all right that I do this on someone else's property?'

I could see this was making him anxious so I said to leave it for now.

When I went in, I found Phyllis had rung. She had already left several messages which I hadn't answered because of the hostile feelings I'd been nursing through having confided in her – a state of mind which was the more unpleasant as there was no one to blame for this but myself. But the following day, guilt finally spurred me into

174

action. And I had questions to which she might know the answers.

It was late afternoon, that moment when the light begins imperceptibly to soften towards dusk. Rooks were cavorting in rowdy acrobatics against a sky of celestial blue. In the field that led to the wood, shoots of tender young green barley were showing. Circumventing the field to mind the crop, I startled a couple of rabbits and watched their white scuts bounce as they raced off.

A lark sheered off so close by my feet that I could see its brushed-up crest, like an untidy schoolboy's hair. It spiralled upwards into the aether and began a fierce, bright carolling.

'*The Lark Ascending*,' my father had said when I asked him what he would like at his funeral. 'No hymns, please. Just the Vaughan Williams.'

The copse had been quietly greening since I last walked there. The floor of the wood, in the light filtering through the pattern of leaves, had been transformed into a miracle of sapphire. Mingling with the seductive scent of blue-bells was a heady smell of garlic from the star-shaped wild garlic flowers. Shards of sunlight, flickering through the shadows, lit up patches of bluebells, making them mirages of cool blue water.

I halted by the pool, where tiny insects were fizzing, and watched a dragonfly, its sequinned twig of a body never quite settling, shimmer just above the surface of the water like a magician's trick. As I watched, an echoing bolt of bright turquoise shot by.

In the days of first knowing Robert, I had looked

eagerly for propitious omens: a black cat, a white horse, a crescent moon to wish on. Now the kingfisher, my bird, seemed to carry some message or sign.

I had with me Dad's old haversack, which I had taken to carrying about to ensure I always had the bird book to hand. It made a useful outdoor cushion and I set it down on a natural seat formed by the humped roots of the big oak and waited.

I sat for some time, trying to ignore the insects whining about my head, first observing a bustling iridescent beetle and then a lettuce-green, angular-backed insect high-stepping fastidiously over the minute white flowers that embroidered the mossy surround. I'd never before taken much account of insects but its intricate form seemed to me now exquisitely delicate and its colouring preternaturally green beside the green of the moss. *Yet it's part of nature so it can't be unnatural*, I thought.

A tiny snail with a translucent violet-and-yellow-striped shell, climbing over a rotting log, began to fascinate me. I diverted myself by searching my mind for other unnatural-seeming natural things: lightning and peacocks, stalactites and red-spotted toadstools, duck-billed platypuses and mistletoe, which last unfortunately led to a recollection of a stolen Christmas Eve with Robert, when Laura's flight was, as luck would occasionally have it, delayed, exactly the kind of recollection that I was trying not to have. I was distracted from this recidivist line of thought by the sight of a nuthatch making its way headfirst down another of the aged oaks and then by a chestnut wren which began to thread bobbin-like through a thicket of blackberry. And all of a sudden, a thrush on an overhanging rowan, its pale, freckled breast puffed out, started up a refrain: *Pew, pew, pew – pee-ewe, pee-ewe, pep-ewe.* Some way off, another thrush chipped in with an answering call.

'But, Dad, what about readings?' I had asked.

'"The Darkling Thrush" if you must read something. I like that one. He knew his birds.'

As if in response to the thrushes, a yellow bill poked out of one of the hazel bushes and a male blackbird hopped out. It cocked its head on one side consideringly, then flew up to a blossoming bough of wild cherry, paused for half a beat and then began a melodious counterpoint to the thrush duet.

But the silent imperial kingfisher having once revealed itself remained aloof.

I awoke with a start, wondering where on earth I had been until I felt the damp moss beneath my hand and the oak burl digging into my shoulder. The gold shards of sunlight had dissolved into a soft silvery fan of fingers and the drifts of snow-white wind flowers had become puddles of ghostly pearl. The sky, through the lacework of foliage, was trailing ribbons of dark rose. From the echoing calls of the homing rooks I deduced I had slept for over an hour.

I had dreamt. There had been voices, a strange chanting. But as I tried to catch hold of it, the dream, already a fading echo, slid away from me, a mere tracery of notes, into the gathering dusk. For one of those moments which seem afterwards – when summoned back – to have slipped outside time, I felt I might go after it, as though if I set off at once and followed the will-o'-the-wisp dream I might find out some great, undisclosed, elusive secret . . . and then the moment passed and I was alone in the darkening wood.

In the chequered half-light, I stood wondering whether to turn back or go on to Phyllis's, as I'd set out to do, havered, then decided to go on. Dew was beginning to fall as I crossed the second field to the village so that my bare feet in sandals grew wet and cold. The sheep were already pale huddles in the twilight, beginning to hunker down, fretfully summoning their lambs to their sides. I could see the crenellated shape of the church tower against the gold-and-scarlet-and-indigo-racked sky. The sun, now a burnished coin, was dropping down into a cleft in the ridged outline of Wenlock Edge.

A whisper of the vanished dream wafted tantalizingly back as if to tease me – the faintest ringing in my ears, not an especially tuneful sound, more like the far-off *clink clink* of the bells worn around the necks of mountain goats, which I have heard at times echoing on Mediterranean hillsides – and then, as if the goats had passed on, over to other pastures, the sounds drifted away again.

Fret not after knowledge . . . Who was it who said that?

14

I was used by now to finding the green door in the thatched porch open and, when I knocked and entered, the fire was burning and Phyllis was in the rocking chair. Her glasses were askew, a dribble of spittle was visible at the corner of her open mouth and she was snoring. As I stood wondering what to do, she gave a loud snort and opened her eyes.

'Sorry if I woke you. I can come another time.' I was quite glad for an excuse not to stay.

'Was I asleep? How are you? Is it time for a drink?'

'I'm fine, I think. Yes, please, to a drink, if you're sure. But I can get it.'

'Sit down by the fire, child, you're shivering.'

It was true I was extremely cold. I stooped to hold my hands to the warmth and as I did so into my mind there came a strange image of a stook of barley.

Mags came sidling up and began to polish my calves with his soft fur.

'Hello, Mags. You've grown.'

'I would say he's missed you; but unlike humans cats sensibly don't go in for missing. Here.'

The sight of Phyllis's hands, the skin freckled and transparent over the veins, as she passed me one of her grandmother's green glasses, prompted compunction. 'Crosspatch' my mother used to call me. I resented the term the more because I knew I was being compared to Margot, the supposedly sunny-natured one. My annoyance with Phyllis arose from no better reason than that I'd confided in her.

I sipped the wine. 'What is it?'

'Dandelion. My 2014 vintage. What do you think?'

'It's not like anything I've ever drunk,' I said truthfully. The wine was rather thick and syrupy. 'Come, Mags.' I patted my lap and the kitten leapt up.

The cottage was very quiet. The only sounds were the occasional spitting of the fire and the slight squeak of the timbers of the rocking chair as Phyllis rocked back and forth. I stroked the kitten's jet-black fur, feeling the lean ribs rise and fall in their own rhythm beneath my hand. *How fragile life is*, I thought. The tiny warm form began to vibrate on my thighs like a small, efficient motor. The kitten suddenly arched his neck luxuriantly and began a throaty, contented purr. *Yet how strong life is too.*

Outside, a red van shifted gear loudly as it laboured uphill and a dove fluttered down past the window. The white bird was framed for a second by the pale-yellow blooms of Phyllis's banksia rose. What did one dove signify? Peace and an olive branch after the flood.

'Phyllis,' I broke the silence. 'You said – is that

right? – you had some ideas about Knight's Fee's name? Hey, stop it, Mags!' as the kitten began to treadle.

'Mmm?'

'I've been reading the file the vicar lent me – gave me, I should say. Nelly East didn't want it back.'

'She wouldn't.'

'Why not?'

'I've read my former pupil's paper. She was a bright girl, Christina, but not a scrap of imagination. It's full of Gradgrindish facts. There's nothing wrong with facts except that people cling to them and they are so often found to be tommyrot.'

'What *is* tommyrot?' I asked, wandering off on a moment-ary tangent. My grandmother, my mother's mother, was fond of this expression but she was not someone whom you could ask questions of. She was the one who asked questions. When we visited, she would say, 'Well, Halcyon, what have you been up to?' which I found very disagreeable and quite unanswerable.

'Now you ask,' Phyllis said, 'I haven't a clue. We can look it up later. Nelly believed that the name went way back, to the days of the so-called old religion. "Fee" refers not to a reward –'

'I know,' I interrupted. 'It's folly. It was Wight's Folly.' She looked at me sternly. 'Sorry. Go on.'

'That is one theory. But there are others. A "fee" was the kind of wise old woman who brewed herbs and simples and made remedial potions. But it's also a synonym for a fae or fairy. And then "wight" is the old word for an immortal being. It was Nelly's belief that her, sorry, I should say your garden was carved out of the fields and woods around the house and that these were the domain of the old people – what are known now as elves and fairies, though they were nothing like your Elfine. In Nelly's view, that was the true origin of your house's name.'

She thought there were fairies at the bottom of her garden, the blonde brat had jeered.

'I've had a horrible thing happen,' I said and described the girl and the distressing encounter with Murat.

'That will be Penny Lane.'

'She's not really called that?'

'She's officially Isabel, but her grandmother, who pretty well brought her up, called her that from the start.'

'Her grandmother hasn't brought her up very well then,' I said, indignation reviving.

'Don't be too hard on Penny. She's no father worth speaking of, a drunken ne'er-do-well who was a one-night stand. Her mother had a post-puerperal breakdown and left the grandmother, who's not the easiest soul herself, to cope. It's not a history likely to breed goodwill unto men.'

'Where's the mother now?'

'She's around but pretty hopeless. She spends half her time in bed with psychosomatic complaints. I gather Penny has to look after her.'

I remembered how the child had spoken of her mother's migraines. 'Still, the girl can't go round making accusations like that.'

'Sue, the grandmother, is still mostly in charge. Would you like me to have a word? I know Sue and it might go down better coming from me.'

'No,' I said. 'If you tell me where she lives, I'll talk to her. I'll be diplomatic.' I owed it to Murat for exposing

182

him to the insult and I wanted to stand by my new-found colleague in abandonment.

'As you wish. But you may find you've entered a lioness's den. More dandelion?'

'Please.' The wine had improved with drinking and there was more I wanted to ask.

On our way back from the garden centre the day before, after finishing our salmon sandwiches, I had asked Murat to drive us to the church by the pub where we had eaten the inferior lunch. I wanted to take another look at the inscription I had found under the yew tree.

The vegetation had grown thicker around the tree's roots since we were last there, so it took some parting of ferns and pulling away of ivy to locate what I had surmised was an old well.

I had brought paper and a soft pencil and by lying on my stomach was able to make a rough rubbing of the inscription. 'See, Murat, it's a name.'

He nodded, politely unenthralled, and asked if he should take a picture.

'Yes, please do, and then send it to me if you wouldn't mind. I'm sorry, I haven't brought my phone.'

That evening, over supper – beans on toast with brown sauce – I re-examined the maps and drawings in the manila file.

I've always liked maps. One of the few subjects I excelled at, other than English and Art, was Geography, mostly because Dad taught me at an early age to read Ordnance Survey maps and to spot where glaciation and other geological formations that moulded our landscape had occurred. The file held a copy of a beautiful manuscript map of Shropshire, or Salope as the map named it, commissioned during the reign of Elizabeth I by Lord Burghley, showing the principal towns, some with castles indicated by two towers connected by crenellations, and the River Severn, marked as Sabrina F. In addition, there was a copy of another seventeenth-century map (1672) of the road from Ludlow to Church Stretton, from a John Ogilby's *Britannia*, and a copy of a 1610 map of Salope by a William Hole. There were also several sheets marked 'Taken from Tithe Maps and Apportionments' on which parcels of land around Hope Wenlock were named.

Taking care not to drip baked-bean sauce on the paper, I made out *Clover Meadow*, *Rushy Field*, *High Field*, *Long Meadow*, *Stony Piece*, less prosaically *Raven's Waste*, *Cow Coppice* and then, a little way from the village, two plots both marked *Wight's Field* and one marked *Long Barley*. At the top end of one of the fields there was an outline of a dwelling and beside it, in small script, the name: *Wight's Fee*.

At the other end of the field a stream, which ran into a wooded area, was marked *Milburga's Brook*. In the middle of the wooded area there was a pool and beside it a name. It was the name I had read on the stone tablet by the yew tree. *Milburga's Pool*, the script said.

The fire was dying down and Phyllis got up to put on another log.

'I can do that,' I offered.

'I'm not so infirm that I'm unable to tend my own fire.'

I was used by now to a certain bracing acerbity from

Phyllis but there was an edge to this which was new. *She has missed me – she* was *hurt*, I thought.

'The wine's delicious,' I said, trying to be conciliatory. 'I always wanted to try cowslip wine when I was a child.' I had been fond of the *Little Grey Rabbit* books in which Grey Rabbit makes a cowslip ball and Moldy Warp the mole brews cowslip wine.

'This is dandelion.'

'Yes, you said. It was an association of ideas. But perhaps it's illegal to pick cowslips now?'

'It's illegal to uproot them. One may pick them still.'

'Oh, right.'

Phyllis, having replenished the fire and poked it so the flames grew brighter, returned to her chair and resumed the steady rocking. 'But I'm not up to gathering the amount required for wine.'

Ordinarily I'd have suggested that if she wanted to make cowslip wine, I would help pick the flowers for her. But for some reason this subject was not going down well – or else she was just in a bad mood. Instead I said, 'I wanted to ask you, who was Milburga, do you know?'

'What do you want to know?' She sounded curt.

'Anything. I came across the name yesterday.'

'She was a princess who became a saint, whatever that means. One of the daughters of a minor king of Mercia.'

I was completely ignorant about early British history. I had no idea what the dates of anything around that time were and said so.

'People talk about an Anglo-Saxon heptarchy of seven

kingdoms, because of Bede.' She had adopted her school-marm voice. I never much minded this. In fact, it amused me. And on this occasion I welcomed it: I was ignorant and interested in learning more and by now I knew enough of Phyllis to be sure she would know what she was talking about. 'But there were many more little king-doms, basically local tribes, most of which converted, or, more accurately, *were* converted, to Christianity in the sev-enth century – or in some cases, I should say, were converted back, because of course by the fourth century the Romans were officially Christian, though there remained pockets of the old pagan faith, especially here on the borders. If you're interested there are plenty of books on the subject on the lower shelf in that bookcase by the door.'

'And Milburga? When was she?'

'She's late seventh to early eighth century. She became abbess of a monastery in Much Wenlock. There are some remains, if you want to go and look, though what's extant is from a much later priory.'

'So was it originally a convent?'

'One that housed nuns and monks both. Women were regularly in charge of religious houses of both sexes and many of the royal houses of Europe had women as rulers. The so-called Dark Ages weren't so dark.'

I detected that she was about to mount a hobby horse and I tried to steer her back. 'But Milburga was local?'

'According to the stories. There's a little effigy in the church thought to be her.'

'The one high up by the bell tower?'

'That's the one. Who knows who it really is?'

'I couldn't tell,' I said, 'whether it was a man or a woman. There was nothing about it in the guide.'

Phyllis gave one of her barking laughs. 'Don't talk to me about that guide. *Mis*guide, more like. It was compiled by the churchwarden who's in love with Peter and doesn't know a Saxon from a Saracen. It is certainly female because the hair is bound. As I used to say to my pupils, when it comes to hair it was the other way about from our day. Or I did until the seventies, when our male youth went in again for long hair. I rather miss that.'

'Plenty of men still wear their hair long,' I pointed out.

She nodded, adding, 'I'm quite taken with this new fashion for man buns, on the right person of course.' She seemed to have recovered her temper.

'Another thing, Phyllis – who owns the land next to ours, where the stream flows? I wanted Murat to clear it but he doesn't like to if we don't have permission. He's very cautious about breaking any rules.'

'Understandably. They're careful not to show it to me – they know they'll get the rough side of my tongue – but there's plenty of prejudice round here. If he stepped out of line, he'd cop it.'

'Peter said so. But Murat is so helpful and courteous.' *Beautiful too*, I thought. 'He couldn't be more law-abiding. People must see that.'

'People!' She sounded unusually cynical. 'People aren't rational. Surely you know that by now? One reason I play backgammon with him, other than for my own pleasure, is to indicate my approval. He was reluctant to play with me at first – in the culture he comes from it's a man's game and he feared for his *amour propre*.'

'How did you persuade him then?'

'I played the solitary old woman card. He unbent out of good manners. But I think he quite enjoys it now. You really should try it. It's a splendid game.'

I'd explained more than once my attitude to games, so I just smiled and said, 'Maybe I'll get round to it.' It was easier at times to go along with Phyllis. 'But the land where the stream flows past our garden, who owns it?' I asked again.

'That's Knapp land. Young James Knapp – so called to distinguish him from Old James Knapp – was a contemporary of Nelly's and, following his father, farmed all that land. He died around the same time as she did but there were no heirs. Or none that were acknowledged. Whoever inherited doesn't farm. It's tenanted now by a family near Ludlow.'

'So they wouldn't mind my clearing the stream?'

'I imagine they'd be grateful.'

'And the wood? Is that Knapp's?'

'That too. And happily it's protected. That wood is as old as the hills. No one can touch it, thank the gods.'

I would have liked to ask more but the church clock began to chime eight. 'I'm sorry, Phyllis. You'll be wanting your supper.' I half expected her to invite me to stay but she continued to rock back and forth in her chair. There was something private about this and, not wanting to intrude, I asked if she could lend me a torch. 'And may I really borrow some of those books?'

'Take whatever you like, my dear.'

I picked out some books, as many as I could fit into Dad's haversack, promising to be careful with them. I knew her to be fussy about her books.

But she surprised me by saying, 'Keep them, if you wish. At my age I know all I need to know and I'm unlikely to read them again.'

As I was lifting the latch of the front door, she called over her shoulder, 'Christianity chased all the native gods and spirits into hiding or forced them into disguises. But they haven't gone. Remember that.'

Darkness had fallen but my doze in the wood had left me with a desire to walk home that way. Any town-bred apprehensions had evaporated and the wood had become a place where I felt welcome, even at home. I walked down the road from the village, climbed the stile and crossed the field of slumbering sheep. Lambs let out little quizzical bleats as I passed and the ewes made reassuring rumblings; but I felt the sheep were no more fearful of me than I of them. I was wearing only a thin cotton frock; my legs were bare and the grass was wet so my feet and ankles were cold but the rest of my body seemed to have adjusted to the temperature.

As I approached the wood, I felt if anything excitement at the idea of being there alone at night. Any ordinary feeling of trepidation was more about finding my way as Phyllis's torch suddenly flickered and died. As usual, I hadn't brought my phone.

Luckily, there was a moon. It moved with me as I moved through the trees, colourless in the dark. By the moonlight filtering through to the wood's floor I could make out the track that led to the pool. I plunged on, relishing the cool night air on my face, undeterred by the various night-time noises: the crackles under my feet, the slight snapping of dropping twigs, the faint rustlings of nocturnal creatures and the shifting of branches over-head, caused by the fidgeting of roosting birds. Had I thought about it, I might have been a little frightened of bats. But I didn't think about it and there were no bats, or anyway none that I saw.

Night scents of leaf sap and bracken and damp earth and something else, wilder and more feral, filled my lungs. I could sense from the way the shadowy columns were beginning to open out that I was nearing the heart of the wood. Ahead of me lay the pool, darkly gleaming like tarnished silver. But before I quite reached it, I stopped still.

There was someone there before me. By the light of the moon I could see a shape. As I stood, I saw there was not one but two or three figures, maybe more. They were moving like quicksilver in the moonlight and suddenly I heard a voice. It sounded almost like a child's voice, a clear, high-pitched, not entirely tuneful sound, more like a chant than a song.

The note changed and seemed to become a dirge or a lament. There was some sort of nocturnal event going on, perhaps a wake for someone in the village. I remained where I was, wondering if I should join in, but as I hesitated the figures moved away out of my line of vision.

I felt they must have seen me and I was interrupting a private affair. Having got so far, I was at first unwilling to retreat and was wondering whether to press on when I was overtaken by a blinding panic and I turned and fled, stumbling back along the track where nettles seemed to have sprung up to sting my bare legs, ran, heart-in-mouth, across the field of drowsing sheep and scrambled under the barbed-wire fence, which tore viciously at my bare arms.

I trudged home by the road, which was not at all exhilarating in spite of the journeying moon that raced across the sky, tracking me feverishly all the way.

15

I was looking forward to settling down with Phyllis's books but when I got home Margot was there.

It was over a fortnight since she'd been back at Knight's Fee and my response to seeing her was outrage that she'd given me no warning. But even as this reaction overtook me, I was aware that I'd no right to it. So I said, trying not too successfully to sound welcoming, 'Hi, how are you?'

'Not great,' was the reply.

Because my sister was always well turned-out and impeccably made-up, I hadn't immediately taken in her appearance. But I now saw that her face was uncharacter-istically puffy and lacking the usual make-up and her clothes were rumpled as if they'd been slept in.

'What's up?' I asked.

'Jules had a meltdown. We're done. Where've you been? You look as if you've been dragged through a hedge backwards.'

I didn't bother to answer this. 'Oh dear, I am sorry about

Julian,' I said and I wasn't being entirely hypocritical. This would mean more of Margot at Knight's Fee, a prospect that didn't greatly please me. 'What happened?' I felt it was OK to ask as Margot never minded revealing all aspects of her private life – indeed, she seemed to relish it.

But she only said, 'It's not important.'

I had never picked up on her suggestion that I might have expected more of Dad's money to come to me. There was a reason for this. When I examined her remarks later, I was ashamed to find that she was right: I had at some level supposed he might reward me for coming to look after him. Margot was better off than me, and I realized I had nursed a hope that he might even up our financial situations. The revelation had left me feeling guilty and I had an instinct that the row with Julian had some connection with this. But I said no more than, 'Shall I make you a cup of tea or would you prefer something stronger?'

'Is there any of that fancy Scotch left?'

The 'fancy Scotch' was an insanely expensive single malt, brought at Easter by Julian. There was plenty left: I dislike whisky and Margot as a rule doesn't drink spirits because, she says, she doesn't want to acquire a bulbous red nose. I fetched it for her and went off to apply ointment to my gashed arm and badly stung legs – the nettles were ferocious. She appeared to have either forgotten or ceased for the moment to care about her nose as when I returned she was draining a large tumblerful and immediately poured another. She looked forlorn in her crumpled blouse with her messy hair and for the first time in years, maybe ever, I felt a pang of real affection for her.

I had poured myself a glass of wine so that she wasn't drinking alone.

'Marg?'

'What?'

'You know what you said about Dad's will and thinking that maybe I thought I should have been left more than you?'

'Don't bring all that up again now, Hass.'

'You were right, though. I didn't realize till you said so but at some level I did think that.'

She shrugged and said, 'Big deal. I'd have thought the same in your shoes.'

'That's nice of you to say so. I've been thinking too about what you said about leaving home because of Mum.'

'I did.'

I'd never considered that. In fact, what I'd thought at the time was that this was more attention-seeking on her part. 'You were always her favourite. So why?'

We had gone through to the sitting room, where Margot had lit a fire. She was better at fires than me – mine tended to fizzle out – and logs were ablaze in the grate we'd found hidden behind a crude piece of painted hardboard. When we first arrived, there had been a dodgy-looking electric fire that, sitting in the handsome, stone-carved Jacobean fire-place, had appeared most anachronistic, so it was cheering to see the fireplace restored to its original state and to smell the pleasing scent of applewood from the dead tree that Murat had felled.

Margot had stretched out on the sofa, balancing the tumbler of whisky on her stomach. She's proud of her stomach which I needn't say is very flat. Now she sighed and said, 'It's extraordinarily naive of you to imagine being the favourite is desirable. It may have been for you with Dad, but Mum . . .? I mean, think what she was like.'

I knew what I thought our mother was like but I'd assumed that Margot, having had such different treatment, would hold a different view. 'What was she like, then? For you, I mean.'

'No different to how she was for you, at a guess.'

'But she adored you,' I objected. 'She didn't like me. I irritated her.'

Then Margot came out with something that really made me think. She said, quite mildly, even a little amused, 'You know your trouble, Hass? You overrate being adored.'

I was so disarmed by this that I said nothing. Then she said, 'I'm knackered. Jules and I were up rowing all last night and I haven't slept, so I'm off to bed.' She got up from the sofa, came over to where I was sitting and kissed me. 'Sorry, I didn't clean my teeth this morning. I expect my breath smells foul.'

She was wrong about that: as usual, she smelt gorgeous.

That night I lay awake with all the adoring words I had heard from Robert churning through my mind: 'You're the love of my life', 'my girl with the air-blue gown', 'my kindred spirit', 'my soul mate' . . . any number of endearments which left me feeling that only I truly counted, I was the centre of his heart and so his life. They sounded hollow now. Hollow? No. But overblown. Because in the end it was Laura who must have counted most, Laura whom he wasn't even sure he had ever been in love with, or so he said.

And then I remembered Phyllis's words to me in the garden: *love is a flexible matter at best.*

I had been so sure. So sure of Robert's love for me. And then so sure that I had misjudged it. It was only much later that I began to see that what I had misjudged was not his love but how far love is sovereign. There are other emotions, less obvious, that may have a longer reach. Loyalty is one; habit another.

What did begin to dawn on me that night was how little I knew my sister. That she too may have been wounded by our childhood was a revelation. I began to consider all the oddities I'd dismissed as attention-seeking. Turning down Cambridge had seemed to me a kind of showing off – 'Look at me, I'm so superior I am not even flattered by winning a place at Cambridge – in fact, it matters so little to me I can give it up.' Only now did it strike me as a bizarre piece of self-sabotage. Then there was her preoccupation with my appearance, which had always irked me. Since she was the acknowledged beauty in our family, I had deliberately downplayed my appearance all my life – except with Robert, when my looks bloomed. Margot's constant reproving comments infuriated me. But that night, I began to wonder if her nagging was not, as I always assumed, a device to emphasize my inferior looks, or social embarrassment at my often shabby appearance, but a kind of compensation for our mother's favouritism.

The birds were singing before I fell finally into a dream-ridden sleep but although the dreams were disturbing I had no recollection of them in the morning.

*

Margot was still in her room when I rose much later than usual. With her in the house I would probably not have followed my usual dawn ritual. But in any case it was well past dawn when I went downstairs to make coffee.

The late-night conversation with my sister had put out of my head my earlier conversation with Phyllis but seeing her books on the table reminded me of what I had set myself to do. I made a second cup of coffee to fortify my spirit and then started out for the village feeling determined.

I didn't take my usual route through the woods but walked along the road. By the map, the road was quicker, so this might have been to get the self-imposed task over, though in practice, thundering traffic meant that for safety's sake you often had to wait for vehicles to pass, which could make the road route longer. But I had not recovered from the panic I had experienced in the wood and maybe going by the road was an inner preparation for what I suspected would be a tough encounter.

Sue Lane, Penny's grandmother, Phyllis had told me, lived in the same terrace of pebble-dash houses as Debs, the handicrafter. Her house was two doors down from Debs' and, I could see as I approached, much less well cared for.

There was a 'Beware of the Dog' notice on the gate, which had swung off its hinges, and a number of chewed dog toys and dog turds on the scrubby lawn. As I walked up the concrete path, I could hear loud barking inside the house.

There was no bell or knocker so I flapped the letterbox a couple of times and waited. The barking became more violent but no one answered the door. There were alleyways set between the houses and I guessed they led round to the back gardens.

The back garden, though larger than the front, was even scruffier. There was a tumbledown shed, a child's trike, a red pedal car, a pram, a deflated paddling pool, many plastic toys strewn about and, apart from some leggy privet and a desiccated lawn, nothing visibly growing.

A woman was sitting in a deckchair, smoking.

'Hi,' I said. 'Are you Sue?'

Her face when she turned to me was not unlike her granddaughter's: pale and sharp-featured, with a wary look in the eyes, and painfully thin, though she must have been a pretty woman once. 'Who are you?' The tone wasn't promising.

'I'm Hassie,' I said, smiling hypocritically. 'Hassie Days from Knight's Fee. I wonder if I could have a word?'

'I cannot for the life of me imagine,' Margot said – she was up but still in her dressing gown when I got back – 'what on earth you thought you would accomplish.'

Our conversation the previous evening had encouraged me to explain where I had been. As a rule, I would have kept the encounter with Penny's grandmother to myself.

It had not gone well. In fact, it had gone about as badly as it could, barring the two of us getting into a fist fight. From the start, the atmosphere was charged with hostility. Sue Lane argued the way I've noticed is practised by the not-quite-clinically mad, which is to say that she picked up on things I hadn't said, or wholly irrelevant matters, and furiously refuted them while completely ignoring my actual complaint.

The gist of her response to my suggestion that Penny had made a very serious accusation using racist terms – which I only managed to get out by shouting over her – was that Penny had done no harm in the potting shed – something of which I had neither accused the child nor even mentioned – and the children had had a talk at school and been warned about 'this sort of thing', by which she clearly intended paedophilia. Penny was only following what the school had ordained and should, she implied, be congratulated for her rule-keeping rather than taken to task by uppity incomers with London ways.

'I can't believe the school warned the children against Muslims, though,' I protested, a little shaken by this extreme ferocity.

Here Sue Lane adroitly shifted her ground and began citing recent allegations in the press about a supposed Muslim network grooming underage girls.

'As if that had anything to do with poor Murat,' I said to Margot, still indignant. 'She carried on as if I had endangered the little liar and it was I who should apologize.'

Which was when Margot asked what on earth I imagined I would accomplish.

'You don't seem to get it,' she said. 'You've probably made Murat's position worse. Now this Lane woman will really be against him. And you'll be for it too for criticizing the granddaughter. I've told you, it's pointless trying to suck up to the locals. They'll like me better, one, because I don't try to hobnob with them and two, because quite frankly I don't give a fuck what they think.'

'Oh give me a cup of coffee and stop preaching,' I said morosely. I had a nasty suspicion that she was right.

Drinking the coffee, which was Margot's London blend and very welcome, I had a thought. 'D'you think Mum preferred you because you didn't care what she thought and I did?'

'Probably. She was a bully and you must never suck up to bullies. You have to show them you don't care.'

'And didn't you care?'

Margot got up to pour herself more coffee. 'To be honest, I don't know. I suppose it's like evolution: as a child you try out various forms of behaviour and you end up sticking to the ones that are successful – or seem to be so at the time. I guess not seeming to mind what Mum thought worked for me when we were small and it became the way I handled her. It got so I really didn't care.'

'But you did think she was a bully . . .?'

'Only later. I witnessed her bully Dad and then she turned on you. She bullied me too but differently.'

'How? You struck me as spoilt rotten.'

'Yeah, I know. I was aware of that at one level and being a selfish little cow I enjoyed it, for a while. But I worked out that the way she bullied me was with praise. It was praise that was completely self-referential.'

I'd never considered this.

'Look, apart from my refusing to kowtow to her,' Margot continued, 'I resemble her – resembled, I should say. I inherited her genes. You inherited Dad's. By the time you came along she was obviously pissed off with Dad and, being a narcissist, was always keen on herself. I was built in her mould, so far as looks go, so naturally I was her favourite. You looked like Dad, tall, dark and bony, and were therefore her natural whipping boy – girl. It was horrible. I don't say it's the only reason I ran away, mind, but it had a role.'

'Where did you run to?' I asked. She had never told me and always laughed and brushed me off when I tried to probe.

'I stayed with Alison.' Alison was a friend who had left school before her.

'Where? Why?'

'Didn't you guess? I was pregnant.'

'Christ, Marg! Who by?'

'Actually, by the father of one of my other friends.'

'Jesus, Marg! Who?'

'It's OK. It was consensual, as we now say. Mind you, he was pretty shit when I found I was up the spout.'

'But this is awful. You had to cope all on your own?'

'Alison helped. And the shit paid for the abortion. He was in a terrible state, worrying I'd tell on him and his marriage would collapse, plus which, although I wasn't underage, he was twenty-odd years older. So . . .'

'But who was this creep?'

She shrugged and said, 'Look, I said I'd never tell and, you know . . . I siphoned a shedload of money out of him for keeping my mouth shut. I kind of justify that by sticking to my side of the bargain.'

'My God, Marg. You don't need to justify anything.'

'It's how I had the deposit for the flat. Did you never wonder how?'

'I supposed you'd enough money from your job in the bank.'

She laughed. 'You're so deliciously naive. No, the man gave me fifteen grand, on condition I scarpered and never told. I took it willingly, I can tell you.'

'And the baby? Didn't you mind?'

She shrugged. 'Not much. Sometimes I wonder. But I'd make a terrible mother. I haven't the patience. I'm like Mum in that.'

'And Cambridge? Is that why you didn't go?'

'No, I could have gone. I'd had the abortion. But I liked the idea of making money more and since I'd got double A-level Maths, as well as Physics and French, jobs weren't hard to find. Bright numerate women weren't applying for positions in finance. We aren't that common even now.'

'Oh Marg. Why did I never work all this out?'

'I don't know. It's not exactly rocket science.' She began to laugh.

'Why are you laughing?'

'I'm laughing at you trying not to tick me off for saying "rocket science". You're sometimes endearingly predictable, my dear sis.'

I felt quite humbled. 'I'm sorry to be so picky.'

'I don't mind. I quite like it. I like teasing you. But listen. First off, Mum's apparently preferring me was only a version of her obvious preference for herself. So it didn't amount to much. Second, this business about me being the beauty and you being the beast. It's nonsense. I was a stereotypically pretty blonde kid with china-blue eyes and I've grown up a kind of poor imitation of Marilyn Monroe.' This wasn't the case at all; if we're talking film stars, the star she resembled was Reese Witherspoon. 'You have far more distinguished looks: tall, elegant, wand thin with that divinely straight nose – mine's all upturned and piggy.' *How funny*, I thought, *that she should rate my nose, which Robert always liked*. 'But you deliberately downplay your looks. It annoys me partly because it makes me feel guilty, as if it's me that's to blame for your insistent dowdiness.'

What was going through my mind, all the while she was talking, was that I always forgot how bright Margot really is. It wasn't a fluke, that Cambridge scholarship. She was clever but she was also canny. For some reason, she hid it. And for some possibly connected reason, this recognition made me bold.

'Marg, the row you had with Julian was about me, wasn't it?'

It was my turn to surprise her. I could tell this by her silence.

'Well?' I asked. 'I'm right, aren't I?'

She sighed and said, 'Sort of. But don't take it on your-self. It was my row.'

'Why? What was it about?'

She sighed again. 'It's a boring story but, to cut to the chase, Jules asked me to marry him.'

I didn't at all relish that idea but neither did I care to think that my dislike of him had somehow come between them. 'You don't mean you're not going to marry him because I don't like him?'

'I'm not that loyal. He wanted a prenup, because of what he went through with Nadia, and I said –'

'That's disgusting,' I interrupted. 'What a – I don't know – arsehole!'

'No, no. I was fine about the prenup. Perfectly sensible request. But I did say that as I only have my flat, I'd like the security of a prenup promise of something more that I could rely on – not a lot but, given I was throwing in my lot with him, something in case we did split up and –'

'But hang on. You don't only have your flat,' I said in some alarm, suddenly seeing the ramifications of this. 'You own half of Knight's Fee.'

'Mmm,' Margot said, and paused. She got up to fetch the coffee pot to refill her cup.

There was something in the set of her shoulders that made me nervous. 'So?'

'Well, yes, I do. Jules pointed that out.' She sighed and then, vehemently, 'And *I* said I couldn't ever think of selling here, even if I needed to, as it's half yours and all you have and I wasn't going to have you turfed out simply so he could be spared the hardship of offering an absolutely *minute* – given his pots of money – financial guarantee for the woman he had just asked to be his wife. I mean, Jesus, come on!'

I was about to trot out some twaddle along the lines of she mustn't consider me but only think of herself and her own future blah blah, when she hurriedly continued, 'He said – well, never mind what he said, the point is the whole discussion ended in a God Almighty row and I told him he could stick his prenup up his arse and incidentally he was so tight-arsed it would take a major operation to get it out and that I hoped he would need a colostomy after-wards if he ever wanted to take a shit, which he would need to do as he was fucking well full of the stuff. Then I left and came here.' She was flushed and her eyes shone when she was recounting all this. She looked very pink and lovely.

'Marg,' I said. 'I am so sorry.' I was. But I was also relieved that she had thrown off the meek-housewifely mantle I'd observed when she brought Julian to stay. She could never have kept it up.

'Don't be. He's an arsehole. I always knew him for an arsehole – but I get on with arseholes, probably because I am one. My only regret is we were going to start a gallery together, which obviously he was going to finance. I was going to run it while he collected artists. I'd've liked that. He's got superb taste in art and I like that too. But there we go . . .' She looked at me as she said this because this is another phrase I would normally have objected to and we both laughed.

'Anyway,' she said, 'I've taken some leave and I'm going to get the house into shape. I've got loads of ideas. It's time we took up all those terrible carpets, there's a running conference of dust mites meeting in them, and we should get the floors sanded – I've been checking and I'm pretty sure the boards are elm – and paint all the rooms. You can get your terrorist to help if you like. It'll be fun, you'll see.'

16

Margot was as good as her word. She set off for Shrewsbury the following morning and returned with a forbidding-looking industrial sander, which she'd hired along with various other tools, and many litres of paint, including some cans of whitewash. 'You were right about this. It'll suit your attics.'

She took a carving knife to the stair carpet.

'Marg, that looks wildly dangerous.'

'Don't fuss, Hass, I'm just using it to prise up the edges. It's stuck down with something lethal.'

'Shouldn't you wear a mask? You always complain about your dust allergy.'

'It's OK, I've stuck Vaseline up my nose.'

The house with my sister in residence was a changed place. I was glad of the conversation that had led to our becoming closer, but I still preferred my own company. The other thing I'd forgotten about her is that while for ninety per cent of the time she's lazy as hell, for the other ten she's a Trojan. (Dad told me once why it is that people who work hard are referred to as Trojans but I've forgotten what he said.) Margot in her unflagging mode was exhausting.

She set about work in a pair of painter's orange overalls and her yellow DMs. With a scarf twisted into a turban to protect her hair and her face plastered with various beauty aids – masks for lines, masks for sunspots, masks for I don't know what – she cut a bizarre figure. And she wasted no time recruiting Murat's help.

The stair carpets were energetically sliced and dragged out in sections, then wheeled to the bottom of the garden where Murat said he could use them to suppress weeds in the new vegetable plot he was planning. He seemed pleased at being invited to take over the sanding machine and proved most competent with it. He and Margot became quite pally. I could hear her tone becoming flirtatious and I began to feel a twinge of my old jealousy.

Come on, I reproved myself. *You should be glad she's willing to see Murat's virtues*. But I couldn't help feeling that he was my friend: I had hired him, I had paid him – and over the odds – *and* I had defended him against both Margot's and the horrible Penny Lane's racist slurs.

I noticed too that he was rolling cigarettes for Margot. I was aware he smoked and was perfectly happy about this since he only did so outside. But once, coming back into the house after a walk, I smelt dope. Several of my friends still do weed but, other than coffee and alcohol, drugs have never appealed to me. I was annoyed and I challenged Margot.

'Should you be encouraging him, Marg? It's OK for

you, if you must, but legally he's an alien and it can get him into serious trouble.'

'Calm down, Hass. No one cares about the odd spliff these days. Not even the police. A guy I know in the force smokes it himself and says that loads of them do. In fact, I'm going to buy that greenhouse and suggest he grows it here.'

At that I did put my foot down. 'Absolutely not. Whatever your pal says, it's technically illegal. I don't want any hassle with the police and you could get Murat deported. So, no way with the weed. OK?'

Trying not to sulk over this, or seem to sulk, while the two of them got on with their sanding and sealing, I took to going on extended walks or retreated to my attic room where, in between desultory sketches for Elfine, I began to explore the books I'd borrowed from Phyllis.

My finances were down to a few hundred pounds, so I couldn't really afford to be spending time on studying pre-Christian habits of nature worship. But the more I read, the less this became yet another addition to my long list of displacement activities and the more I found I wanted to know.

I discovered that long before the country was Christianized, before the Romans first arrived, trees and groves and springs were worshipped. And I began to have a better sense of what Phyllis had intimated: all the sacred trees and groves were chopped down, axed by Christianity's cruel reforming zeal, while the sacred springs and pools became 'holy' wells, colonized by upstart saints. As if 'holy' somehow trumped 'sacred'.

One afternoon, sick of Elfine, I walked into the village up to the church and found Peter in the graveyard. 'Paul's off with one of his backs.' Paul was the handyman hired by the church and prone to having 'backs'.

'You should sack him, Peter. It's daylight robbery. But you enjoy being acting gardener, don't you?'

'How well you know me, Hassie. How are you?'

'So-so. Margot's embarked on an extensive programme of restoration so I'm escaping.'

'Who was it said all change is for the worst?'

'I thought I'd come and take another look at the stone figure in the niche,' I explained.

'Well, churches are nothing if not time-honoured places of sanctuary.'

He came with me into the church and together we stood inspecting the blunt little stone figure ensconced on what looked like a child's primitive high chair.

'Phyllis says she may be Saint Milburga,' I said.

He nodded. 'So I gather. It's possible. Milburga was certainly in evidence hereabouts.'

'She seems to have been a famous miracle worker, bringing the dead back to life, curing all manner of ailments. Mind you, from what I've been reading, that was standard form. All the saints seemed to be at it.'

'Yes, I fear our modern Church is a toothless lion by comparison. We could use some miracles.'

'I thought only Catholics had those.'

'You know, Hassie, in my view we left quite a bit behind that we should have hung on to from pre-Reformation days. I blame Cromwell. The Mantel one, who has a lot to answer for, as well as puritanical Old Ironsides.'

'Where was this found, d'you know, Peter?'

'Ah, now, Audrey could have told you that. She did an

archaeology course run by a chap at Loughborough. My recollection is that it was found in one of the fields around here. I have all Audrey's archaeology notes at home if you'd like to look.'

'I'd love to. She seems . . .' I considered the little stone figure, 'I don't know, calm,' I decided. 'Calm and dignified.'

'They can be saintly characteristics, I suppose.'

I left Peter clipping the long grass, called by at the shop for stamps and chatted to Hayley, whose mother had acquired a boyfriend. 'She calls him that – I said, "Mum, at seventy-two he's no boyfriend," and she giggled like a teenager and said, "And I'm no spring chicken." She's wearing nail varnish too. Dad wouldn't have liked that.'

'I think you should be glad for her,' I said. From what I'd heard from Hayley, I'd warmed to her mother, who sounded to me like a force of nature.

'So long as she doesn't go marrying him and leaving him all her money. It's not for myself I mind. She's always said it's to go to the kids.'

I didn't want to get back to the house while Margot and Murat were still at work, so I bought a malt loaf and walked up the hill to the house with the green door.

Phyllis was watching a Ginger Rogers and Fred Astaire film. 'You've caught me indulging in one of my weaknesses,' she said, getting up to turn off the TV. 'I always had a yen to tap dance. Not that I would have been much cop. I was a chubby child.'

'I don't know,' I said. 'Tap rather suits plump people. I've brought an offering but don't let me interrupt.'

Phyllis said she knew the film so well she could

practically do all the dance steps. She made tea while I sliced and buttered the malt loaf and filled her in on Hayley's mum. As ever, she had a view.

'She misses Hayley's father. Diane's one of those women who function better as part of a dyad. People don't like to imagine their parents having sex, especially not with those who aren't their parents, but Hayley'll come round. She's a kind-hearted girl and her mother is lonely.'

I almost risked asking what I'd often wondered, if Phyllis ever felt lonely. But its only purpose would have been to leave me feeling less so myself, so I told her how I'd been reading her books. I didn't reveal that they had become my own refuge from loneliness.

'There seem to have been a tremendous number of miracle-working saints back then.' I'd not really taken in before that it's miracles rather than self-sacrificing or noble behaviour that's required to achieve sainthood.

Phyllis laughed. 'It was an age of saints and miracles. Funny how rarely miracles happen these days, unless you count technology. That *is* miraculous. Although,' she amended, 'perhaps that is more like wizardry. Did you make anything of Milburga?'

'I liked the story of her hanging her nun's veil on a sunbeam,' I said. 'That seemed like fun.' There was a devil-may-care insouciance about it lacking in the worthy miraculous cures. For some reason, I didn't feel like disclosing my discovery of Milburga's name inscribed by the pool on the old map of the lands around Knight's Fee. 'And she seems to have had a special relationship with birds. I liked that too.'

'That will be the geese. She persuaded a flock of geese out of a field of barley before they destroyed the crop. I can't say I would count that as much of a miracle. More like plain old-fashioned common sense.'

I described the well by the yew tree and the dismal pub that I had found with Murat.

Phyllis knew it, of course. 'That was almost certainly one of the sacred springs reputed to cure long before the Christians got to it. It's possible the water itself contained some efficacious mineral or element but you know, Halcyon, belief is itself a powerful remediant. Perhaps the most powerful. People forget that.'

I stayed and drank a glass of dandelion wine and borrowed a few more books. By the time I set out again, the air was filled with the haunting aura of night-scented stocks, which grew in the crevices of Phyllis's garden path. The sky had turned green, the cow parsley, now high in the ditches along the hedgerows, was giving off a ghostly glimmer in the vanishing light as I walked along the road and climbed the stile. The dew-drenched field as I crossed it was a lucent pearly grey.

I had not walked late through the wood since the night Margot fled from Julian. On that occasion, I had turned back in a panic and gone the long way round by the road. This time, I decided, I would press on regardless.

The birds were making their gentle off-to-bed noises, different in tone from the bolder sounds with which they greet the renewing day. The quality of light too was different. But, as with the dawn, the effect of the twilight was to blur my own boundaries so that I felt strangely loose-limbed and set free.

Overhead, the branches of the trees sighed and whispered as if they too had been freed to release their deeper secrets. I followed the familiar path by sense rather than sight until I reached the pool. There was no one there but, as I approached, a bird in the nearby undergrowth let out a churring, rattling noise and I wondered if it might be a nightjar.

The air was soft and balmy and the midges were out in force. I hunkered down on Dad's haversack. Luckily, I'd brought a cardigan with me, because I had to put it on and clutch my skirt around my knees to save being savaged. There was something hypnotic about sitting there as the light imperceptibly drained and the foliage took on a faint lilac hue, dimmed but not obscured. I began to remember how, as a child, I was told that the earth's centre was molten fire and I had imagined the planet taking great deep breaths, in and out, so that each evening, as I saw it, light was drawn back into the earth's lungs and then slowly expelled again in the form of the dawn. It felt to me now just as if the earth was very, very slowly breathing and I began to breathe deeper in concert with it.

As I sat, I was infused with a sense of radiant calm, a sense that all I had so long and so sharply felt, all that had agitated and perplexed me, was draining away with the light, that my former troubles no longer mattered, or not at that moment. And then, some way further into the wood, I saw a tiny dot of light, moving about like a firefly, and again I heard that high-pitched, silvery, piping chant.

Margot was outside sitting in the garden smoking when I got back. She had enfolded herself in a pale silk shawl which cast a pearly aura around her and made her look exotic and mysterious.

'Mosquitoes,' she said, waving her cigarette at me. 'I had to light up to keep the buggers at bay.'

'How did it go today?' I asked. My resentment over the improvements had evaporated.

'We sanded the hall and dining rooms but we've still all the upstairs corridors to do. I have to hand it to your terrorist, though – he can work.'

I didn't bother to reprove her. In that second, I caught a glimpse of how much I prompted these goading responses, how this need to provoke me was just a habit she'd got into and how, if I made no protest, she would drop it.

'Blow some smoke in my direction, will you?' I said. 'The blighters have been feasting on me like mad.' Blighters was one of our father's expressions.

'Have one,' Margot suggested. 'You needn't inhale.'

It was years since I had given up smoking and when I did smoke it was mostly a cover for nerves. But to sit quietly smoking in an evening garden with my sister seemed, at that moment, what I most wanted to do in the world. We sat together as stars emerged, piecemeal. A pale moth veered towards the flame from the match with which Margot lit my cigarette and fluttered off again. A single bloom on one of the elegant old garden roses had opened and in the dusk light I could still make out the grey-green foliage and delicate white petals. Its sweet-violet scent mingled with the smell of tobacco smoke.

'Smells take you back even more than taste does,' Margot remarked.

I'd forgotten that she got an A for French at A level and for all I knew might have read Proust. I didn't ask what it was that she had been taken back to. I had a sense that by remaining in our private worlds we were closer.

17

That night I slept deeply and dreamlessly and woke to a dark green and russet sky. For the first time since Margot's return I went outside and observed as the green became teal and the russet turned to coral and watched the swifts high, high up, wheeling and shrieking as they swooped down in pursuit of flies. It crossed my mind then that I should like to be a swift. Swifts sleep on the wing and once out of the nest never willingly touch ground. It must be the closest thing to being an angel.

Deep apricot rambling roses entangled with apple-scented eglantine were tumbling over the grey stone wall into the long flower bed. A crimson tree peony had appeared out of nowhere and shot up above the spires of sapphire delphiniums. Bees were already busily prospecting in the freckle-throated foxgloves.

I padded barefoot down to the stream, which still fumed night mist. As I approached, out of the corner of my eye, I half saw, half sensed a shape move off into the thicket at the borders of our land.

I called out 'Hi!' but no one answered. It was that liminal time, the hazy hinge between night and day, and no doubt this was a trick of the light playing games with my vision.

Walking back past the potting shed, I collected scissors and stopped to cut a single bloom, one of the garden's old cream roses with a heavenly scent. Then I made coffee, filled a bowl with Margot's cereal and her oat milk and carried a breakfast up to her bedroom.

She was awake and consulting an interior design magazine. 'What have I done to deserve this?'

'I don't believe in just deserts,' I said sententiously. I did of course; I suspect most of us do.

'Thanks anyway. I was just wondering if I could woman up and haul myself out of bed.'

'You've made it lovely in here,' I said.

Her taste fitted the house better than mine. I liked to think of myself as the sensitive one but my sister had her own sensibilities. She'd imported a Jacobean four-poster with tapestry hangings, and her bedding was topped by a silk quilt the colour of old gold. The walls, as she had planned, were a dusky yellow, the floor was covered with oriental rugs of muted colours, on an antique chest a Chinese bowl full of aromatic herbs scented the air and the heavy draped curtains were of a copper-coloured taffeta. In its way, Margot's bedroom resembled Phyllis's sitting room and I took a certain malicious delight in the suspicion that neither would have welcomed the comparison.

'I'm going to have to clear all this stuff out to sand the floor,' she told me. 'It's a bore – but it'll be worth it. This rose smells divine, by the way. Is it one you planted?'

'It's an Alba rose. One of old Mrs East's.' A thought struck me. 'I meant to ask before, don't we need planning permission? I seem to remember from the report that it's needed even for internal work.'

'I've a contact who lives with a planner in Shrewsbury. He said not to quote him but what the eye doesn't see . . .'

'OK. But on your head be it if we're fined. I'm not going to pay.'

'We'll only be fined if we sell or someone blabs. Why d'you think I'm employing Murat? He's not going to blab. He's terrified of any authority, poor darling.'

I was right. Once I stopped protesting, she dropped the terrorist joke. This is a hard lesson to learn and I mention it only in case you find it useful, though I suspect it's a lesson you only learn through experience.

I had reached a point with my work where I had to force myself to get on. The publishers had moved the publication date and as a result the deadline had been extended. This, unfortunately, had only extended my periods of procrastination and even by my lax standards I had made slow progress. My resistance to drawing the elf and her noisome little pals was expressing itself psychosomatically in a sensation of having physical weights hung on my wrists; every illustration, as well as leaving me mentally depressed, left me physically depleted. But by now I was perilously short of money and other than borrowing from Margot, which I had vowed never to do, I had no resource, nor prospect of one, but Elfine.

And yet with necessity the reluctance to continue with her increased. That morning, when I had ground out a drawing of a beleaguered hedgehog called Henry, I pushed away my drawing board in exasperation and hurried downstairs past Margot, who was trying to manoeuvre the sander along the corridor.

'No sign of Murat and he's not answering his phone. Have you heard from him?'

'No,' I called back. 'But he'll be here. He's completely reliable. Can I borrow your bike?'

Margot had brought her bike with her on her flight from London and I had begun occasionally to use it. I loved my walks but the bike was handy too. I was kidding myself that I was going to take a quick break by biking to the shop for a few non-essentials before getting back down to work.

Hayley was talking on the phone, so I read the headlines: TRUMP DUMPS IRAN NUCLEAR DEAL, *The Times* announced; BOJO FINDS HIS MOJO, the *Sun* informed us. *Bully for you*, I thought sourly. *I wish I could find mine.*

Hayley came off the phone flushed and excited. 'That was my mum. Sue Lane's been attacked in her own home.'

At once I felt alarm. 'How? Who was it? Do they know?'

'Mum says she's unconscious. The police are up there now.'

I hared along to the Lanes' house to see what was up. A young woman in a long, drooping skirt, with Penny at her side, was talking to a police officer. So this was Penny's mother. An ambulance was pulling away, bearing, I guessed, Sue. Debs, in her front garden, was enjoying these events over her fence along with various other neighbourly spies. I spotted Jade, whose husband I'd met on my first visit to the shop, with baby Molly in her arms.

'Sue surprised him robbing the house and got lammed over the head for her pains,' Debs said. 'Shocking, isn't it?' It was apparent that she was vastly elated at the drama.

'Do they know who it was?'

'Penny, the granddaughter, says she saw him.' She paused and a shadow crossed her eyes. 'She says – but you know, it's just her word – it was your Albanian.'

'Where is he?' I asked, ignoring the suggestion that he was 'my' Albanian.

'They're looking for him now.'

Across the gardens I could see Penny's white, vindictive little face. While her mother's expression was anxious, Penny was looking well pleased with herself. 'I wouldn't believe a word she says,' I said angrily.

'Pardon?' Debs turned from delivering another update to a few more villagers who were expressing their concern with excited gleeful chatter.

'I wouldn't jump to any conclusions,' I amended swiftly. 'Our experience of Murat, mine and my sister's –' I wanted to distance myself from the notion that he was 'my' Albanian – 'is that he's very decent and utterly reliable.'

'You never know with them, though, do you?' Debs said. 'Not that I've anything against them but you know what I mean?'

Margot was almost as indignant as I was when I biked back with this news. 'That's bonkers. Murat isn't violent.'

'You suggested he might be a terrorist,' I reminded her.

'You know that was basically a wind-up. They can't really imagine he'd brain an old woman. He's a pussycat.'

'She's not that old,' I observed irrelevantly. 'And he's vanished, which they'll assume is a sign of guilt.'

'I expect he's frightened. I'd be if someone accused me of mugging some mad old woman.'

'She's not that old,' I said again, feebly.

'Do they imagine a jihadist would be wreaking revenge on the Christian world by planting fucking pumpkins? I mean, Jesus!'

'Not pumpkins,' I said. 'I didn't want pumpkins.' Anxiety had rattled my wits. 'And we may see that it's ridiculous but Sue was whopped over the head with some blunt instrument and they were hinting about Murat's access to garden tools. They kept looking at me, and Iris from "A Stitch" actually said, "Doesn't he have the key to your shed, Hyacinth?"'

I half expected Margot to remind me of how she'd counselled me against giving Murat the key but all she said was, 'Stupid cow can't even be arsed to remember your name.'

'Where can he have got to?' I wondered. 'Where's he sleeping?' I had an image of the cold and bedraggled homeless, bundled up in dirty sleeping bags, whom I used to see depressingly often on London streets. Murat probably hadn't even got a sleeping bag.

'Your pal Phyllis might have an idea. Why don't you go and ask her? In fact, I'll drive you over. It'll be quicker and I can't do anything here without Murat. If they've bloody well driven him away, I shall personally throttle that kid with my bare hands.'

Margot dropped me at Phyllis's and drove on up the hill to turn the car round. The front door was, as always, unlocked and Alfred came bounding out when I opened it. But there was neither sign nor sound of anyone else, not even Mags. I knew Phyllis tended to take naps at odd times and, not wanting to disturb her, I left. Margot picked me up on her way back down the hill.

'Not in?'

'Not that I could see. She may be asleep.'

'How about trying the vicar then?'

She shot down the hill and along the high street past the snicket to the church. 'You should go some time,' I said, 'now you're back here more.'

She didn't bother to answer this but turned smartly into the rectory drive, braked hard, hopped out and strode ahead of me to bang on the front door. She was always bolder than me and the Murat affair had galvanized her.

Peter's usual easy-going expression when he answered the door was overwritten with concern.

'It's about Murat,' I said and he nodded.

'I wondered if you'd heard. The police were here. They want to interview you.'

'Why?'

'Because he works for you. I said what I could in his favour, that he had always seemed to me a hard-working, honest lad and has done the odd job for me. If he contacts you, and he might, it would be wiser for him to come forward voluntarily. Try and persuade him to if he turns up.'

'I don't know,' Margot said. 'There's prejudice everywhere, including the police.'

This struck me as a bit much coming from her but Peter said sadly, 'I'm afraid you may be right.'

'I have an impression that he may not be legally here,' I said. 'In which case, he's probably afraid of the police, even if he's innocent – which I'd bet my half of the house he is.'

We got back to Knight's Fee before the police arrived to question us both: how long had we known Murat, when had we seen him last and what could we report of his character? They interviewed us separately but, comparing notes afterwards, it sounded very similarly, except that the police officer who questioned me asked quite pressingly about the nature of our relationship.

'I had a weird feeling she was fishing to see if we were lovers,' I told Margot.

'Oh yeah, mine asked me if you were "intimate". I said that was rubbish and you had a lover in London.'

'Bloody hell,' I said. 'Where did that idea come from?' I was twenty years older than Murat and the idea was preposterous. 'Anyway, he's married,' I pointed out, which, had I thought about it, was daft coming from me.

'Your precious villagers' gossip, I imagine. I've always said not to trust them.'

'Thanks for the London lover, anyway,' I said. 'Lucky I don't have to produce him.'

'I was thinking of Aitken,' Margot said. 'You were his lover, weren't you?'

Among the many shocks of that period of my life, not least was the discovery that Margot had known all along about Robert. My response was to blush furiously, which made any denial pointless. Two mugs of strong coffee later, I asked how she had known.

'It was blindingly obvious the moment I saw you bound like a fawn off his boat. And you kept shooting surreptitious glances at him all the time he was talking to Nadia. Besides which, he was plainly stark naked. Anyone could see that.'

'So did you all discuss us afterwards?' Upsetting thought.

'Nadia, she's a bitch by the way, was all agog with it. Jules couldn't give a monkey's – he's not a one for tattle and by then they were hardly talking – and I said I hadn't noticed anything as I hope you'd expect. I could tell Nadia was dying to out you both. She was pally with his missus.'

'Laura?'

'My guess is she was sent by Laura to nose.'

Which had been my guess too. 'Marg?'

'Yep?'

'What's happened to Robert? Do you know?'

'Do you care?'

I wished that I didn't but the truth was I did, so I probably made some non-committal gesture.

'I can find out if you really want to know. I could have asked Jules. I never mentioned him because of you. But I know enough other arty people in Aitken's circle.' She was silent for a while and then she said, 'Look, Hass, I know it's none of my business but all of that left you trashed. Dad kind of hinted that you weren't in great shape.'

'Dad said that?'

'Yes. He was worried about you. I was too if it came to that. We spoke a few times on the phone while you were with him.'

I was beginning to feel very stupid. Not only had I foolishly prompted the false accusation against Murat but I'd been so blind about my sister. 'I didn't know you'd rung,' I said humbly.

'I said not to tell you. I could see you wanted to lick your wounds in private. But look, hearing about Aitken from Jules is what made you ill after Easter. I'm sorry about that. I would have alerted him but I honestly thought it best to say nothing. He's usually not much interested in other people's lives. But I don't want to be the messenger with news that sets you back again now.'

'I don't believe it will,' I said, without any real conviction. 'I think it's called closure.'

She shot me a surprised look – 'closure' is the kind of word I dismiss as psychobabble – and then she laughed, catching my tone.

Although I was meaning to sound ironic, the laugh should have been on me as closure was exactly what I was hoping for.

18

So many things happened in quick succession around this time that I may have got the sequence confused. There continued to be no trace of Murat. The police questioned the Ludlow wife, who apparently claimed not to have seen him for over a fortnight. I was intrigued to learn from this that they still met. Several weeks earlier, I had spotted the two of them together. I had run out of my drawing ink and Margot, rather grudgingly, had driven me into Ludlow one Saturday to buy more. I didn't introduce myself as I felt it might embarrass him. She was a pretty dyed blonde, with a neat figure but a hard face. Her voice sounded harsh – you can tell a lot from the timbre of a voice. And it was better that I hadn't made myself known as his expression when they talked had seemed very downcast. Recalling this, I tried to steer clear of the gossipy villagers as much as possible.

I couldn't altogether avoid Hayley. Although Margot was now buying most of our food in Shrewsbury, I had still an occasional need to shop. And besides I liked Hayley. She and Russ had befriended me and I didn't want to lose that friendship. Knowing my concern, she tried to sound sympathetic. But the situation was not helped by the *Sun* around this time running prominent headlines about gangs of Albanian drug dealers controlling Britain's organized crime. Half the village, according to Hayley, were swapping horror stories about Albanians and I was consumed with a new distaste for village life.

I did my best to counter this trend. 'As my sister says, what kind of terrorist or gang leader hides away in a Shropshire village doing badly paid gardening jobs? I mean, think about it, Hayley. It would be daft.'

'I suppose he might have come here to hide, to avoid being found out for what he was, if that *is* what he was . . .' was her response. 'Not that I'm saying he is. But to be fair, as Russ says, we don't really know much about him.'

Nor was the news of Sue Lane reassuring. She remained in hospital, still unconscious. No progress had been made on discovering the identity of her attacker; the police were still searching but Murat had not been found.

In his absence, I did my best to help Margot; but I made a poor substitute. I was neither naturally handy nor interested in acquiring practical skills. But useless as I was for Margot's purposes, it provided a displacement from Elfine.

One afternoon, when I'd been more despondent than usual about the thankless nature of my work, Margot said, 'If you were to sell that painting you could survive quite a time on what you'd get for it and then you could afford to dump Elfine.'

I knew at once what picture she had in mind but to give myself space to think I acted innocent. 'Which painting?'

'The only one you have worth anything: the Gabriël Metsu. I assume Aitken gave it to you.'

The prospect of selling my girl in the air-blue gown was so radical I went physically cold. 'I'm not sure –' I began but she interrupted.

'Look, it's your call. I'm just saying. You'd get at least thirty grand for it, maybe more. It would depend on the auction.'

And quite suddenly this novel possibility seemed the potential end I'd been looking for. If Margot was right about the painting's value, and if I was willing to surrender my last relic of Robert, the proceeds could be spun into at least two years of freedom. Possibly more if I was frugal. I could say good riddance to Elfine and her like and draw whatever I wanted. I could, in short, be free of the pressure of material necessity – or free, anyway, for a time.

'OK,' I said, making up my mind in a flash and consequently feeling braver. 'Next time you go to London, take it with you and get it valued for me. And thanks, Marg,' I added. 'I'd never have thought of this myself.'

'You can pay me back by helping me strip off that godawful paper in the hall. Old Mrs East, or whoever was responsible, ought to be hung, drawn and quartered for it.'

'It's hanged,' I corrected her. 'Hanged, drawn and quartered. Pictures and wallpaper are hung. People are hanged.'

'Hassie,' Margot said, 'if you don't watch it, I'll pour this bucket of whitewash over your head and then go outside and trample on Murat's precious seedlings.'

*

In Murat's absence, Margot's work on the house stalled. She left for London, taking with her my girl in the air-blue gown, protectively swathed in bubble wrap. I let her go with an easy heart. *You've been a companion and a colleague*, I told the girl, *but now you must be my meal ticket.*

Although I remained concerned about Murat, the prospect of a coming freedom lightened my mood, so I was able to tackle Elfine more readily and completed almost as much in days as I'd managed in months. Penny Lane's elfin features had etched themselves in my mind and I hit upon the notion of using her as a model for Eloise, which allowed the double satisfaction of venting my spleen on the human child while at the same time giving scope to my dislike of Elfine's obnoxious little companion. And when Travis the Troll acquired the gnome-like features of Paul, the handyman who was supposed to tend the churchyard, I found I was enjoying the work and stuck at it with far fewer breaks.

By the end of the first week of Margot's absence I had almost finished the illustrations and had only a couple more to complete. With my increased consumption caused by late-night work, I'd run out of coffee, my muscles were tight from the extended periods of concentration and I felt I'd earnt some air and exercise.

The barley in the field was high and there were three larks singing their hearts out in a sky that was the colour of the wild blue flax which had shot up amid the crop. The story of Milburga and the geese came back to me and I remembered how the strange image of a stook of barley had come to mind that evening at Phyllis's. Suddenly, I was quite sure that the little stone effigy had been found in this very field.

As I rounded the edge of the field, I saw a man by the track to the wood. A youngish man with a red kerchief round his neck. He looked very sunburnt and his hair was the colour of the ripening barley. It struck me that this must be the tenant farmer to whom the Knapp heirs rented their land and I waved to indicate I'd like to speak to him. But as I walked towards the top of the field a grouse whirred up in front of me, obscuring my view, and when I looked again he had gone.

Perhaps, I thought, *he is getting in firewood, or seeing to the coppicing*. I hurried up the field after him but there was no sign of anyone and when I called out only my own voice came echoing back to me through the trees.

I'd not spoken to Phyllis since Murat had disappeared. I had rung and left a couple of messages but she didn't always listen to these – or perhaps she was paying me back for the messages I had left unanswered. In any case, I decided I must call on her once I'd bought my supplies. I was about to enter the shop when I spotted a familiar pair of pink shorts.

'Penny,' I said, grabbing the child's thin shoulders and turning her forcibly round to face me.

She wriggled like an eel. 'Get your fucking hands off me. It's illegal.'

'Nothing to worry about, Penny,' I assured her, removing the offending hands, though I'd dearly like to have shaken her till her teeth rattled. 'You know that I'm an artist? I draw for the Elfine books, you may know them, and you are just the spit of one of the elves I have to draw.'

'What's spit?' she asked, very suspicious.

'You look very like I imagine this elf. She's called Eloise and if you let me draw you, I'll pay.'

This gamble paid off. 'How much?'

'Five pounds,' I said, preparing to go up to ten. But she agreed, a little sulkily, to these terms, only stating that she'd have to tell her mum first.

We found her mother in the garden, hanging out some tired-looking sheets. She nodded distractedly at my proposal and asked, 'Can you keep her with you till teatime? I have to visit Mum.'

Hayley raised eyebrows when we called by the shop for a Magnum and a can of Fanta. I explained that I was helping Penny's mother out. There was a tricky moment when Penny began to protest that she was only with me because I was paying her. Rather unfairly, because this was after all true, I winked at Hayley and whisked the child away.

When we got home, I left Penny in the garden while I went inside to fetch my sketch pad. I found her, when I came out again, down at the stream. It occurred to me that any inquisition might be more productive after tea, so while she went on splashing about, I made a few swift sketches of her face and hair. I could see this might be genuinely useful: there was something truly elfin about that dandelion-clock hair.

'D'you fancy tea yet, Penny?' I called.

She nodded so I shouted, 'See you up on the lawn in ten minutes,' and went to make sandwiches.

When I came out again, she had picked a bunch of flowers from the long flower bed.

'For my nan,' she announced defensively.

'Very nice,' I said. 'You've made a nosegay.'

'What's that?'

'Like what you've picked. A bunch of flowers that smell nice. Your nan will be pleased.' She stared at me as if to say *Don't imagine I'm taken in by your crap* and I felt the moment had come to put my proposal to her. But it required a cunning to match hers.

'It must have been horrid for you, Penny, seeing your nan attacked like that.'

Her mouth was stuffed with a Marmite sandwich but she gave a non-committal nod.

'Were you actually with her when it happened?'

'Can I have a biscuit? I don't like these.'

I obediently fetched a packet of Jaffa Cakes, which I'd bought in a mistaken fit of nostalgia, and the fruit bowl. 'I expect you heard her at least when she was attacked.'

She looked at me suspiciously. 'Why?'

'I was thinking you must have had to be very brave. Would you like an apple?'

'I don't like fruit.'

'Have another Jaffa Cake.'

'Have you got any other biscuits?'

There were some custard creams in the pantry which I'd bought for the removals men. By this time, they must have been rather stale but they seemed to go down well with Penny. I waited while she polished off two. 'Can I have some more Fanta?'

'I'm afraid that's all I have.'

'Milk then?'

'In a minute. Do you know what perjury is, Penny?'

To my surprise, she said, 'It's when you lie in court.'

'But you wouldn't do that, would you?' I suggested.

'I can't go to court. I'm a minor.'

'You're very well informed. Let me get you some milk.' As she downed the milk, I asked, 'How old are you, Penny?'

'Why?'

'I'm just impressed. You're clearly extremely intelligent.'

I hoped that might soften her but she just said, 'I'm eleven in August.'

'That's a difficult time to be born.'

'S'not,' most indignantly.

'I didn't mean to disparage you. I only meant that you must be one of the youngest in your class.'

I could see her mentally assessing 'disparage' but she only said, 'I'm older than Stephen Hicks. He's thick. He's special needs.'

It was not the moment for an improving lecture. 'Penny?'

'What?'

I shut my mind to the image of my father's unimpeachably honest face. 'If I gave you ten pounds instead of five, would you tell me what you really saw when your nan was attacked?'

She appeared to be considering this. 'I don't remember.'

'You don't remember what? What you saw?'

'I don't remember now what I said, what I saw, I mean.'

'You said you saw my gardener, didn't you? Or . . .' I left a gate open for her.

'Could've been one of the Travellers.'

'Oh?'

'There's a Traveller in my class this term. It could've been one of them.'

'OK,' I said. 'Look, it's perfectly OK to change your

mind. No one is going to tell you off, in fact, they'll be really, *really* pleased that you've thought it over and are being responsible.' I was visited by a sudden troubling vision of some innocent Traveller replacing Murat as scapegoat. 'But it's best not to say who you think it was if you can't remember now. Maybe you could just say, if this is the truth, of course –' I looked at her levelly – 'something like you've been going over it in your mind and you don't now think it was Murat after all. It was a mistake. It's easy to make mistakes when something horrid happens. You can say you were upset. You must have been very upset, Penny. I expect you're upset still.'

She had pulled apart a custard cream and was examining the content. I'd rarely seen anyone look as thoroughly unperturbed.

'No one will blame you,' I pressed on. 'Suppose I came with you?'

At this she looked so alarmed I quickly amplified. 'I would just be there to see no one was cross with you. They won't be, I promise. I'd make sure.'

She made no answer but began to scrape the cream from the biscuit with a fingernail.

'If I come with you, Penny, do you think you could go and say all that about maybe making a mistake to the police?'

'You said you'd give me a tenner.'

'Twenty,' I said, forestalling any bargaining. 'Twenty for being brave, once you've corrected your account. But listen, Penny.' Clear grey eyes gazed up at me with angelic-seeming attention. 'This is payment for being my model for Eloise. I'm not bribing you.'

For which I was treated to a look of well-deserved contempt.

There was no police station in the village. For that we had to get to Shrewsbury. I considered ringing Phyllis to ask if she could ferry us there in the Mazda but Peter was closer and seemed a safer bet. I rang and gave him the news of Penny's apostasy and he said he'd come over at once.

'Your car's dirty,' Penny advised him, when ten minutes later the Morris van appeared.

'I keep it that way,' Peter told her. 'It puts off thieves.'

I doubted if any thief would deign to steal the van; the body was liberally dented and scraped, there were browning banana skins and discarded sweet wrappers on the back seat and dried bird droppings across the windscreen; but it shut Penny up. She was very quiet all the way to Shrewsbury and when we got to the police station said aggressively, '*He's* not coming in with us.'

'Don't worry,' Peter said. 'I don't wish to. I'm actually going to the hospital to see how your grandmother's doing. Shall I take her your flowers?' I'd wrapped them in cooking foil and tied them with some Christmas ribbon I found in Dad's desk.

Penny snatched up her nosegay. '*I'm* taking them to her.'

'Fair enough,' Peter said cheerily. I wondered if he and Penny maybe had past form. 'I'll wait for you both at the hospital, shall I, and give you a lift home?'

Although I did my best not to show it, I was most uneasy about this ruse of mine. For one thing, I could not be certain that my bribe would hold Penny to her word; for another, I wasn't sure the police would consent to talk to her without her mother. In the event, the whole transaction was rather easy. I explained that Penny's mother was at the bedside of her own mother, and since Penny had confided in me, I had considered it right to bring her to explain at once before she lost her nerve. She was, I added, playing to the gallery, extremely concerned that she had unwittingly misled the police, was most anxious now to do the right thing but was understandably nervous. I had reassured her, I smoothly added, that the police were very kind and that they would judge her a highly responsible and sensible girl.

Penny remained mute while I spun this confected version of her volte-face. Her slight physique and angelic fairness worked in our favour. As I produced my account, she stared at her feet, giving a convincing impression of meekness and modesty. I inwardly congratulated the girl: for all my dislike of her, we made a good team.

The police, one a female constable, one a male sergeant, went out of their way to reassure. They produced milk and a chocolate biscuit for Penny and for me a cup of tea and questioned her with immense professional tact. They did ask, but most gently, why she had named Murat.

'I heard people disparage him so I thought at first it must have been him, but then I thought they're just being racist.'

Wow, Penny, I thought. *Clever girl.*

'I only seen a man's shape,' she continued, fixing the sergeant with her candid grey eyes, and then, with perfect timing, hung her head again.

'So you saw nothing but his shape, Penny?' the constable asked.

Penny persisted dumb and the sergeant asked, 'What kind of shape, Penny? Was he my build, for example?'

Penny gave an appraising look and said, a little disdainfully, 'He was tall,' at which the sergeant smiled. He was a rather short, chubby, amiable-looking Asian man and I'd caught him raising his eyebrows at his colleague at Penny's reference to racism.

When they were satisfied with our story and I explained we were going on to the hospital so Penny could visit her grandmother, the sergeant drove us there in a police car. As we got out of the car, he offered his opinion that Penny was 'a little sweetheart and very smart'.

And when we found the way to Sue Lane's ward, it turned out that the revision of Penny's statement had been unnecessary after all. Sue had come to her wits and had stated categorically that her assailant was Penny's father, who had arrived out of the blue, blind drunk and demanding to see his daughter. Stoutly, if rashly, Sue had declaimed he would do so over her dead body and he had bashed her over the head with the tool he'd used to force open the back door and then made himself scarce.

When Penny asked for the toilet, I took the opportunity to escort her there and hand over a twenty-pound note. She pocketed it with a cold stare. We were not to be friends but I felt fairly confident she would calculate that she'd come off well from the whole experience, both from our financial transaction and in her successful handling of the police. She was a shrewd minx, and it was in her interests to stick to our story.

I left her at the hospital with her mother and grandmother discussing the errant father. 'They'll put him away

237

for sure now,' Sue was saying as I left. I got the impression that she felt being bashed over the head was worth it if this was to be the outcome. No doubt this man had a major part to play in the kid's semi-delinquent nature but I hadn't then the emotional energy to care.

Driving back to Hope Wenlock, I reminded Peter, 'You mentioned I might look at Audrey's archaeological findings?'

'Surely. Come in for a drink.'

'Where *can* Murat have gone?' I wondered again as, back at the vicarage, Peter poured me one of his lethal gin and tonics. I felt too ashamed to confide my fear that it was all my fault.

'I expect he'll turn up once he gets word he's no longer a suspect.'

'Do you think that's why he disappeared?'

'Gossip flies fast in the village and if, as you intimated, he is not legally here, then once the police were involved he probably thought it best to take to the hills. You can't blame him.'

'I don't,' I said. The whole episode had gone to strengthen my feeling that Murat and I were colleagues in misfortune.

At Peter's invitation, I stayed for supper, a dismal pizza dredged from the depths of his deep freeze. The plates bore marks of dried food, the wine glasses were bleared and the kitchen table needed a scrub. But the wine looked very grand.

Peter filled my glass. 'I'll be frank with you, Hassie, this is a 2015 Margaux. Not one for every day but we must celebrate the fact that Murat's name has been cleared.'

'You know, Peter,' I said later, running the plates under the hot-water tap, preparing to wash up, 'it's very nice for a woman to have a good male friend.'

He smiled a little bashfully. 'Leave those. I do them in the morning. Shall we sit more comfortably for coffee? And I'll dig out Audrey's notes for you. She'd be pleased for them to find a sympathetic reader.'

He insisted I go into the sitting room and appeared with two cups of coffee. While little islands of undissolved coffee powder spun in the lukewarm water, I watched a daddy-long-legs high-step under the piano. The legs of the grand were laced with fantastic cobwebs; a small fawn-coloured moth had got itself trapped in one.

I'd always supposed the piano was Audrey's but that evening there was a score open at the keyboard. 'Do you play, Peter?'

Up until then I had seen only a diffident Peter, but now his face lit up and I saw another side.

'That's my sad story. My ambition was to become a professional musician but my father, also a priest, had set his heart on having his only son ordained. I should never have complied, I'm not one of God's naturals, you've noticed that, I dare say, but I was devoted to my father.'

'Oh dear,' I said. 'That seems a shame.'

'Perhaps I would never have made it beyond the second violins. Not that I played the violin.' He laughed his uncertain laugh. 'I was always a pianist, though I dabbled with the oboe for a while.'

'I'm sorry,' I said. 'It's awful how we can't escape our parents.' I think about this a good deal now.

239

'I can't help feeling I might have served God better by playing His music.'

'Yes,' I said. 'I can see that too.'

'Music is how I met Audrey.' His eyes were filling. 'Our jaunt to London for an opera was her annual treat. It was then I used to buy her scent. It will sound silly, I know, but I have some still and I sprinkle it on my pillow at night. I don't know what I'll do when it runs out.'

'When it runs out, we can go to the opera together,' I declared. 'And you can replace the Mown Hay.' I yawned. The wine had made me sleepy.

'You're tired, my dear. I'll run you home.'

'I'll walk. You're over the limit and we can't have Hope Wenlock's vicar on a drink-driving charge.'

I was about to set off with Audrey's file when he laid on my forearm a gently detaining hand. 'Audrey always said if anything happened to her, she would want me to be happy with someone else. She would have liked you, Halcyon.'

For a second, I missed his meaning; then I saw the look in his eyes.

Help, I thought, frantically trying to compose a tactful reply.

'That's very flattering, Peter. But . . .' What to say? That there was no answering spark? Kinder to lie with a version of the truth. 'The thing is, I'm not free.' There was a truth in this, of sorts. I was never going to be free of this disabling love for Robert. 'I wouldn't want to raise false hopes. I'm sorry, Peter, really.'

I was sorry. But also a little annoyed. Inwardly, I cursed Margot and bloody Julian for being right. It was as if the Margaux wine by some sympathetic magic had summoned up Margot's influence. The day's events, Penny's recantation, Sue's statement, relief over Murat and the effects of alcohol had lent an unusual warmth to my words. And no doubt the wine had in turn loosened Peter's inhibitions, which had led to this unforeseen declaration.

I needn't have worried. He was gracious in his reply. So gracious that I wished for half a second that I had it in me to please him. It would have been a solution for us both, of a kind.

'No, no, don't be sorry,' he said, hastening to absolve me. 'I am not at all surprised that some eminently sensible bloke has snapped you up. You'll forgive me for throwing my hat into the ring? There are not many people I would care to live with after Audrey.'

'I'm honoured,' I said. 'You're a good man, Peter. Audrey was lucky to have you,' and I meant it.

Walking home, I pondered on why it seems to amuse nature to construct humankind to want what it has determined we can't have.

19

I wasn't entirely surprised when the following morning I found Penny Lane paddling in the stream. She started when she saw me and began to wade away.

I shouted, 'Hey, don't go.' We had become, in a sense, partners in crime and I felt I owed it her to call a truce.

She stopped and turned back, doubtful.

'Penny,' I said, an idea coming to me, 'Miss Foot says your real name is Isabel. Is that right?'

'Why?'

'No reason. I only wondered if you might like me to call you by your real name.'

'My nan calls me Penny cos of the Beatles. D'you know who they are?'

'Yes,' I said, slightly offended. 'And I get that. It's a song. A song I like and I imagine your nan does too.' She stared up at me mistrustfully. 'It's up to you. I don't mean to presume.'

Frowning, she said, 'I don't presume you,' which made me feel fonder of her.

'My real name is Halcyon,' I said. 'You can presume to call me that if you like.'

I hoped she might produce her inevitable 'why?' so I could recount the story of my name. But she only said, 'Can I have a custard cream?'

'I wondered,' I said carefully, after I had found the custard creams and she had put away the last of the packet, 'whether you might like to help me.'

'What with?'

'The stream. I want to clear it and I wondered if you'd help.'

'How?'

'I have tools. You're small, smaller than me, so if you go ahead of me along the bed of the stream and cut away the lower brambles and overhanging branches, I can follow behind and clear the higher ones as we go. Might you like to do that? I'll pay you.' Obviously that had to follow.

'How much?'

'A fiver.'

She considered this and then said, 'Yeah, all right.'

We repaired to the shed where I furnished her with the smaller pair of secateurs and myself with the tree loppers for the tougher vegetation. Together we waded along the stream. Penny snipped away most efficiently with a savage determination; I followed, taking out the tougher hawthorn branches and brambles, and by and by we came through to the pool.

'I've been here before,' she announced.

'Really?'

'With my nan. When I was little. It's called the ladies' pool. I made a wish.'

'Did it come true?'

'My nan says to give it time. She came here with her nan and her nan came here with her nan to get a baby.'

'I wonder how that worked.'

She looked up at me, scornful at my ignorance. 'Babies aren't made like that these days. They don't come here now. Can I have my five pounds?'

'Penny,' I said, producing a note.

'What?'

'Should I call you that or Isabel? You didn't say.'

She appeared to consider. 'Don't know.'

'OK, I shall call you Isabel Penny or maybe Penny Isabel if that's all right with you?' She made no reply, which I took as assent. 'Thank you, both of you, Penny and Isabel, for helping to clear the stream and for telling me about the pool.' She stood, apparently lost in thought. 'We could make a wish. What d'you think?'

'You have to have a pin.'

I had some of the nails Murat had removed from the attic in my pocket. They had flat heads and shaped shanks and I was keeping them because I thought they might be Jacobean. 'I have these. They're quite like pins.'

'Those look old. My nan gave me one of her safety pins.'

'They are old. But old's good. The pool's old.'

'All right.'

She took one of the nails, which indeed looked very old, and stood, cupping it in the palm of her hand. It was a very small hand, scratched, and her fingernails, on which the blue varnish was peeling, were bitten to the quick.

'There's no hurry,' I said. 'We have all the time in the world.'

'I'm thinking.'

'Sorry.'

We stood side by side and minutes passed. Water boat-men skimmed over the water and tiny insects whizzed round our heads and I thought how odd it was that the presence of this child, whom I had really quite hated, seemed not to disturb the feel of the place which had become for me such a sanctuary. Penny's eyes were scrunched tight shut and her lips moved as she murmured wordlessly to herself. Quite suddenly, she tossed the nail high in the air. It fell right into the very middle of the pool with a tiny *plip*, producing a series of rings on the water's surface. We stood watching as they expanded, shivered and finally disappeared.

'All done?' I suggested.

'It didn't come true last time.'

'Remember your nan said to give it time.'

She didn't reply but she favoured me with an almost grin.

I watched her scamper away through the wood and stood there a while longer, watching a mayfly skim over the water, admiring the delicate lace effect of its fragile wings. Then I shut my eyes and threw my own nail into the pool.

Later that afternoon, I was lying on the lawn when a shadow fell across my eyes. I opened them to see Hayley's Russ standing over me.

'Hayley said to come. Miss Foot's had a stroke.'

I was already on my feet and hurrying into the house to collect my bag. Russ drove me to Shrewsbury, where

Phyllis had been taken to hospital, explaining on the way what had occurred. A neighbour had heard Alfred barking and had gone in to find Phyllis hanging half out of bed, unable to speak and paralysed down one side.

'That's the second person from Hope Wenlock in hospital,' I commented and Russ remarked that things went in threes and he wondered who'd be next. He went on to say that Hayley had suggested that I was the person Phyllis would most want to see, which left me feeling guilty. When I looked back over the past weeks, I recognized signs in her of failing health.

Phyllis, I was informed at the hospital reception, was in one of the geriatric wards, which made me feel ten times worse. While technically geriatric, she had never seemed to me old. So the sight of her, crushed, yellow-skinned and shrunken, lying mute in a metal-framed hospital bed – these always put me in mind of cattle stalls – was disturbing.

But I tried to not show how distressing I was finding this. 'Phyllis, I came as soon as I heard.'

The nurse on the desk had warned me that she couldn't speak. 'But she's having physio and she's got a pad and a pen and she's keeping us on our toes.' It was a left-hemisphere stroke, the nurse advised me, which meant it was her right side that was affected. She was lucky, the nurse said, in being left-handed.

Phyllis's expression showed she had recognized me, which was a comfort. She reached for her pad and wrote *Take Mags?* The writing was shaky but clear.

'Of course. I'll be glad to.'

Keep in for 3 weeks. Butter paws before outside.

'Understood. What about Alfred?' I felt I should offer but I greatly hoped Alfred could stay elsewhere.

Hayley Russ she wrote.

While her left arm still functioned, it was apparent to me that the act of writing was taxing her. 'Don't wear yourself out,' I said.

She started to form an M and I guessed she was about to ask about Murat but she wrote *Mazda. You use. Key in desk.*

'Thank you. But I'm not insured.'

Insured for other drivers she wrote and then laboriously scrawled a note to say I had her permission to drive the car.

'Thank you,' I said. 'It's very kind of you to think of me when you're . . .' I didn't like to say 'so ill', so I said 'laid low' instead. 'It will be handy to have the car to visit you here. I'll stay a while longer but please rest now. I'll just sit here by you and be quiet.'

She nodded slightly, closed her eyes and seemed to sink back into herself. This reminded me so much of Dad in the days before he died that I became tearful, though I kept the tears back. I knew her well enough to know that tears would not be welcomed.

After a bit, the nurse I'd spoken to at the desk came by. 'Maybe enough for today. We don't want Mrs Foot over-doing it,' which I could tell irked Phyllis from the way she twitched the working side of her mouth.

'How about if I came tomorrow?' I suggested.

She made a feeble gesture of assent with her hand and then waved it to indicate she had more to say.

Murat? she wrote.

I had not wanted to distress her needlessly but when

I began to convey the bad news she waved her hand again to indicate that she was wise to it.

Tell him to stay in my cott. she wrote and lay back, looking bone-tired.

Russ was waiting for me at the hospital entrance. 'I popped in on Sue to see how she was coming along. They're keeping her in while they do a few more tests but she seemed fine. Sharp tongue all present and correct. She was the same year at school as my dad and to be fair he says she was a little cat then,' which reminded me that I had to collect Mags.

Mags was far from biddable and I would be needing a means in which to transport him. 'Would you mind if we called by Knight's Fee, Russ, and then went on to Phyllis's to collect her kitten? She's asked me to look after him but I'll need a basket and there's one up in our attics.'

Russ accompanied me up to the attics. 'Want me to help carry this other junk down?'

Margot had plans to sand the floors, so it was an opportunity to get it cleared. Russ carried down the tin trunk with the old tennis rackets and a box full of dusty papers inside.

'Want me to bring down the horse and fire screen and the kiddie's desk too? You can probably get something for them. People go crazy for this old stuff these days.'

He was welcome to them, I said, as a thank you for his help. Loading the desk into the van, he said, 'Maybe I'll pass this on to Steve and Jade for when the little one's bigger,' which seemed fitting, as Steve, when baby Molly had just been born, was almost the first person I met when I came to Hope.

Mags was skulking by the fireplace when we came through the door but bolted smartly into the kitchen. When I approached, making encouraging sounds, he shot behind the fridge and even when I tried tempting him out with cat treats he refused to budge but crouched there, lashing his tail from side to side.

Russ shifted the fridge and when I finally grabbed hold of Mags' skinny body he writhed around, kicking violently with his back legs, clawing and biting until my wrists and hands were covered in reddening scratches. Beads of bright blood were issuing from a wound on my palm.

'You'd best get that looked at,' Russ advised. 'Cat bites can turn nasty.'

It was not a peaceful journey back to Knight's Fee, with Mags yowling furiously at his enforced confinement. I'd collected all the tins of cat food I could find at Phyllis's, so I was able to offer him some once I'd released him from the basket. He sidled out, very small and intensely cross but rather magnificent in his way. He was not unlike Penny – small and fierce, but with a certain aura.

I left him overnight in the scullery with an old cushion in the pantry to sleep on and plenty of food. When I came down to make my morning tea, I found he'd ignored the cushion and made a bed in the box of papers that Russ had brought down from the attic. I'd forgotten how cats love boxes. I scattered some treats by the box, along with his food and water, and went back to bed to remind myself about Much Wenlock, which I planned to visit later that morning.

St Milburga [I read] *was a powerful princess and a devout abbess.*
In the 680s a monastery was founded by her father, Merewald, King
of Mercia. Milburga was placed in charge of a double house, with
separate provision for monks and nuns. By the time of Milburga's
death she commanded extensive lands and had a reputation for
performing many miracles.

By now, I was familiar with these 'many miracles', so
I skipped over the account and went on to the history.

The monastery was probably sacked by the Vikings and her shrine
was lost but the ruins were rebuilt as a minster in 1040 by Earl
Leofric. In 1101 two boys were playing in the ruins of the earlier
nuns' quarters, today the church of the Holy Trinity, when the
ground gave way and they fell into a pit revealing the saint's bones.
The water in which the bones were cleansed became a potent source
for miracle cures and the bones were reinterred in a shrine in the
third religious foundation built on this site, a twelfth-century
Cluniac priory.

I'd promised to visit Phyllis in the evening but there
was time to walk over to the village, pick up the Mazda
and drive the few miles to Much Wenlock. It was the first
real outing I would have made in months, other than my
trips with Murat to the garden centre.

Recalling Murat punctured my mood. He had not reappeared and by this time I was feeling really stricken,
imagining him fearful and lying low, as if he were a real
felon. In tackling Sue Lane over Penny's childish insults,
I had stirred up a hornet's nest through a picture of myself
as someone doing good. 'Do-gooders? Spare me!' as

Margot once said, when we were having an argument about Mother Teresa. 'More like old busybodies.' She had been right about my thoughtlessness in approaching Sue Lane.

It was mid June, the day was warm; a blazing sun was working its peculiar inverse alchemy, making the sky a cerulean blue in which scimitar-winged swifts circled and soared. I had packed sandwiches and a thermos flask, and the sense of freedom as I bowled along the roads, with the roof back and my hair blowing behind me, was intoxicating. For all my self-reproaches, I was elated to find I had not lost my driving skills and I was excited at this venture. Research can make you proprietorial; I had become a little so with Milburga and was hopeful that this expedition would yield more historical information – or at least give me a better sense of what kind of woman she might have been.

Much Wenlock is prettier than its cousin, Hope Wenlock. More of the houses are whitewashed and timbered, it boasts two 'holy' wells and an impressive Saxon cross, eroded by time, still stands in the churchyard where the first nuns' quarters once stood. There are historically authentic inns and the remains of the twelfth-century priory, built on the site of Milburga's monastery.

I parked, paid my entrance fee and walked into a grassy area.

What I saw was immediately impressive. The priory had fallen foul of Henry VIII's pettish Act of Dissolution and the lofty and extensive remains of the twelfth-century buildings possessed the peculiar charm of ancient ruins. Robert and I once visited Chartres and I remember how aghast I was when he told me that the sober interior of the ancient cathedral, which induced such a sense of grave and majestic harmony, would in its heyday have been adorned with gilt and gaudy colour. The high-arched remains of the Cluniac priory, the weathered stone, softened by weeds sprung up in its crevices, set off by the surrounding yews discreetly laced with scarlet berries, were lovely in their austere grandeur. Impossible not to be reminded of Shakespeare's bare ruined choirs . . .

It is debated whether Shakespeare's sweet birds were the feathered kind, or his poetical image for the departed chanting nuns and monks. My guess is both. Through the frame of the storeyed Gothic windows I spied a single kite and around it a company of rooks, swooping and tumbling, and I wondered if I would have liked all this as much when it was a new-build, designed to shut in the pious chanting human choirs and shut out the singing birds and the soaring sky.

I paced around the area where the saint's bones were said to have been reburied. There were very few people about and, on an impulse, I knelt down and murmured, 'Help me, Milburga. Help me find Murat and put things right.' A middle-aged man wearing a dog collar approached and as I struggled up, feeling ridiculous, he bestowed on me an indulgent smile, as if to reassure me that I could rely on his discretion to keep my eccentric behaviour to himself.

Strolling around the site, I began to imagine how I might draw this former princess, capably ruling over her order of monks and nuns. In my mind's eye, Milburga was a low-sized, sturdy woman, with a firm, uncompromising gaze and slightly protuberant gooseberry-green eyes. Her wiry red-gold Celtic hair I saw pulled tightly back under her wimple, revealing a naturally high, smooth white forehead (I decided that for whatever reason – a lingering vanity? – she didn't shave her head), innocent of lines. My Milburga was resolute, industrious, impatient with diffidence, disinclined to bother with trivia and not at all given to being fanciful. But in my image of her I could summon up nothing in the slightest mystical or other-worldly.

It was not quite midday. As a rule I lunch later, sometimes not at all, but I suffer from an irresistible greed over picnics, so I settled myself on a handy boulder and ate my sandwiches and drank tea from my thermos, enjoying the sunshine and the surroundings.

As I sat absorbing the outward environment, I began to consider my response to it. The place, the site of three historical layers of spiritual aspiration, was undeniably beautiful: the architecture was an impressive testament to humankind's yearning to rise above the quotidian, the building, in its dilapidations, was appealing and, for all my worry about Murat, my mood was for the most part contented. But as for any sign or sense of sanctity or lingering holiness, I felt not a jot nor a whisker.

I was quite ready to suppose that the lack lay in me. I had never been of a religious disposition, never been in the habit of seeking out spiritual beings or places, other than with Robert, purely for their aesthetic beauty, so I had no inner sounding-board with which to locate any such response. Nonetheless, I had from time to time felt intimations of – what shall I call it? – some telling moment of access to a mystery, such as when I stood at dawn on the grass in the garden or sat under the oak by the pool in the wood. Yet here I was, experiencing nothing more than an ordinary simple pleasure in sun on stone and the reliably satisfying taste of ham-and-mustard sandwiches.

My kneeling gesture and muttered plea was a sham. I had performed this more as a test, an ordeal I was putting myself through for my part in the Murat debacle. I had been embarrassed at being seen by the touring cleric but the embarrassment served as part of a self-inflicted punishment, a penalty for the damage caused by my righteous indignation. As far as making touch with another world went, it was a hollow gesture, a laughable fraud.

At this moment, the wandering cleric reappeared and, no doubt prompted by his having witnessed my seeming devotions, remarked that this was – didn't I just feel it? – a holy site and wasn't it the case that you could apprehend, for all they were long gone, the almost palpable presence of the holy sisters and brothers?

I smiled cordially, while agreeing with none of this privately, and made a performance of packing up my picnic. He was a lonely man, I sensed, liable to seek to prolong this conversation and I didn't want to get drawn in. Also I badly needed to pee.

I waited till he'd taken himself off and then nipped behind one of the higher walls, reflecting amusedly, as I pulled down my knickers, that this was the second time I'd found myself peeing at one of Milburga's holy sites, and trusted that she wouldn't take it as a personal slight or act of sacrilege. If she was the sensible, practical woman of my imagination, then I felt sure she would be fine about it. Indeed, I could see her pulling up her skirts and squatting down to urinate without the slightest fuss or false modesty. I imagined that they didn't bother in those days with drawers.

Although both Murat and Phyllis were still on my mind, the freedom allowed by the Mazda was too tempting to forgo an exploration prohibited by my former carless state. From Much Wenlock, I drove up to the Long Mynd, past ranks of dark-pink foxgloves standing sentinel beneath hedgerows bound in honeysuckle and laden with creamy elderflowers, to where the sheep, livelier-looking than their lowland colleagues, were grazing the high, unfenced pastures.

I got out and surveyed the landscape spread below. It doesn't surprise me that revelations come to people standing on high ground. For all my anxiety about my friends and my possible part to play in their misfortunes, I felt my shoulders palpably relax and my spirits rise. In the clear late-afternoon light, with the unpeopled hills rolling before me like mighty waves frozen for all eternity under some wizard's cosmic spell, I saw for a fleeting moment how small we mortals are, how puny our power and how, somewhere, somehow, without our efforts or aid, matters may still turn out well.

I can't pretend this mood stayed with me long but I can recall even now the sense of release.

I wandered along one of the tracks and paused to watch a curlew's flight, delighting in the elegantly curved bill and plaintive cry; and going back to the car, I stooped to collect a small hank of sheep's fleece, caught in the heather, and wondered why daydreaming is known as 'wool-gathering', for surely wool-gatherers were thrifty housewives, prudent and industrious rather than dreamy.

By the time I got home it was almost time to set out again to the hospital. I would have carried straight on to

Shrewsbury but I was anxious to see how Mags was doing. I was met, when I opened the door into the scullery, by scuffed, paw-marked papers all over the floor. At the sight of me, he shrank away.

'It's OK, Mags,' I assured him. I badly wanted us to be friends again. He fixed me with his luminous green eyes and I knelt down on all fours to be at his level and looked straight into them. (I assure you, this works with cats.) Then I said, 'Darling Mags, please be happy here. I promise you are quite safe,' which may sound even dafter than kneeling to the bones of a seventh-century saint but was more sincere on my part. My tone must have somewhat soothed him as he consented to nibble two treats from my palm. I took a picture of him on my phone to show to Phyllis and left him tormenting a hapless handful of fleece.

Phyllis already had a visitor when I arrived at the hospital: a gaunt elderly man, a little unkempt and shabbily but not unattractively dressed in a tweed jacket which had seen better days but looked as if it had class. He introduced himself as her brother, Philip, and before I had time to say who I was launched into an account of how all the Foot siblings' forenames began with P.

'She was incorrigibly stingy, our mother. Her first child was a Penelope Elizabeth – she died young of meningitis – but Mother had laid out on a special offer of Cash's nametapes, so we all had to be P. E. Foot.'

I could see from Phyllis's expression, which I could read, even with her face awry, that she was impatient at having to suffer this well-worn family anecdote. Nevertheless, I felt it polite to respond. 'How many P. E. Foots are you? Were you?' I remembered Phyllis mentioning a sister who'd died.

'Five, if you count Penelope. Patience Evelyn, who has gone before, this one here, Phyllis Elspeth, I'm Philip Edward and the youngster of the family is Piers Ernest. Patience was the religious one, Piers is the practical one and Phyllis here is the brains.'

'How about you?' I asked. 'I'm Hassie, by the way.'

'Yes, I know who you are. Me? I'm a star gazer.' (I learnt later he had been a respected astronomer.) 'You illustrate books. Phyllis has mentioned you when we've talked on the phone. I was pleased for her that a kindred spirit had turned up. Hope Wenlock society has a limited appeal.'

I explained that I was just back from a trip to Much Wenlock. 'In fact,' I said, remembering, 'I went there in what I think is your grandson's car. Phyllis has been kind enough to loan it to me. But maybe you –'

He interrupted. 'Feel free. I don't drive myself and Orion won't be back for months.'

'Orion? That's on a par with Halcyon.'

'Technically Oliver, but he goes by Orion in the family. There's a story there.'

But I felt that were I to encourage the telling of this story Phyllis would have another stroke. Instead I described my impressions of Milburga, which I hoped might entertain her.

Philip anyway was entertained. 'Yes, I can just see her. A bustling, no-nonsense sort, with the kind of super-abundance of energy that's wearying for us lesser beings. I've often thought these so-called saints were probably rather unsympathetic people, impatient with ordinary mortal failings.'

Having to lie mute while this animated conversation took place was, I sensed, a torment for Phyllis. I felt it was time to leave her with her brother, so I said goodbye, assuring her I would come again soon.

The Lexus was parked in the drive when I pulled in and Margot appeared. When I explained how I came to be driving the Mazda, she said, 'I'm sorry the old bat's been struck down but cool that she's lent you her wheels. Classy ones too. Where've you been with them?'

I wasn't about to share my investigations with Margot, so I merely said I'd done a little local exploring and she asked for no details. She was too full of news about the girl in the air-blue gown.

'Bonhams are putting it in their early September fine art auction with a reserve of fifteen grand but the guy I dealt with reckoned it could go for double that. The Dutch are back in fashion, he says, because modern artists have reached such silly prices that the less well-off collectors have reverted to the seventeenth and eighteenth century. So your painting should attract interest.'

To my surprise, she took to Mags. 'He's a sweetie, though you'll have to hang a bell round his neck if you want to protect your precious birds.'

I explained he had to stay inside for three weeks before he could be allowed out.

'Phyllis won't be in hospital that long. These days they kick 'em out soon as. Unless she's planning for you to keep him for good.'

The nurse had told me Phyllis might have to go on to a rehab centre for further physio, so it was likely she was including that in her calculations. All the same, Margot's words did make me wonder. Phyllis had seemed most intent on my buttering those paws.

20

For some weeks I had been sleeping with my window open, the better to hear the dawn chorus. The promise of birdsong is a potent soporific, but long before first light I woke at another noise.

A weird sound seemed to be coming from the garden, so I got out of bed and went downstairs to check that Mags was safe.

He had made himself at home in the box of papers which I had left for him in the pantry, with the door to the scullery open for him to roam. When I put on the light, he was sitting upright, paws neatly together, on the mat by the back door.

'Do you want to go out, little one?' I asked.

His green-glass eyes looked reproach at me as if to say: *I would have thought better of you than to deny me my feline rights.*

'OK,' I said. 'But I'm putting you on trust to come back.'

Margot's goat butter, which I felt more appropriate

than cow, was in the fridge. Mags was surprisingly docile and hardly struggled – though I took the precaution of putting on gardening gloves – while I liberally smeared the soft pads of his paws. Paws well buttered, he punctiliously licked them clean, rubbed his skinny ribs briefly against my ankles and streaked past me the moment I opened the back door. I followed him barefoot into the garden.

In the shadowy flower bed the blooms glowed like fireworks, vivid and strange. A gibbous moon hung low in the sky amid multitudinous particles of ancient light.

> *Look at the stars! look, look up at the skies!*
> *O look at all the fire-folk sitting in the air!*

Thanks to Robert, I had come to see the stars as an image of all our illusions, shining in the lonely reality of our darkness yet in substance absent. But now I began to see them differently: as signs that while the past has seemingly gone for ever, it is with us still. Nelly East must have stood, as I was standing, and gazed up at the same night skies; and before her, so must all the other residents of Knight's Fee, right back to the Wight who built the first house here and marked out his territory from the uncharted wilds. And the starlight, that had met us each in turn, in turn had come from way, way back, long before any of us existed, before our ancestors existed, before there was mortal life on earth.

The stars that night, as I stood in the hallowing darkness in which Knight's Fee is couched, seemed brilliant points of conjunction in a vast and invisible net; and gathered within it were all our histories down the ages, right back to the very beginnings of time.

See, see, the stars soundlessly sang, *you are not alone. All and everything that came before you is here with you now.*

After a time, for all these lofty thoughts, I began to feel chilly and went back inside and made a brew of extra-strong tea. Mags had tipped over his box again, so I decided to leave it on its side and remove the encumbering papers. I dumped them in the kitchen to look through later, propped open the back door and returned to bed.

That night I dreamt I had lost Mags and, with that sense of powerless anguish, the hallmark of nightmares, was frantically hunting for him in a garden, which was both my garden yet resembled no garden I have ever known or seen. There was a pond with goldfish and lily pads and by the pond a sundial. Some words were carved on the sundial, which in the dream I recognized but had escaped my mind when I awoke in a fright, with the dream kitten still missing, and, nearly slipping in my socks, I rushed downstairs to check on whether the flesh-and-blood Mags was back.

I was relieved to find him curled up, a neat fur rosette, in his box, and when I stroked him, he opened a fraction of one green eye and shut it again. His small pink tongue unfurled from a yawn exposing exquisitely pointed white teeth. He arched, stretched and then settled contentedly back down.

That Mags had accepted the hospitality at Knight's Fee was heartening. I stepped outside, where the scent of the old roses mingling with honeysuckle and lilac on the fresh morning air was so delicious it seemed almost dangerous.

My head felt clear but strangely empty, as if my brains had been tipped out and my voided skull had been thoroughly rinsed and cleansed. The long flower bed was a tapestry of blues, reds, yellow, orange and white, and the ancient quince, which Murat and I together had laboriously liberated from its ivy fetters, was alight with blossoms of incandescent pink.

But the sight of the tree prompted sobering thoughts of Murat. I decided that if he didn't show up soon I would drive into Ludlow to track down his wife.

Margot had come down when I went back into the house to make coffee.

'Your cat has pooed in the corner.'

'He's just making himself at home,' I said, getting some kitchen roll to clear it away. 'And he was out last night so from now on he'll do it in the garden.'

'He'd better. I don't fancy coming down each morning to a cat latrine. And what's all this?' she asked, pointing to the pile of papers.

I explained they had been in the box that Mags had corralled and that I was planning to sift through them before consigning them to the recycling bin.

'Well, hurry up. They're making me sneeze.'

I lugged the papers outside with a tray of coffee. Margot came and sat on a rug beside me. 'What are they?'

'Mostly stuff about the house. Look at this – a 1960 bill for a chimney sweep, 15/6d. And here's an invoice for removing starlings' nests from chimneys.'

We found various other items of interest: a 1902 bill for two flat-top hives and two bee skeps, cost £3 17/9d; another dated 1923 for a hen coop and netting. 'I can see you as a hen wife,' Margot suggested. 'There was a story about one in that Rackham book of fairy stories you nicked from me. What happened to that?'

'I hid it in the garden shed,' I said. 'It scared me. I couldn't confess to you I'd pinched it, so I hid it under some sacks of compost and, when I went to find it, it had gone mouldy.'

'Bloody hell, Hass. That was a first edition. What did you do with it then?'

'I wrapped it in some newspaper and put it at the bottom of the dustbin.' After all that time, I still felt guilty about this.

There were other invoices for plants and gardening paraphernalia and, towards the bottom of the pile, some exercise books.

Margot opened one. 'It looks as if it's about the garden.'

It was an old-fashioned exercise book of the kind once used in schools, with paper lined in blue and margins marked in red. The first pages were lists in a neat ink script of the vegetables that had been sown and a pencil sketch of what I recognized as our vegetable garden. There were notes indicating where various seeds had been planted out. It was a competent sketch, signed N. East and dated 1949. 'You know, Marg, I think this is Nelly East's record of the garden. She must have begun it when she married Arthur.'

'What happened to the parents?' Margot wondered. 'I mean, did they all live here together or did the parents tactfully move or were they booted out?'

'I'll ask Phyllis. She knew them.'

'How's she doing?' Margot asked. 'When are they allowing her home?'

Phyllis was not recovered enough to manage life alone in her cottage. I explained I was due to collect her from the hospital and take her to the rehab centre.

'That's nice of you but watch out, she's not your responsibility. She's got family, hasn't she? A brother?'

'I know but . . .'

'This tendency to take on other people's problems. It doesn't pay.'

It was true I'd been chastising myself about the dangers of too much 'care'. But this was different. Phyllis was a friend, a good friend who had been good to me, who was ill and in need. I was about to protest when I had a sudden insight. Margot was jealous of Phyllis. It was a radical notion, but it felt true enough for me to hold my tongue and say, 'Her brother seemed pleasant but he didn't strike me as terribly effective. Not everyone has a competent know-all sibling like me to look out for them,' which I could tell pleased her as she said, 'If you have a stroke, don't think I'll be coming to your rescue. It would serve you right. Your diet's a disgrace. Can I stick these papers in the recycling now?'

She stuck out her tongue when I said, 'You can and you may,' though I added hastily, 'but not those old invoices for the bee skeps and so on and definitely not the exercise books. We should keep them; they're a kind of history of the garden.'

In one of the books there were a number of pencil drawings. 'Look here, Marg. It says Midsummer Eve 1956.

Phyllis said that Nelly used to hold a Midsummer party. D'you think we should revive it?'

'What have I said about sucking up to the village? I'd've thought the experience with that Lane woman would've cured you. Anyway, Midsummer's any day now, isn't it? We wouldn't have time to arrange it.'

Some mornings later, Mags was not in his box. I'd been leaving the scullery window open for his night-time prowls and so far he had always come home. Although I was a little alarmed, it wasn't till later that afternoon that I really began to fret.

'Where has he got to?' I asked Margot, not expecting an answer.

But she sensibly suggested that he might have returned home, so I drove over to Phyllis's to check. There were no signs of either human or animal habitation in the cottage, other than the spiders, which Phyllis regarded as valuable dust gatherers. 'If people only left spiders to weave as they will there wouldn't be half as much cleaning to do. There's nothing like spiderwebs for trapping dust,' she told me once, in one of her pedagogic moods.

Recalling what she had intimated about Murat using the cottage, I wrote a note for him on the chance he might show up there and left it, where the key was always left, under the water butt.

When I got home, Mags had still not appeared.

'Don't get your knickers in a twist,' Margot said. 'He'll turn up. Cats have nine lives.'

'But he's not mine. I'm in loco parentis, remember.'

'Just as well you don't have any real children if you're in such a dither about a cat.'

'He isn't a cat,' I said. 'He's a kitten.' I was half in tears; I wasn't quite aware of how attached I had grown to Mags.

'That's like those people who have bumper stickers announcing they have a baby in their car,' Margot said. 'As if babies matter more than any other human being.'

By the evening, I was frantic. I was in the scullery about to dig out a torch and go on another hunt when a small dark creature darted across the front lawn. It was running towards the bottom of the garden and I was visited by a recollection of a woman in our street at home, who drowned the superfluous kittens born to her large pro-miscuous tabby. Shoving my feet into boots and grabbing the torch, I ran into the garden.

The moon was at that stage when you can't tell if it is full because it never does seem to make a quite perfect round. It hung in the sky over the far hills, a child's yellow balloon, casting light enough to make my torch unneces-sary as I hurried down to the stream. Once there, I began to wade along the stream bed, shining the torch into all the crannies and holes in the bank. The light from the moon became dimmer as I stooped lower and lower in my search, and my hair escaped from its ponytail and trailed in the water. Either the brambles on the banks had grown back or Penny and I had missed a few, for vegetation seemed to whip out maliciously to scratch my arms and face as I pressed on, calling, 'Mags, Mags.' Nothing. Only the faint night noises and a weird echoing of my own voice.

And then the narrowness widened and I was out among the trees.

I was standing in the pool in an aqueous light. The still-ness was almost palpable. All of a sudden, a clatter of wings like a gunshot made me start violently. I lost my balance, dropped the torch, attempted to catch it, fum-bled, slipped and slid down in the water, banging my bottom on something sharp and submerged.

Soaked and muddy, my bottom bruised, my face and limbs scraped with briars, I scrambled up and stood there, my arms strait-jacketing my shuddering frame, tears and snot streaming down my cheeks and chin. Another bird made an explosive hysterical cry, shocking me so the nerves down my arms ran like a freezing current. Above, through a black fretwork of branches, the moon shone sinisterly yellow, cold and baleful. An annihilating sense of the abso-lute indifference of all around suffused my being, a great tide of sorrow rose up within me and I cried aloud to the vast unfeeling nothingness of the universe, 'Whatever's the point? There's no bloody, goddamned point in anything, anything at all.'

At length, when it seemed I had cried all the tears in the world clean out of me, some seventh sense alerted me.

Deep in the shadows surrounding the pool, a shape detached itself from the darkness. I might have thought it part of the vegetation, a branch of yew, a holly bough, a hazel bush stirring in the chill night breeze. But as I stared, drenched through, sore and utterly lost to hope, I made out a figure. I stood there, emptied of all feeling, as the figure began to move slowly towards me . . .

PART III

21

When I woke in my bed the following morning, a sun-beam was gilding my pillow and a soft weight plumped down beside my head and began to nuzzle my ear.

'You *bad* cat! Where on earth have you been, Mags?'

For reply, he jumped on to the sheet over the region of my stomach and began to treadle with his claws, which was painful as I was naked. I sleep naked when it's warm.

Mags had returned in an affectionate mood. He now began to wind himself around my bare feet and lick my toes with his rasping little tongue. I lay enjoying this atten-tion until the desire for tea grew stronger, and I slid out of bed, threw on an old dress and went downstairs with Mags tripping lightly down beside me. Unlike most cats, he never got under your feet.

Margot was already up. 'Hello, Sleeping Beauty. I was about to come and see if you'd died on me.'

'It's not late, is it?'

'It's gone twelve.'

'Blimey,' I said, amazed.

'Well, you were out till God knows when. What time did you get in, finally? I thought you must've gone to some village Midsummer Eve rave. Oh, and you'll be pleased to hear our gardener is back.'

I opened the back door and there was Murat weeding the long bed as if he'd never been away.

When I came in, after Murat and I had been three times around the garden together, Margot had made me brunch, scrambled eggs with smoked salmon on rye toast, which was kind of her as I was ravenously hungry. But I was learning that she could be kind.

She said now, 'Where did Murat go? Did he say? Hey, stop that!'

Mags, bless him, had chosen that moment to attach his claws to a long thread dangling from Margot's skirt and was busy unravelling the hem, which allowed me time to consider my answer.

'He's staying at Phyllis's,' I said. Which had the virtue of being true.

'All that time?'

'If you're so curious, you ask him.'

'I did and he just smiled. He's very handsome when he smiles. I suppose he's been with some girl and didn't like to say. And we were so worried! That's men for you. By the way, I've put those old exercise books you wanted to keep up in your room. They were making me sneeze.'

Later that day, I sat on the window seat, where Nelly East had once sat, looking over the garden, and read the modest school exercise books, which proved to be rather more than simple garden records. They turned out to be records of her private inner life, journals in which she had chosen to pour out her heart.

As many women down the ages have done, she wrote to express feelings she was unable or forbidden to voice, in her case thoughts about her husband. I didn't care for the sound of Arthur. Apart from the admittedly unconventional act, for someone of his class, of marrying a working-class girl from Bethnal Green, he sounded to me a stuffed shirt, with regressive notions about a woman's place even for that time.

Poor Nelly. I felt for her. The journals say nothing of her treatment by the Easts as a child evacuee but as an adult woman she sounds to have been nagged, scolded and lectured by her husband pretty well morning, noon and night.

The early journals were accounts of her strategies of escape.

Today I said I must go to the village to see about the milk which has twice been off when delivered and A made a fuss over. He offered to drive me, this being a reason for me going out he cannot object to, but I said I would walk, stating that the air does me good, as he allows. There is a nip in the air at present and A said Mind you wrap up warm now. You have had so many chills these past months. The truth is I've had none to speak of but have used them for an excuse not to sit in that damn church catching my death. I do miss choir, though. I like to sing and A doesn't like me singing round the house. 'Church is the place to sing,' he says. Oh is it? say I, but I don't say it aloud.

*A was fussing me to be up and go with him to church. I laid
in pleading a headache. Oh, you and your heads, he said, quite
nasty. I don't know if he believed me. Thinking he would be
gone at least two hours I got up and went to the woods. I was
back in bed in time for him to tell me the sermon. Very dull it
sounded about Paul who sounds to me too full of himself and
angry, much like A in one of his turkeycock moods. I made
out how sorry I was not to be there to hear it and A said It
would have done you good to hear, my girl, which he says when
he wants to lord it over me. Then I see my skirt on the chair
by the window has sticky-burrs all round the hem which would
give me away as having gone out, so I shut my eyes and made
a sigh as if I was going back to sleep and he left me before he
noticed the burrs, thank the Lord.*

Nelly's only source of respite was that even as a young
man Arthur retired early, leaving her the evenings to herself. Increasingly, as time passed, he left her the nights free
too. At some point in time in the course of writing these
journals she decamped from his bed to my L-shaped
room, where she had a view of the garden.

The garden was Nelly's real love. My guess is that it was
the garden and not Arthur she fell in love with as a child
and that was how she came to marry him. A mistake – but
for the garden. So maybe not a mistake in the end.

If I didn't take to Arthur, I did take to Nelly. For a start,
she came from Bethnal Green, where I had had my flat.
But beyond the shared locale, I couldn't claim much other
kinship with her, or not anyway on those grounds.

She was a proper East Ender, brought up just off the
Roman Road. Along the way, she must have had a good

schoolteacher because someone had encouraged her interest in ancient history, starting, maybe because of the proximity of the Roman Road, with the Roman occupation of Britain. In my mind, this teacher had something in common with Dad; Dad was first-generation university, and his father, our grandad, while smart as paint, left school at fourteen. So Dad always took especial pains with children from less advantaged backgrounds.

I could see why Phyllis and Nelly had become friends. Inspired by this teacher, but I guessed too as solace for her barren marriage, Nelly began to explore the history of the area. Her findings were personal rather than academic, but it was she who had tracked down the maps that Peter had passed on to me. She was especially interested in the tithe map of the old parcels, or 'hides', as she called them, of land around Knight's Fee when Wight's Fee, the house with its much older and ambiguous name, stood here.

Today I discovered the pool in Knapp's wood was named for Saint Milburga. I took a hanky to hang on the hazel bushes, as is the custom I learned, and prayed to her, Please spare me A in my bed. I cannot take much more.

My illustrator's imagination, as I read this, was picturing a square-faced, sandy-haired man with brutal red hands and Victorian mutton-chop whiskers. But when I came across a tiny black-and-white snapshot of Arthur, he appeared to be a short, pallid man with one of those egg-shaped English faces and a mean mouth and nasty, squinty little eyes. There was certainly a cruel element to his character. Who knows if it was Milburga's doing, or some other force of nature, but it seems Nelly's prayer was granted. Once she escaped Arthur's bed, he looked elsewhere in the village for sexual satisfaction in what sounded to be a revoltingly crude squire-of-the-manor way.

And from here on, what Nelly writes begins subtly to change.

> *There's a barn owl calls across the fields at night which for the second time woke me. Up I got in my nightgown and downstairs and out into the garden in my bare feet, like the raggle-taggle gypsies-O and along the stream I went.*

> *I was singing by the stream late this evening when I heard someone singing downstream and thought it must be young James Knapp.*

> *I saw him today in the field by the wood. The barley was coming on and later I found a basket by the stream with white violets from our grove and a note 'For you the first violets'.*

I had seen the descendants of those white violets in the wood and, reading Nelly's cryptic words, I got out my sketchbook and began from memory to draw them.

The summer passed with me rooted in peace: lazing about, gardening, reading and paddling in the stream. I'd submitted the illustrations for Elfine and was paid, so for the first time for many months I was free to draw what I chose. I began to make careful sketches of plants and leaves and flowers, at first from the garden but then, more often, from the wood. My wood, as I had begun to think of it. I spent many contented hours lying under the oak tree or leaning against the trunk, the mossy burl pressing reassuringly into my shoulder blades, as I studied and sketched the insect life which collected in the rotting logs and in and around the pool.

The fruit and vegetables and salad stuff that Murat had planted flourished and every day he proudly brought me trugs full of produce. A raging appetite had overtaken me, I became greedy for these gifts of our garden (for by now it was Murat's garden as much as mine) and although it was an almost entirely vegetarian diet that I feasted on, for the first time in my life I began to put on weight and even had to shift the buttons on my skirts and trousers.

One day he arrived and presented me with a parcel.

'What's this, Murat?'

'Open and see.'

I opened it to find two tiny, brown-glazed coffee cups. 'For Greek coffee, until you come to Corfu. Some sweetness is good for you now.'

Over the weeks, Peter and I slowly recovered our friendship. For a time we were both shy with each other. Then one day, when we'd met outside the shop, he said, 'I meant to ask, did you find anything of use in my wife's archaeology notes?'

'Oh Peter, I am so sorry, I should have told you. According to Audrey's tutor, who sounds as if he knows what he's talking about, it's likely the effigy in the church wasn't Milburga at all but a much older figure of pagan worship.'

It was the case that it was found in the barley field near Knight's Fee. I was a little smug at discovering my hunch had been correct.

After this, all was OK between us, which was as well as he could never have got over the fear that in loving someone else he would be betraying Audrey and in me he had a good friend. So good that one day he felt able to confide, 'To be frank with you, Hassie, I have been having serious doubts about the existence of God.'

And I felt able to say, 'If there is a God, Peter, then I feel sure It would not be the kind to be bothered about a bit of doubt. And if there isn't, then what's the harm?'

'You don't think I need to resign my position?'

'I think it would be daft. What would Audrey say? I am sure she would never have allowed you to let a little thing like doubt get in the way of doing a good job.'

'She did always say that I should have been named Thomas rather than Peter.'

'The village loves you and look at all the other things you do for them, apart from marrying and burying them.'

'And christening them, Hassie. That I do like. Anointing the babes' soft heads always gives me joy. It was a great sadness to me and Audrey that we could never have little ones.'

It was some weeks after Murat's return when I met Sue Lane in the High Street. She acknowledged me with a stiff nod and was about to go on but I stopped her by saying, 'Sue, I wanted to say how grateful I was to your granddaughter. It was sweet of her to help me clear the stream.'

She visibly relented at this and said, in a not unfriendly tone, 'She's not a bad kid.'

'Penny mentioned that your grandmother knew the pool up in Knapp's wood.'

'What about it?'

'I'm interested in it. I gather it's very old. I wondered, did your grandmother ever mention Saint Milburga?'

'She always called it the Ladywell. I never heard mention of any saint.'

One Friday in late August, Margot, who had arrived from London that evening, opened her post and said, 'Oh look, your picture's coming up for sale. Do you want to go?' And there, looking out of place as a postage stamp in a glossy brochure, was my girl in the air-blue gown.

To see her reduced to what amounted to an advert was unsettling and I did suffer a swift but swingeing pang. But the prospect of the money she might bring was an immediate consolation and I was a little abashed to find it remained no great hardship to let her go.

But whether I wanted to be present as she was unsentimentally flogged off was another matter. 'I don't know,' I said. 'I'll let you know nearer the time.'

However, the night before the auction, when Margot was due to return to London, I gave in to curiosity and travelled there with her in the Lexus. I'd not set foot in London since the day I left for Sheffield, the day I had left Robert behind.

Margot's tenant was at home in the flat, so I bedded down on the sofa. Marg offered her bed to share but, closer though we had become, for me that was a step too far. And although I heard one o'clock strike, it was excited anticipation over the coming sale, rather than any physical discomfort, that kept me from sleep.

Margot went in to work early but we arranged to meet

at the auction house that afternoon. I rose late, breakfasted on several cups of coffee from her espresso machine, took a shower and then, prompted by the sight of Margot's extensive wardrobe, went out and recklessly spent some of the money I didn't yet have on a frock I saw in a shop window, a moss-green dress which I bought because . . . maybe for no better reason than that it wasn't blue. I imagine I wanted to mark my parting from the girl in the air-blue gown.

'All I can say,' Margot said when she met me, 'is you'd better come to London more often.'

The auction was nerve-racking, increasingly so as the auctioneer moved down the catalogue, and by the time my painting came up I was feeling sick. Bonhams had placed a reserve of £15,000 and for the first few minutes, as I dug my nails into sweaty palms, there was no advance on this. Then, somewhere behind me, a hand must have been raised because the bidding began to take off.

Someone was bidding by phone. At every stage, after the opening bid, the phone bidder was ahead of the others and now, on top of the nausea, I began to feel faint. Finally, the bidding came to a halt at £37,000. The phone bidder had bought the painting and in a flash of insight I knew who this phantom bidder must be.

Robert had seen the sale catalogue and was buying the picture in order to give me the funds. He was trying to make good the hole he had made in my life. He had been faithless but . . . but I never did learn what followed from that ill-defined 'but' . . .

'Are you OK?' Margot said, frowning. 'You've gone very pale. Shall we go outside?'

Outside, exhausted from the emotional toll of the sale and feeling giddy from the heat of the saleroom, I was leaning against some of the black railings that decorate the streets of Knightsbridge when a familiar voice sounded close to my ear. 'Hassie?'

He was almost the Robert who lived in my mind. Maybe a little leaner, the face more lined, his dark hair more brindled with grey. But the eyes with which he gazed down at me were the same grey-blue of the sea he loved to sail.

Margot moved, a little theatrically, to my side, linking her arm through mine. She asked what he was doing there and the tone with which Robert answered was light. 'I was interested in a Craxton but it went way over my limit,' and laughingly added, 'Intriguing to see the girl with the air-blue gown.'

He was not my fantasy bidder after all. (That turned out to be a couple who had bought a grand house in Durham and wanted to deck it out with old masters.) Robert and I talked for a while, perfectly civilly, in something like our former concord and yet not like it at all. Margot maintained an attitude of undisguised hostility until Robert remarked that he must be going, pausing only to say that I was looking well and that life in the country must suit me.

Later I wondered how he had known where I had settled but at the time I was feeling nothing more than *Thank heavens I am wearing a new frock and that I thought to tidy my hair.*

Margot hustled me over the road to a pub, where she proposed buying me a double brandy. I was shaking and she said later she was afraid I was going to pass out. What she couldn't know was the trembling arose partly out of a mounting need to vomit (which I did discreetly in the Ladies) and partly out of something like astonishment, because for all the daft build-up and the shock at seeing Robert – for whom I once would have given my life – I felt next to nothing, almost nothing at all.

'Actually,' I said, when I emerged from the toilets feeling wonderfully cleansed, 'I don't think I want brandy. Tomato juice with lashings of spice, please.'

With the fantasy of the bidder blown, it was as if the last of my attachment to Robert had been blown away too. He had stood there before me, as attractive on the face of it as ever; but that invisible tie that had bound my heart to his had finally attenuated, broken and drifted away.

I was curious about the reasons for his dereliction but I found, when I came to inspect it, that my heart was intact. The only damage was to my pride, and I knew, even as I sat in that very ordinary pub, drinking nothing stronger than tomato juice, that this trivial loss of face would be quickly overcome. I was even a little amused by my own defection. The only regret that touched me at all was the thought that he never did teach me to sail.

'Hass,' Margot said in the pub, once she was satisfied that my shaking had not been the onset of another nervous collapse, 'there's something I need to say.'

Relief at my release from Robert made me belligerently cheerful. 'What?'

She fiddled with her bangles. 'Jules,' she said at last. 'So, Jules and I are kind of back together.'

'Fine,' I said briskly. 'No skin off my nose.'

'It is in a way because . . .'

'Oh, I see,' I said, ready for some new attack from fate. 'You're going to tell me we have to sell?'

'I'll get us another drink. Wine?'

But I needed no alcohol to lift my spirits. She returned with a second large brandy for herself and for me another tomato juice and a packet of crisps. My stomach was empty and I felt the need for ballast.

Margot placed her glass down carefully on a beer mat and appeared to study it. It had nothing more oracular on it than *Carling Premier*, so I presumed that whatever it was she had to say was giving her difficulty. I was right about that as after a moment she said, 'Now listen and please don't interrupt,' assuming the serious expression she adopted occasionally and which always made me want to smile. But I didn't smile. I was feeling very fond of her for her demonstration of loyalty during the surprise encounter with Robert. 'Leaving Jules to stew worked,' she said now. 'He came round. You know I said we'd planned to run an art gallery? I found somewhere perfect in Fulham, with a flat overhead, and he's putting the lot in my sole name. So if it all goes down the plughole, I have capital. But my guess is it won't. He's not in great shape – skin cancer, too much lying in the sun at his place in Antibes – and he seems to have acquired a weird idea that he needs me. I'm not arguing. But even if he kicks me out, or I decide it's not for me after all, with the income from the gallery and my own flat to let out I'll be well off. And I've no plans to have kids. So . . .' She paused, appeared to consult her glass of brandy and then swigged the lot down. 'So . . .' she said, wiping her mouth with a napkin.

'So?' I said. 'So what . . .?'

'So, I've no need to take my money out of Knight's Fee. In fact, consider my half yours.' She said this last very fast and I felt even fonder of her because I was sure the reason she was gabbling was that she was getting this said before she could have second thoughts.

'Steady on!' I said. 'There's no call for that.'

'I shan't need it. And I think it's what Dad would have liked. It was you who looked after him and my guess is he didn't leave you the lion's share because he knew I'd kick off. And I would have done. Like mad. I reckon he'd have liked us to be better friends. And we are now, aren't we?'

She looked quite pleadingly at me and I found that my jealousy seemed to have vanished along with my passion for Robert. I felt suddenly proud of my beautiful sister.

'I can always visit you and I won't bring Jules,' she continued. 'He's frightened by the country, poor darling. When I took him for a walk when he was down, he trod in a fresh cowpat and that was that. Which is good cos I'll be able to get away alone to see my sister in her bucolic bliss.' She paused, then added, 'It was a fantasy of mine, living in the country. It doesn't really suit me. I'm a town mouse. But it suits you. You've bloomed there. You even look different – I can see that.'

'I can see that I've been a crap sister.' By now I was feeling very ashamed.

'So? I have too. That was our mother's doing. But don't forget that living together was my idea. Remember how I had to talk you into it?'

She had a right to look pleased with herself. I'd been within a whisker of rejecting the move to Knight's Fee. 'I'll keep your half safe for you,' I assured her. 'You might need to take sanctuary some time.' I was not at all sanguine about this decision to live with Julian. 'You're not going to be rid of me that easily.' I could feel my eyes pricking but I knew she would dislike tears. In some ways she was really very like Phyllis, my sister. It still amuses me how little they would each recognize that.

She grinned and ruffled my hair, and I understood that she understood how I had always disliked this and that she was doing it now because she also knew I would no longer mind. 'You can keep my room for me, if you like. It'd be a shame to move the four-poster and the curtains will never fit anywhere else. They cost a king's ransom so they may as well stay there. But the rest of the place is yours to spread where you like. You might need to. Oh, and by the way. I found this you've been going on about in a second-hand bookshop,' and she handed me a parcel.

I opened it to find a handsome old cloth-bound herbal.

22

That might seem to be the end of the story – but it isn't.

One clement afternoon in September, when the swifts had already departed, the swallows were assembling in rows along the telegraph wires ready to make their long flight back to their winter quarters and the roses were in their second flush, Phyllis and I were once more drinking tea in the garden.

Murat had mowed the lawn and Mags was skittering around our feet, chasing wisps of new-mown grass. He was living with me now – Phyllis felt it would be too hard on him to move him again and from the night of his first venture out he seemed to regard Knight's Fee and its garden as his domain.

Murat, in turn, was living with Phyllis to help her out until she was able to cope alone. Her right arm had remained paralysed and her mouth since the stroke retains to this day a slight lopsided twist, but her speech was as fluent and her mind as acute as ever. She was on the mend.

'Better each day, thanks,' she said, in answer to my asking how she was progressing. She always made light of her infirmity. 'But I don't know where I'd be without Murat. He has been a godsend.'

'Yes.'

We sat for a while in companionable silence until she sat up in her deckchair and said with sudden energy, 'Murat understands hazard. You turn up your nose at backgammon but I assure you it is more than just a game. It's about the connection between fate and chance. All experience is pervaded by chance – that's our fate – but it can be – *is*, in fact, whether we choose to see it or not – transformative. Peter supposes I'm against the precious God he's in such a tizz over. I'm not, as it happens. Or rather, I'm against his idea of God. I dislike the insulting image of God as a vast security blanket, some sort of promise of eternal harmony, which – if we're lucky enough, or *good* enough – we get to be swaddled in. If that young radical was here for anything it was to offer us an example of how to live with no clue about what might happen next. The best thing he ever said was "Fear not". Jesus didn't give a tinker's cuss about security and he must be spinning in his peculiar place in eternity at the notion he was here to sell us that tinsel, gimcrack idea. If there is divinity in the universe it surely manifests in the uncertain and unstable, in just those things which we humans, for all our so-called "knowledge" and for all the advance of science – I'm not against that either, Peter is wrong about that too – cannot predict. The lion shouldn't lie down with the lamb. It's the lion's business to devour the lamb, there will always be plagues, if not of locusts then other natural phenomena inimical to humankind – and by the way, why shouldn't a locust have as much right as any one of us to exist? –◦ and there never was and never will be peace on earth. Peace is the reward for dying. Only the dead are peaceful.'

This speech, long even for her, was delivered with unusual vehemence. She slumped back in her chair, frowning.

'Perhaps you'd better teach me backgammon then,' I said. 'I'm beginning to realize there's no point in trying to escape your fate.'

'In that case, isn't it Murat you should play with?' The flash of fire in the hazelish-green eyes had reverted to an amused glint.

I ignored this. I hadn't told her of my chance meeting with Robert, though she knew about the auction.

'You remember the other man I once told you about?'

'I remember your being annoyed that you had told me.'

'I'm sorry,' I said. 'It was myself I was annoyed with really.'

'That's all right. Being vouchsafed a secret is like receiving any other gift: liable to be followed with an invoice.'

'I'm sorry,' I said again. It made me think of Margot's gift of Knight's Fee. She has never invoiced me for it, which is another example of how wrong I was about her. 'Anyway, I met him when I was in London at the sale.'

She said nothing to this but looked enquiring.

'It was funny – not funny, why do we say that, I wonder? – unexpected. I felt next to nothing when I saw him. It was a shock, meeting him like that, but once I'd got over the shock there seemed nothing left in me to feel.'

'That doesn't mean there was never anything there.'

'No. I can see that. What happens, do you think? How is it that we can care so passionately about someone and then it can all in a trice disappear?'

'I'm no expert, as you know, but I imagine love, like everything else, needs attention. I doubt that it goes in a trice, or only if it was never there in the first place. But if it is given no attention, then, like everything else, it will wither and die – an unwatered plant.'

Months later, when I had had time to ponder my long relationship with Robert, I found that while I never learnt what had happened when he and Laura parted, I hadn't relinquished the belief that he had genuinely loved me. As Phyllis had said to me, all that time ago in the garden, love is a flexible matter at best. What had transpired with respect to his attachment for me I never did find out. Perhaps merely time passing had loosened the bond – perhaps his need for Laura was stronger than either of us had supposed and without her he couldn't, or didn't, function as he had. Very likely he never quite knew himself what had happened or what he felt or why.

And recently, maybe only a month or so back, I remembered how, when Phyllis had also said to me in the garden that the minds of men were often opaque to women, some words had lit up in the back of my mind. As a modern woman, versed in the doctrine of equality, I had resisted that idea, though I hadn't bothered to voice this at the time. But the words that had come to me unbidden were Feste's to Orsino, a man who epitomizes the incalculable shiftings of the impassioned heart: *Thy mind is a very opal.*

I find this image best explains Robert to me, though what it explains I can't put into words.

But I have since often reflected too on what my sister said to me that night when we first began to understand each other: 'You know your trouble, Hass? You overrate being adored.' Margot was right: I had overrated being adored. I had grown up seeing her as the adored child and I had craved what I believed she had had and I had lacked. (Dad's undemonstrative love of me was always tempered by his own diffidence.) Robert had offered adoration. But adoration only goes so far if it is not attended by other, more resilient, attributes and perhaps it is only gods and babies who rightly should be adored.

But that particular day in the garden there were other loves I was more interested in.

'Who was young James Knapp, Phyllis? Were he and Nelly lovers?'

'Arthur supposed so.'

I had told her what I had discovered from reading Nelly's journals. I reckoned that Phyllis probably knew already what was in them; Nelly had been her friend and in speaking of what I had divined I reckoned there was no betrayal. I had come to feel that Nelly and I were kin and that I could speak for what she would or wouldn't mind.

'But you . . .?'

'You've read her journals.'

I had read all that long summer how Nelly walked in the wood alone and bathed in the pool, my pool – which had also been her place of sanctuary. And how she had begun to walk there with young James Knapp, who was 'brown as a berry' with 'hair the colour of ripe barley'.

But I had read this too:

I met with them at long last, after many evenings waiting. I came upon them dancing and singing and making their strange chant. They stopped as I came near and to my sadness fled but the next night I came again and stood awhile and then they graciously let me stay.

I danced with them in my bare feet, like the raggle-taggle gypsies. All night long we danced till the dawn light came and then they left me by the pool to go back to the other world. I did so long to go after them.

'She saw fairies in the wood.'

'Certainly she believed so. Though she never named them as such. The *other people* is what she called them. I have always imagined they were elves.'

'Did you ever see them, Phyllis?'

'I doubt I have the sight. But I believed that Nelly did. I am sure one needs a certain gift. But I have a feeling that it is the house, or more properly the grounds it stands in, the wood and here, the garden, that allowed her to see them. From what I have read, it is the place that counts and there are places still, pockets of the old country, where they have never entirely gone.'

'And she wasn't mad?'

'I've often wondered how we moderns have the nerve to consider ourselves so superior to, for example, Shakespeare, to whom worlds besides ours were second nature. Nelly was a down-to-earth East End Londoner, not at all given to moonshine. No, it was Arthur's ill-treatment that scattered her wits; she was perfectly sane before.'

'And her baby? She did have a baby, didn't she?' The journal became suddenly very confused and obscure.

'That was a tragedy. It was what cost her her mind.'

'But she lost the child?' What I was able to piece together from a few incoherent entries had made distressing reading. From that point on, Nelly had written no more in her journal.

'Arthur made her give the baby away. He knew it couldn't be his. She never got over it.'

'Do you know who the baby went to?'

'I don't. I think she tried to find out. I never liked to enquire. I never even knew if it was a girl or a boy child.'

'And the father . . .?'

I glanced over at Murat, busy in the long bed, deadheading the roses. He must have felt my gaze as he straightened up from tending the old Alba rose, which had produced a glorious second flourish of scented white blooms, and stood looking back at me with his topaz eyes.

Phyllis glanced in his direction too and then averted her eyes to a clump of mauve Michaelmas daisies, where some goldfinches were savaging the fluffy seed heads. I began to study their distinctive markings and to wonder, not for the first time, why a flock of goldfinches is known as a charm. They're really quite aggressive little birds.

Phyllis seemed to be considering. Then she said, 'Who's to say?'

There was a silence. Neither of us spoke. Somewhere a thrush sang. Then I said, 'What a sad story.'

'It was, is.'

'And the child? I wonder how the child turned out?'

'I imagine such children are invested with their own magic.'

She said no more, and we passed on to other matters.

A week or so later, as the October mists were beginning to shroud the early morning garden in fine white gauze, Phyllis rang me. 'Can you come for supper? I've a favour to ask, so be warned.'

'So what's this favour?' I asked, over one of her root-vegetable stews.

'My brother Philip, whom you've met, is selling his house. He's tired of ownership and wants to simplify his life and rent from now on. He suggested coming to live with me but I couldn't hear of it. Anyway, with Murat here there's no room.'

Murat was planning to return to Corfu but I said nothing of this. It was not my place to tell Phyllis and besides I suspected she wanted an excuse not to offer her brother a room.

'And . . .?'

'He wondered if you would consider renting him a room at Knight's Fee. I warned him that you would very likely bristle at the suggestion but he says to say that if you were willing, he would pay to put in a separate bathroom and lavatory – a separate entrance too if you are concerned about your privacy. He would pay a decent rent but of course you must feel free to say a resounding "No". He won't be at all offended. I needn't say that neither will I.'

'Phyllis,' I said, 'that is a simply marvellous idea.'

'Really? I was most reluctant to ask you.'

'No,' I said. 'I mean, yes. I mean, you were right to ask because . . .'

Strange events, the old stories suggest, can fade and vanish from the memory as if they have never been. I am writing this now in case of some accident to me before you are of an age to be told and so that a record is put down while it is as clear as starlight in my mind.

You will meet Murat, who lived all that time in the wood, to whose safekeeping, thanks to my foolish interfering, he had retreated and where he too was found. If by some ill luck I am not around, he can tell you – at least as much as I can – about that night by the pool.

And there are Nelly's journals. One day, you too will read Nelly's journals.

Naturally the villagers gossip about how you came to be conceived and by whom. They are almost as curious as I am to see what you look like, whom you resemble, what colour your skin, your hair, your eyes, what shape your nose, your ears. Jade has offered to return the child's desk that came from our attic and Russ is repairing the rocking horse, which he never took to be sold. Penny Isabel has asked if she may take you out for walks. I am not sure I am ready to trust her with someone so precious; but I have been tactful. I have said we must wait and see.

And I have come to think that maybe there is something kindred about Penny Isabel, which perhaps I should have recognized from the intensity with which I hated her, for I believe that she was also granted her wish. Her father was finally apprehended and is now doing time for aggravated assault and for two related charges. So she and her mother and Sue are free of any immediate intimidation.

So you see, Penny Isabel and her grandmother have had a part to play in our story. And a part in undoing my picture of myself which, as your aunt Margot has always hinted, was somewhat awry.

By the time you read this I hope you will have learnt to love Margot, who will certainly indulge and very likely adore you. Like poor Nelly, she too lost a baby and I know that somewhere she minds. She has given up asking questions but inevitably she has her own ideas.

And I hope you will also learn to love Phyllis, whose sharp manner conceals a decidedly tender heart. When I told her about you, she asked no questions – she is naturally discreet but I sensed that she had already understood; or anyway as much as she chose to understand. I did surprise her, though, by saying, 'You can be grandmother,' at which she actually blushed.

'My dear,' she said, 'no one has ever paid me such a compliment.'

'Peter can be honorary uncle,' I went on, enjoying this new-found source of munificence.

When I told Peter, he was so excited he began to plan your christening.

'I shall play Bach, on second thoughts Schubert, no, better Bach because she will be an Easter babe. And, Hassie, frankly, it's an occasion to push out the boat. We'll christen her with my '82 champagne.'

But there will be no christening for you, my daughter. For you there will be a simple blessing with water from the pool. Our pool.

Which reminds me, I should tell you how you came by your name.

Phyllis's brother Philip has moved into Knight's Fee. Like his sister, he's an eccentric, but gentler, less opinionated, and it has been a pleasure to have another intelligent adult around. But that was not the only reason I agreed to his living here. When we met by Phyllis's hospital bed, he told me he was a star gazer and if there has been any guiding light in my story, it has come from the stars. Knight's Fee sits in an area of rare dark sky, which is one of the reasons Philip asked to rent rooms here. On starlit nights, he takes me star watching and I am learning to recognize the various planets and name the constellations. On the night of Hallowe'en, the sky was exceptionally clear – I could make out the dimly sculpted contours of the distant hills against the starry backdrop of the boundless universe. The stars were almost preternaturally bright and, looking up, I saw your name . . .

Best beloved Stella,

It is a year to the day that I came to live at Knight's Fee, when everything began – or maybe began anew, because everything, I now believe, recurs – so it seems fitting to finish my story, which is also your story, here – though no human story is ever truly finished and it is time for you to take the principal part. As I write these words, I feel you stirring in me, preparing to plunge headfirst into a world where who knows what untold strangenesses you may find. Whatever comes, my darling, I believe your wits will be sharp as the brightest star in the night sky; but, more important, I believe you will be happy here, will love the garden, will play there and paddle in the stream.